PRAISE FOR T

"Cannibalism. Murder. Rape. Absolute brutality. When civilizations ends…when the human race begins to revert to ancient, predatory savagery…when the world descends into a bloodthirsty hell…there is only survival. But for one man and one woman, survival means becoming something less than human. Something from the primeval dawn of the race. "Shocking and brutal, The Devil Next Door will hit you like a baseball bat to the face. Curran seems to have it in for the world … and he's ending it as horrifyingly as he can."

—Tim Lebbon, author of *Bar None*

"Tim Curran is one of those guys that people talk about when you speak of ultra-violent and gory horror. Books like Biohazard, or The Devil Next Door are a couple that I've read that made my stomach turn. I was wondering where Blackout might lead me when I got this from the publisher to review…Tim Curran builds on this with every turn of the page. Each of the characters have their own unique perspective and voice of the events, and the group survival mentality is in full effect. He does a great job of getting across just how dire of a situation this is through their actions and dialogue. Every bit of it had a purpose and moved this story forward."

—Reviewed by Joe Hempel, Horror Novel Reviews

"Tim Curran's, *The Devil Next Door* is dynamite! Visceral, violent, and disturbing!"

—Brian Keene, author of *Castaways* and *Dark Hollow*

"Nightcrawlers is a monster story and an ode to H. P. Lovecraft. I would say that this story has two of Lovecraft's in it: The Colour Outer Space and Facts Concerning the Late Arthur Jermyn and His Family. It is also completely Tim Curran. Curran manages to own the story and the monsters within it. But one cannot deny the spirit of Lovecraft…So, having read the rest of the story, I can say that I had a great time reading it. You do get to know the characters more and more the deeper you go in, and one thing that surprised me is how much we got to know one character when she wasn't even in it for very long. Throughout the story, including the ending, Curran shows his talent for creating actual frightening scenes that can linger long after reading them. If you let them. And you should. It is why we read horror after all, isn't it?"

—Darkness Dwells

"Horror is a lot of fun, and Worm is proof of that. If you're looking for very complex plots with descriptive passages that belong in classic Russian novels and characters with full back stories, look elsewhere. However, if you're looking for a taut, fun, grisly read, ignore the stench and sink your teeth into this one."

—Gabino Iglesias, HORROR DNA

"Tim Curran has a way of slinging words to create grotesque imagery that makes you cringe and yet you find yourself absorbed, frantically turning the pages to see what kind of gruesome avenues he takes you down. SOW is a quick and thoroughly enjoyable read. This is eye-popping madness, paranoia realized, body horror most foul. Curran takes what should be the one of the happiest times in someone's life and turns it on its head. Really this is a story for anyone who craves a good, creepy yarn. If you're a Curran fan and you haven't read this one, you'd better rectify that. If you haven't read Curran yet (what?), this is just as good a place as any to start as any. Think Rosemary's Baby dunked in a bathtub full of acid and you begin to touch on the madness that is SOW"

—Robert Essig, Splatterpunkzine

"Okay so I rocked on with this collection, Tasmaniac have kicked a major here kids, and I've found a new must read Writer whose name is now chiselled into my tree of counted sorrows. One of the best collections of the year in terms of quality and content, full recommendation this book is one that you simply cannot miss assuming you can get a copy before the print run is depleted. Take down the name Tim Curran, you are going to be hearing a lot about him in the coming years."

—Scaryminds

BLOODING NIGHT

Trade Paperback Edition

Disclaimer: This book is Extreme Horror and is suitable for adults only!

ISBN: 978-1-957121-21-5

Interior and cover design by Cyrusfiction Productions

Editor and Publisher, Joe Morey

Weird House Press
Central Point, OR 97502
www.weirdhousepress.com

BY

TIM CURRAN

Blooding: *To smear with blood; the act of anointing a novice with the blood of the first kill of the hunt.*

ONE

Chloe woke in a wild panic, gasping for breath and fighting to get free. She was bound and trussed, a gag over her mouth. Struggling, she told herself it was a nightmare and she needed to wake up. She even believed it for about two minutes.

Because it *was* a nightmare.

Only it was real.

She opened her mouth to scream, but closed it as fast. That wouldn't do. Whoever put her here would probably get off hearing her scream. No, she couldn't do that. She had to keep her nerve or she was done.

She started struggling again, pulling and straining until her limbs ached and sweat ran down her face. But she wasn't going anywhere. In the heavy, coveting darkness, she could feel that her wrists were tied behind her back. Every time she tried to move them, it yanked on her ankles. They were bound together, too, a securely knotted cord connecting them to her wrists.

She was hog-tied.

Gagged.

She had no idea where she was. Maybe lying in the cool dirt of a cellar...except she could see light, fingers of light coming through the irregular spaces between planks. Not a cellar; a shack or a shed. She tried to cry out, but she was gagged expertly.

Where the fuck am I? What the hell is this about?

Her mind kept drawing a blank.

Think! *Think!*

She had to calm down and make sense of things. She needed to remember, but her head was filled with a drifting fog thick as cotton. There was nothing but a vague suggestion of a memory that kept slipping away. Trying to make sense of it was like trying to read a blackboard that had been wiped clean.

The shack creaked.

Chloe tensed.

The shack creaked again.

She was breathing so hard she thought she might asphyxiate. The gag felt tighter than before. It was hot and clinging with the moisture of her breath. Trying to blink away droplets of sweat, she shifted in the dirt. Her limbs felt numb, her muscles aching. She was almost certain that someone was out there, pressing themselves against the shack.

It creaked again.

A shape moved past the spaces between the planks. A shifting, furtive shadow and nothing more. Squinting, she peered around in the darkness. Over there to her left…hadn't there been light coming between those boards just seconds ago? They were dark now.

She waited.

Watching for movement.

There was nothing else to do. She knew very well there was no point fighting against her bonds.

Chloe slowed her breathing using yoga exercises, calming herself inch by inch. There. That was a little better. Carefully, deftly, she began moving her wrists using her sweat as a lubricant. Side to side, twisting back and forth, working it. After a few minutes of that, her bonds already felt a bit looser. She was far from being free, but at least she was able to shift her hands and arms a bit. The change in position brought the feeling back into her fingers. After a few minutes more, they were no longer tingling.

Keep going.

She began moving her ankles in a likewise manner. By starting with very short, slow movements as she did with her wrists, she was able to get some feeling in them. She tried not to think about how many hours if not days it might take to slip free because it filled her with panic. Somebody brought her here and she knew damn well they did it for a reason. There was no way in hell they were going to give her the time she needed to get free.

Don't think about it.

Concentrate.

Yes, she had to be hard-nosed and practical now. It was a matter of survival. There was nothing else. But as she worked, her brain fought to remember. Things were beginning to come back. Yvonne. Steph. Emma. They were...*camping.* Yes! That was it! She could see the site. The red dome tent. The fire pit. They were getting high and roasting hot dogs—plump and juicy, God she was hungry—and then, and then...

Nothing.

A seamless gray wall in her head.

Listen.

Yes, there was something. A regular, guttural sort of sound. Breathing. There was no doubt of it. Someone was out there. Someone with deep, ragged breathing. She was certain for a moment or two she could smell their breath—hot, salty, and rancid. The stink of meat that had gone bad...no, the breath of someone that had been *chewing* on meat that had gone bad.

And they were right outside.

Their physical presence was nearly crushing.

Chloe tried to remain absolutely still and absolutely quiet, but a low frightened moan came from deep within her throat. She shifted. Off to the left, that's where the breathing man had to be. She focused her eyes, trying to see between the planks, but she couldn't see anything. A new smell filled the shack—something like blood and wet leather.

The shape out there moved.

It pulled away from the planks.

She saw a single bloodshot eye staring in at her. It was wide, gaping, and insane-looking. It did not blink.

Chloe screamed.

The effect was instantaneous. The breathing man began breathing even faster, practically panting. He rattled the shack. He shook it back and forth, grunting and squealing like a wild boar. The shack was in motion, dust filling the beams of lights, splinters of wood dropping down. He was getting more and more excited, more frenzied. She could hear a juicy sucking sound as if he was trying to control the gushing saliva in his mouth.

He stopped beating on the shack.

Now he was clawing at the boards as if he was trying to dig his way in. After a few frantic moments of that in which Chloe's heart felt like it would stop in mid-gallop, he began sniffing between the planks as if he was trying to get her scent. He must have gotten it because he went into that same primal mania again, beating at the boards, pounding and kicking. By that point, she was nearly out of her mind, drowning in the sweat of her terror. Huge, filthy, completely misshapen fingers gripped one of the planks and wrenched it free.

And then—

Nothing.

She saw a hulking shape move past the missing board—dear God, it was grotesque and shaggy, it couldn't possibly be a man—and then it was gone. She heard it retreating, heavy footsteps moving through crackling dry leaves. Then there was only the silence of the forest, birds chirping and insects buzzing, a light breeze fluttering in the treetops.

Trying to control her own breathing, Chloe waited.

Five minutes.

Ten.

Still nothing.

Whoever or whatever had been out there was gone. She was alone again and somehow that was almost worse.

Steph's memories were coming back.

They weren't quite there yet, but they were definitely on the way. In her head, she saw many of the same things that Chloe had. They had gone camping. It had been Steph's idea. She borrowed all the stuff from her suite-mate, the tent and coolers, cook stove and lanterns. And it was Labor Day weekend and no one had classes, so why not?

It beat the hell out of staring at one another or—*gag*—studying.

No one had anything else to do or anywhere to go.

Steph could remember that much, but the rest of it was still a little on the blurry side. Yet, she kept getting distorted images of a face she thought she should recognize. Someone familiar. Someone friendly. Someone she thought she could trust.

Fuck!

It kept fading.

There and then gone.

Maybe you might want to worry about that later, she told herself. That was sensible, but the memories were still important. If she could only clear her head and remember, then her predicament just might begin to make sense. Maybe not the why of it, but at least the how.

She gritted her teeth.

It felt like the rope was cutting into her wrists, burning right into her skin. She tried to shift herself, but it did no good. Her own weight was the enemy.

Like Chloe, she was gagged so there was no point in crying out or screaming. Besides, that would only get her worked up and make it that much harder to breathe. Craning her head back, she looked up. She was in some kind of well or cistern, a circular shaft made of mossy, crumbling bricks. What she could see of it looked like it might collapse at any moment. High above, at least twenty feet, was the opening. There was a metal grating or lid up there. The rope that painfully bound her wrists together was tied off to it and from it she swung.

There was a dark streak at her left forearm.

Blood that had run from her wrist and dried.

She was hanging from above, but she was knee-deep in oily, dark water that stank like sewers. It was her only saving grace, displacing her weight somewhat. Maybe not much, but a little was better than nothing. She didn't know what would be worse—hanging there until her arms pulled out of their sockets or sinking into the dark, leaf-covered waters below. She could just imagine the black mud and slime at the bottom and it gave her the chills.

When she first woke up, she freaked right out.

She twisted and kicked and contorted…but that only punished herself. It tore her wrists, filled her shoulder joints with fire, and in the end she was still partially submerged in the dirty water, swinging slowly back and forth.

She kept wondering how long it would be until her shoulders were pulled out of joint and how much longer after that until she sustained permanent damage.

Her only relief was to spread her legs and brace her hiking boots against the walls. When she did that, she could lift herself a few inches. But she could only balance herself in that position for maybe five minutes, ten at the outside, and when her wrists again took her full weight it was agony. The momentary relief was barely worth it.

"How long?" she muttered beneath the gag. "How long can this go on?"

As if in answer, she heard a scratching sound from above. It sounded like a knife was scraped over the lid.

Steph craned her head back again.

Yes, someone was up there. A shadow pulled back from the grate.

A few flakes of rust fell down. She could see them drifting downwards in the dusty beams of sunlight. Someone had been up there watching her. She tried to call out through her gag, but succeeded only in making muffled noises.

All she really wanted to know was if someone was there and if they could help her.

Fat fucking chance, she thought.

Because, really, it was a topic she was avoiding, but the truth of the matter was that this was more than a simple, twisted prank or hazing.

Think about it. You've either been brought here to be raped or tortured or killed, maybe all three. There can be no other reason. The entire point of hanging you like this might be to take the fight out of you, to soften you up so you'll be a more willing slave.

That was the stark reality of things, like it or not.

Drip.

A drop of water struck the top of her head.

Another fell into the bog that sluiced around her knees.

Was it raining? Was it—

A stream of water rained over her, soaking her hair and running down her face and washing down the back of her neck. It was hot and sour-smelling.

Urine.

Somebody up there was pissing on her.

Shock and disgust became rage. She fought and twisted on the rope, kicking out against the walls, splashing and stirring up the stinking water below. The barely-clotted wounds of her wrists tore open and fresh blood seeped down her forearms.

"I'll kill you! I'll fucking kill you!" she shrieked behind her gag.

The rage spent itself quickly enough.

In the end, she was more miserable than ever. Her wrists were on fire and her shoulders filled with needles. One way or another, she was going to get out of this and when she did there would be hell to pay.

Goddamn yes.

THREE

Yvonne came out of it slowly, very slowly, muscles bunched and limbs cramped. She hadn't felt this worn and badly-used since that time she and Sterile Daryl had tripped on mescaline for three days straight. She came out of *that* in a cornfield, naked and dirty, wilted wildflowers in her hair and a hammer-and-sickle tattoo on her left breast. The inside of her mouth had tasted like tar and she had no memory of the previous forty-eight hours...something she was honestly grateful for.

But this...

What the hell was this?

Her memories didn't return as quickly as they had for Chloe and Steph. She was always slow like that. Maybe it had something to do with all the chemicals she had fried her brain with since she was thirteen.

She opened her eyes and it was dark.

Was it night?

She remembered hanging around the dorm with Steph and the others and then...?

Nothing.

Yet, she was almost certain Steph had said something about going camping.

God, she was cramped.

She couldn't straighten her legs and the blankets were wound around her so tight she felt like an Egyptian mummy. That's when she realized she was in a sleeping bag. That made perfect sense. Camping. Sleeping bag. But as she tried to wriggle free, the material did not feel soft. No, it felt kind of slippery like vinyl.

She couldn't poke her head out.

There was a zipper running the length of the thing. She wasn't in a sleeping bag, she was zipped in a body bag. This was when she started panicking. She and claustrophobia went way back and their relationship had never been good.

She screamed.

Unlike the others, she wasn't gagged. Not that it much mattered. She frantically traced the zipper with shaking fingertips, but there was no catch. Nothing on the inside anyway and that made perfect sense—who the hell ever tried to get out of a bag once they were zipped inside?

Panic gripped her and she fought, raged with complete animal fear. The bag rocked back and forth…then fell. It hit the floor with a resounding thud, knocking the wind out of her. Then it began to roll end over end, faster and faster. It hadn't been on a table as she'd thought; it must have been on a ledge.

It was rolling down a hill.

As it picked up speed, it struck rocks and saplings, thumping in and out of dips. Yvonne's head spun with vertigo. Her stomach was in her throat. She saw stars.

Finally, it came to a stop.

She felt the bag settle into soft, moist ground like mud. It took a minute or so for her head to stop spinning. And when it did, she had all she could do not to vomit. Her throat was filled with warm grease. She laid there for a time, stunned and senseless, her body bruised and aching.

The air in the bag was thin, foul, smelling of rubber and sweat.

She began to gasp.

She was suffocating. Dear God, she was suffocating!

She began to fight anew, tearing and beating at the bag whose material seemed oily and hard to grasp, impervious to her attack.

Stop it! a voice cried out in her head. *You're only making matters worse!*

She knew it was true, so finally she did stop, gasping and sweating and trying to think. That voice of reason sounded so much like her mother she wanted to cry. Mom had died three years before, but very often in times of great stress or fear she would hear her voice—calm, reasonable, and solid.

She was hearing it now: *Take a few deep breaths, Yvonne. That's it. Go ahead. In and out. See? It might not smell that good, dear, but you're hardly suffocating. Now trace that zipper. It has to start somewhere.*

Sound advice.

Swallowing, Yvonne traced it with her nails. It seemed hopeless. It was impossible to trace it down any farther than her waist. The bag gave her no quarter. It held her, clung to her. She traced the zipper just above her head. She found where it began but there was no pull tab. Yet, she saw a tiny sliver of light. If light could get in, so could air.

Work it, the voice told her. *Widen it.*

But with what?

There had to be something in her pockets. Coins. Gum. A Bic lighter. *Keys.* That was it. She worked them free and inserted the tip of her car key into the tiny opening where the zipper began. She forced it in there as far as she could and began to pry downwards. The zipper slid down a few notches. It was very stiff, very unyielding. An industrial sort of zipper like the kind used on old heavy-duty canvas tents.

She pried it down a bit more.

The zipper slid down a few teeth.

She was actually going to do it!

Of course you are, said the voice.

Then...she heard the sound of crunching dry leaves.

Something poked the bag. Something like a finger.

She tensed, trying to control her breathing. She was poked again. Whatever it was—finger, stick, or claw—traced its way down the bag to her thigh.

Something sniffed along the zipper like a dog.

Don't move. Don't even breathe. Remember the key.

Whoever or whatever was out there was toying with the zipper pull now, flicking it back and forth. Now the sniffing again followed by a scratching as if fingernails were being drawn roughly down the length of the bag.

They were getting more and more violent.

The voice: *Think, Yvonne. Think! If it's an animal, they sense that you're inside. They smell you. They're intrigued. If it's a person, then they're toying with you, trying to get a rise out of you. Either way, do not give them the satisfaction. Play possum and remember the key.*

Yes, the key or keys, would have been more accurate. Car key, room key, gym locker key, trunk key…there were six of them. She grasped the fob and keys tightly in her fist, a single key protruding between her second and third fingers like a dagger.

She had a weapon.

The zipper pull was being tugged on now. It went down an inch, then another. Yvonne smelled something rank like the musky pelts of animals. It was sickening and warm. The stench seemed to fill the bag.

Then, through the unzipped opening she saw a mouth…a crooked mouth with awful yellow teeth jutting from discolored gums. Then an eye. A bleary eye with a staring, fixed pupil. It pressed in closer and closer right to the opening, trying to see inside.

And as it did that, Yvonne jabbed her key right into it.

FOUR

For the longest time there was only darkness and a cramped, uncomfortable space. Then slowly, incrementally, Emma saw light. Just a weak sliver of it, but it was something. She knew it hadn't been there a few minutes before.

Nothing made sense. At first, upon waking, there was confusion and numb acceptance, a sort of groggy realization that something just wasn't right. Then—panic.

She came out of her fugue, trying to cry out only to discover there was a square of duct tape over her mouth. That could mean only one thing—she was being held prisoner. She had been abducted. These were the thoughts that raced through her mind as she balanced somewhat precariously on the edge of hysteria.

But why me? she asked herself. *Why kidnap me? I have nothing. I have no money. I work four days a week at IHOP just to keep my head above water. I'm worth nothing.*

Maybe monetarily she was a zero, but there were other reasons to hold someone prisoner, particularly a twenty-one year old college girl.

Shit.

Rapist.

Serial killer.

It all went through her mind in a flash and she had to fight against going with it, losing control. Which, of course, would not help her. *Use your brain. You're smart. At least, you maintain a 4.0 in chemical engineering and that's no easy bit. Everyone thinks you've got a brain so use it.* Yes, that was the key to this mess. To think. To reason. She took in her surroundings. Pitch-black, save that sliver of light. Her hands were tied, mouth taped shut, and she was lying on her back. She moved to the right. There was a wall. Another to the left. She brought up her knees and they banged into another surface with a hollow thud.

Buried alive…I've been fucking buried alive.

The panic swelled inside her in hot spikes. She thrashed this way and that, but there was no getting around the awful fact that she was in a box.

Not a traditional coffin from the feel of it but a coffin-shaped box. Okay. Okay. But the box wasn't buried because she could see light. And if light got in, that meant air would, too, so she wasn't going to asphyxiate. She told herself this again and again. *You will not suffocate. You will not suffocate.* It was a mantra she repeated in her head. Finally, she calmed. At least, somewhat.

All right.

Think.

The first thing to do was to get her hands free. Her legs were not bound so that was something and her hands were not tied behind her back so that was something else. She breathed in and out, sucking in musty air, her heart thudding in her chest. She needed to be calm. It was the most important thing. First, her hands. That's where she needed to start. Her wrists were bound, but not too tightly. In fact, not tightly at all. Almost as if…well, as if her captor wanted her to escape.

They were tied so loosely that she could move them somewhat. This was what she did, the cheap nylon rope that bound them digging into her flesh but becoming easier to wiggle the more she tried to work her hands free. The left was already beginning to slip out, greased by the perspiration that was flowing freely from her.

She pulled.

She strained.

She twisted.

This was going to work, she knew with a sudden burst of optimism: it was really going to work. *Okay. Keep going.* Yes, she did it the way she did all things in her life, carefully and methodically. She focused her mind, concentrated with every fiber of her being. She wasn't about to get this close and then lose it all in a moment of panic. The rope was tearing into her hand as she worked it in rough half-circles, lubricated by her own sweat. To the left, to the right, worming her hand free. And then she had it. In the darkness, it was pretty much impossible to work the knots that still bound her right hand, but that didn't matter right now.

Both hands free finally, she pressed up against the lid of her box. It lifted about three inches, letting more light in as well as a fall of thin, sandy soil; the dust of which was gagging. She sneezed. She coughed.

She pushed again, using the strength of her knees as well this time. No, the three-inch limit was it. And she soon saw why. The box was bound with rope. A single stand of it, but still bound. If she wanted out, she was going to have to cut that rope, break it, or loosen it somewhat.

Holding the lid up with her knees, she reached out and grasped the rope. It was thin, about the same diameter as a pull rope on a lawn mower, but it was strong. There was no way in hell she was going to snap it. That meant she had to cut it. She thought of trying to tear it strand by strand with her teeth, but there was no way she could get her head down that far. It was impossible in the cramped box.

Think!

There had to be a way. All she had was a hoodie and jeans. Her wallet was in her pocket. She could feel it there. But there was nothing sharp in it. Credit card. Driver's license. Campus ID. Twenty dollars. Nothing of any use. But wait…just…wait. There was something in her back pocket. She could feel it there.

Concentrate.

Again, that was the key. What was in her back pocket? There was a memory associated with it. The mist clouding her recall began to part somewhat. The camping trip. The woods. The fire. Drinking. Laughing. *Drinking wine…we were drinking wine.* She could see them around the fire, passing a large green jug. The wine had a sweet, fruity taste. Not great, but it brought the buzz on just fine. She could see Chloe handing her something and whatever that was, it was still in her back pocket.

She had to find out.

She squirmed and twisted, arching her back painfully until she could squirm a hand behind her and reach her ass. She pushed two fingers into her back pocket and touched the object. Right away she knew what it was and something inside her leapt with joy. She could remember then. *Emery board.* Yes, she had a nasty hangnail. She was trying to stop biting her nails. Chloe was always filing her nails, perfecting their shape. *Here, use this,* she had said. Emma remembered now. Other things were coming back, too. But she didn't have the time to fool around and examine them one by one.

The emery board in hand, she began filing at the thin rope.

It was going to be work. And if she put too much pressure on it and broke it, then she would be in a real world of hurt. It wasn't a file; it wasn't designed for heavy-duty work. She would have to go at it gently. So this was what she did. Holding the lid up with her knees, she worked the emery board back and forth against the rope. At first, it seemed hopeless, but with some effort she sawed a tiny groove into the strands. She kept at it until her hand was so cramped and her knees so sore she had to stop.

She let herself rest for two or three minutes, then she was back at it again, sawing and sawing. She was a quarter of the way through. It was little gain for all her effort, but it was something. Five minutes later, she was nearly halfway through. This got her excited and made her stronger. She kept sawing and sawing until she was two-thirds of the way through the rope, using different parts of the emery board, bringing to bear what edge she had for the best cutting. All the while she kept increasing the pressure of her knees.

The rope was strained tight and the tighter it was, the easier its strands were to cut through. Finally, it gave. Emma let out a gasp of triumph. Sweaty, covered in sand, dusty and coughing, she had done it.

She pushed the lid up and saw bright sunlight that nearly blinded her.

Then something hit the box, snapping the lid down and knocking her back into its depths.

She was stunned for a moment or two, but not so stunned that she could not hear what pressed down on the lid, breathing with a low, guttural sort of sound.

FIVE

Anger was the thing Steph was good at, so she used it. She let all her rage and fury rise to the surface—something she had spent a lot of years trying *not* to do—and power her. The asshole pissing on her from above was what did it. This was all bad enough without the humiliation of someone emptying their fucking bladder on her.

That was it.

That was the catalyst.

She might have dangled there God only knew how long until her arms popped out of joint or she lost her mind or blacked out, but the piss, in its own demeaning way, slapped her across the face and kicked her in the ass, made all the wrath rise bubbling and hot from the center of her being.

She hadn't been this mad in years. Maybe not since Jenna Cheevers stole her boyfriend in 10th grade and she had waited for her at a low boil outside the door to Bio 2. When Jenna came out—pretty and bouncy, blonde and offensively perky—Steph punched her in the face. Then she grabbed her by her luscious flaxen hair, ramming her head into a locker and then smashing it right through the window of a display case where the science fair trophies were stored. Jenna needed thirteen stitches to close her scalp. Steph was expelled, forced through a degrading series of anger management courses, all of which were taught by a vacuous dumb blonde therapist that looked suspiciously like a thirty-something Jenna.

But it was back.

It was really back.

Her hot-blooded animal rage had returned and with such gusto that she felt no pain. Bracing her feet against the sides of the cistern with great dexterity—this time there was no backing off—she pulled and strained with immense pissed-off strength until she freed one of her hands, jumping up and getting it on the rope about four inches above her bound wrist.

Now she had it.

She tore her gag free and breathed in the dank, terrible air of her tomb.

She pulled herself up, discovering footholds between the bricks of the well. She climbed slowly, but she *was* climbing. The grating was closer now. The rage did not leave her. In fact, the closer the grate became, the hotter it burned in her. She was going to do this. The rope was still knotted around her left wrist, but she was grasping the line with it, her free hand pulling her up and up with aide from her feet.

That's when she saw the ladder.

It was rusty and ancient-looking, bolted to the side of the well. It descended only about ten feet, but if she could get on it, then she would be able to push the grate free.

At least, she hoped so.

But in the dim, black mist of her brain, there was no doubt, only the knowledge that she would do this and when she was free, she would reign hell down on whoever pissed on her. It was an insult and it would be answered in—

Blood. I'll have their fucking blood for this.

Her temper blazing like mushrooming solar flares, she kept climbing, pulling and pushing herself up. In the back of her mind where the kind, calm, extremely stable and rational Steph cowered in a corner, it told her in a weak voice that she would never get away with this. It was hopeless to fight because she did not stand a chance. Her captors would not allow it. Under no circumstances would they let her simply climb out of the well. At the last moment, they would kick her back down into that pit of seeping, sewer-smelling water.

Steph ignored the voice.

It was nothing.

It was no one.

She did not give a damn how mature that voice was or how impulsive it thought she was. It was already defeated; she was not. She was fueled by sheer instinct now that took the form of hatred, that all-warming, all-sustaining emotion that could drive you through the worst tempests.

A few more feet.

Don't think! she warned herself. *Act!*

She climbed higher up the rope until she was within five feet of the grate. She could smell the fresh, clean air above mixing with the putrid stench of the well. Sunlight streamed down in smoky beams. The ladder was right there. She reached out her free hand and touched it. Rusty. Filthy. But strong. The question was: would it take her weight? The idea of grabbing hold of it and having it pull away from the wall, sending her plunging down into the blackness below was her greatest fear.

Do it!

She had to.

There was no choice. The rope was tied to the grate. Hanging from it as she was there was no way she could shift the grate with her weight pulling down on it. Sucking in a deep breath, she reached out and grasped the rungs, pulling herself to them and getting her feet on the lowest one. The ladder groaned but it held. If worse came to worse, she was still tied to the rope.

That was something.

As she prepared to move, she heard a sound which nearly made her fall off the ladder: a scream. A real bloodcurdling, agonized cry that rose up to a piercing volume and then faded away. It made her cringe.

What in the Christ was that?

It didn't even sound human, more like a bestial roar of pain and madness.

She listened.

She heard nothing.

No footsteps. Just birds singing.

Go! Quit wasting time!

Sure, but that cry. It was without a doubt one of the most awful things she'd ever heard. The rational Steph was trembling. Her rage began to be replaced by a cold terror that made chills run down her spine. But she knew she couldn't allow it. She got mad again. She thought of being pissed on. And despite all her years of anger management, she began to boil again with the hot-blooded, irrational need for payback. It had gotten her in a lot of trouble through the years, but this time it was going to save her ass.

Though she wanted to race up the ladder, she did not. Rung by rung, she moved slowly, cautiously, being sure of each grip and each foothold. It took her a few minutes to get up to the top. Then, clutching the ladder, she reached out and pushed up on the grate.

It would not budge.

No, goddammit! No! I haven't come this far to be stopped now!

Maybe it had a lock on it. Then again, maybe it was stuck. She pushed again. Nothing. Bracing her legs and using every bit of strength she had, she pushed again. It moved an inch or two, scraping against its concrete flange. This emboldened her. Now she did not just push, she slammed her hand into it. It lifted up. It was heavy, but not too heavy. She could do it and she knew she could do it. She hit it again and again until it popped up, teetered, looking as if it would fall down into the well and take her with it, then it tipped over into the grass.

Steph climbed all the way up, reaching out and finding something like a stump and pulling herself up into the world of light and out of the subterranean hell below.

It was a bad trip. That's what it was. A bad fucking trip. This was what Yvonne thought after she stuck the key in that horrible eye and heard the resulting screech of anger and pain which threatened to crack her skull open with its intensity. But it worked. Whoever that punctured eye belonged to had scampered away at top speed.

And for five minutes, paralyzed with terror, Yvonne did not move. In fact, she found that she *couldn't* move. Her muscles were bunched and tendons strained. It was as if she were encased in concrete.

She shivered.

She wanted to cry.

Something in her had simply given up. She wanted to close her eyes and make it all go away like a bad dream.

Then she heard that voice in her head, the voice of her mother. It sighed. Mom had always begun her sentences with a sigh, particularly when she spoke to Yvonne. *Honey, listen to me. Listen good like you've never listened before. You've got yourself in a real pickle this time. Pretending and retreating into that jumbled rat's nest you call a mind will not get you out of this. You need to face the unpleasant reality of this situation. Someone out there wants to hurt you, to torment you, to maybe even kill you. You need to act. You need to pull up your big girl pants and do something. Nobody can get you out of this one but you.*

Yvonne found herself nodding, as if Mom was right there with her. It was like the time she got caught shoplifting at Justice. Her friends put her up to it, daring her to take that tube of lip gloss. She did and was caught. The manager took Yvonne to her office. She was allowed to call her mother before the police were brought in. And Mom, hearing her daughter's tearful confession over the phone, sighed—of course—and said, *Oh, you stupid, stupid girl. You got yourself into this and now you have to get yourself out of it. I can't help you. Tell them why you did it, how you were put up to it. Tell them the truth.* So Yvonne did and the manager, moved by her sincerity perhaps, let her go. No police. Only a stern warning to stay out of the store and think before she acted.

And all that for a five dollar tube of lip gloss.

Yvonne knew Mom was right though. She had to get herself out of this one any way she could. The keys were still in her hand, the stabbing key held tightly between her second and third fingers. There was something wet and gooey on it now but she refused to think about that.

She pressed the key against the zipper tab and pulled with all her strength. The zipper came down hesitantly. She got it down near her waist and then she went wild with panic, squirming and worming her way free and crawling through wet, leave-covered humus and squishing a puffball beneath her knee.

But she was free.

She was free.

Like a frightened animal, she looked around. There was no one that she could see, no immediate threat. Okay, okay. She waited. Listened. Tensing, she put her mind out there, searching for telltale signs that she was being observed. Satisfied, she stood up. She was in sort of a gully, a hill sloping up before her. It was covered in yellow leaves, a few scraggly-looking trees above. The air was damp and chill. The key was still in her fist, a ready weapon. Behind her there was a small creek and forest beyond. It looked dark and threatening.

Up the hill, dear. See where you are. That's the first thing.

Swallowing dryly, wanting to sip from the creek to soothe her burning throat, she started up the hill. It was slippery. She clawed her way up it on all fours.

She was going to do this.

She was going to make it happen.

See, Mom? I'm not as completely useless as you thought.

But, boy, that was really stretching it. Her mother had never approved of her lifestyle choices, her recreational habits, her lovers, her worldview. Hell, she even disapproved of her major, English Lit. *For godsake, Yvonne, what are you going to do with a degree in that? Why don't you be like your friends?* Yes, why didn't she major in chemical engineering like Emma or nursing like Steph or physical therapy like Chloe? Because she wasn't them and they weren't her. She told her mom she might end up being a great writer or an editor or a teacher. *That's swell, hon, but to make those things happen, you have to have ambition to do more than get stoned, read and watch TV, and do that snapchatting nonsense.* No, her mother did not and could not understand so many things. She was tough and practical, but like a stone, she did not dream.

What in the hell is that?

Yvonne reached the top of the hill, pushing as quietly as she could through scrub brush until she came into an open grassy run hemmed in by tall oak trees. She was cautious, moving silently. Then she saw what was tucked behind one of the trees.

A cage.

It was a fucking cage. The kind they keep monkeys or bears in in old movies. It was about four or five feet tall, not much more than that in width. It looked old, the bars rusty as if it had been out in the elements a long time.

She blinked.

Something was in it.

Don't look, she cautioned herself. *It's part of all this, whatever this is. Part of the sick game you're caught up in. Do not look in it.*

But she had to look because what if one of the girls were in there, held prisoner as she had been held prisoner in the body bag? Ignoring the warning bells ringing silently in her head, Yvonne went over to it. There was a small form, curled up, facing away from her.

A child.

Just a child.

She was certain it was a little boy.

A rank, savage odor came off him as if he had been rolling in the carcasses of animals.

He was filthy and stinking, naked, shivering in the cage. His hair was long and matted, his skin dark with ground-in dirt, streaks of dried blood, numerous scratches and contusions. There were sticks and leaves in his hair.

A feral child?

Was that what he was?

"Are you okay?" Yvonne said because she felt she had to say something, had to inquire as to his health and well-being, even though his state made such a question absurd.

The boy jerked at the sound of her voice as if he had been kicked. He turned, his face mostly obscured by hanging, stringy hair. There was a greasy shine around his mouth as if he had been chewing on meat. His eyes were huge and dark, oddly shiny like those of a dog.

The very sight of him and the way he looked at her, made something flinch inside Yvonne. She wanted to run. The boy's eyes did not blink. He made a whining sound that was, again, more like a dog than a human being.

"Are you okay?" she said again.

It looked as if he was going to smile at her, but instead he offered her a ferine grin of long yellow teeth, black grit packed between them. His lips curled away from them and he made a snarling noise that made her take a fumbling step backwards.

Then he threw himself at the bars, snapping at her like a wild animal, his flesh seeming to ripple.

If he hadn't been caged, she was certain he would have leaped on her and torn her throat open, lapped up the blood that spilled out happily and hungrily like a kitten with a bowl of milk.

He reached out a hand, slashing at her with black ragged nails, growling and hissing.

Yvonne moved away, half-running and half-tripping, seeing then that there were other cages and in each of them a child, boys and girls…but all of them low and coarse like the boy, wild things that growled and gnashed their teeth, glaring at her with yellow eyes.

She ran blindly off into the woods, tripping over stumps and rotting logs, fighting her way forward as branches whipped her face, laying her cheeks open. Then she found a trail. She followed it as it twisted and turned. Another opening in the trees.

Oh Christ, oh God no.

Yvonne came to a stop because there was a woman there, up against a huge tree. She was naked, contused, deep gashes laying open her belly and breasts. Her head was slumped forward, her arms stretched above her head...and that was because her hands were nailed to the tree with spikes driven through the palms. Blood had run down her arms, drying into a crusty film.

Yvonne began to sob. This was madness. None of it could possibly be real.

The woman lifted her head. She smacked blood-crusted lips. *"Run,"* she said in a dry, cracking voice. *"For God sake, run! GET OUT OF HERE! THEY'RE COMING! IT'S ALMOST TIME!"*

Yvonne was propelled forward by her legs, not thinking, just reacting, driven forward by pure instinctive terror.

SEVEN

Chloe nearly had one hand free now. If she could just get it loose she could probably get out of this damn harness they had her tied in. If, if, if. If her captor allowed it. If it was part of his game. If she didn't die from a heart attack because right now her heart was trying to pound its way right out of her ribcage. It was getting hard to breathe like steel bands were encircling her chest.

But it wasn't her heart and she knew it.

She'd lived all her life with her nerves exposed like bare wires. This was the beginning of a panic attack—shortness of breath, profuse sweating, the shakes, dizziness. Yes, it was coming and she knew it. She'd done so good keeping it under check thus far and that was a great accomplishment when you thought about it, because she was a girl who regularly suffered panic attacks. Things like exams and speeding tickets and lost keys could bring one on. But this, the most horrible experience of her life, had not.

But maybe that was going to change.

Please, not now! Not now! she implored herself. *I can't afford the fucking drama right now!*

Yet, she could feel it coming on, the sense that there was no air to breathe, that she was trapped in a confining space that was shrinking away, ebbing with her strength. She had been diagnosed with a panic disorder when she was sixteen after she repeatedly seized up and fainted. Years of CBT—Cognitive Behavioral Therapy—and plenty of Paxil had freed her from anxiety…now this, now a test that was beyond anything her therapists could ever have imagined.

Right now, if she was in a sane and safe place, she would have been reaching for her Effexor, but there were no medications. There was only escalating fear.

Sometimes it's okay to be afraid, she could hear her therapist saying.

But this was not one of those times. For all she knew, the other girls were dead. She was alone. Alone against the big, bad world that had suddenly become much bigger and much badder.

She practiced her breathing exercises, yoga meditations. It eased her discomfort somewhat. She distracted herself as much as possible by trying to work her hand free. She was certain that if she could do that and get herself untied and ungagged, she would feel that much better.

There was something outside the shack.

She could hear it moving through the dry leaves, closer and closer. With a last surge of desperation, she pulled her hand free. It was red and abraded, feeling as if it had been flattened in a vise. She had curled and compressed it for so long to get it out of the noose that held it, that it was painful to open it and stretch her fingers.

But she did it.

With trembling fingers, she pulled the gag from her mouth. It was damp with saliva and fear-sweat.

Whatever was outside the shack was pressing itself up against it now, flattening itself against it like a spider sucking up warmth. She could see its black shape in the spaces between the planks. And worse, she could smell it: a wet dog smell that riled her belly. And it was humming.

A woman.

It's a woman.

It seemed inconceivable, yet she was certain the voice she heard was a woman's voice. The tune it hummed was nonsensical, off-key, more of a groaning noise than music. The melody was simple, childlike, something composed by a disturbed mind. She imagined that a hyena would hum like that as it prepared to dine on the rent carcass of a wildebeest.

Panic cut through her as she picked at the knots at her ankles. At any moment, who and possibly *what* was out there could burst through the door and that's how it would end.

The woman outside kept humming, pressing herself against the planks as if she were trying to hug them. Now she was scratching around the door, clawing at the boards with doglike nails. The shack trembled. Then there was silence...but not for long.

Now the woman must have been down on her hands and knees. She was sniffing around the bottom of the door.

"I know you're in there," she said in a grating tone. "I can smell you."

Chloe nearly cried out. She couldn't take this. She was riding a rollercoaster of anxiety now, sweat running down her back, the hairs on her arms standing on end. Her heart was pounding painfully and her head was spinning. She was going to lose it. The terror was closing in around her, pressing in from all sides. She began to whimper without even being aware that she was doing so.

And then the voice: "Ssshh...you must be quiet. I can help you, but you must be quiet."

Chloe felt her panic lessen by degrees. That voice, that awful voice. It was scraping and raw, everything wrong about it, yet she wanted to believe that its owner truly wanted to help her even though she knew better.

"Open the door and I will help you," the voice said. "You must open it...I cannot. It is not allowed."

Chloe, her mind rioting with lights as she quivered on the edge of blacking out, knew she must not listen to the voice. That she could not trust it. If she did nothing else, she must keep her lips pressed together.

The woman was breathing with a harsh, phlegmatic sound. "Do you hear me, girl? I know the way out! I know the path to freedom! Open the door and I'll help you!"

Chloe wanted her help. God, she wanted nothing more. But she was too petrified to move. All she could do was shake as tears spilled down her cheeks, hot and cold flashes making her sweat and shiver.

Now the woman out there was getting angry—her breathing was faster and she was making a low groaning sound in her throat like an animal. She beat at the door, clawing at it with her fingers. There was an inch of space between the bottom of the door and the earth beneath it. Now gray fingers pushed through, each of them ending in a black, gleaming hook like the talon of a raptor. They tore rents in the splintered wood at the base of the door.

These were not the hands of a woman.

They were the claws of a beast.

What might have happened next, Chloe didn't want to think about. There was a sudden shrieking voice out there. Not the woman, but someone else. Someone pissed-off beyond reason. She heard the woman run off.

The voice boomed: "WHERE ARE YOU, YOU STUPID MOTHERFUCKER? IF I FIND YOU I'LL RIP YOUR FUCKING HEAD OFF! I'LL SHOVE YOUR BALLS DOWN YOUR THROAT!"

There was no doubt who it belonged to: Steph. And in the sort of mood that made people run for cover. When she got like this, things got broken. Doors got kicked in and windows shattered and people lost teeth.

She kept shouting out her threats, getting closer and closer to the shack and for the first time in what seemed hours, Chloe did not feel like she was going to pass out.

EIGHT

Some minutes before Steph went on her tirade, Emma shook inside the box as someone laid on top of the lid. Though they made no sound, she could feel them up there, pressing down with their weight, some sadistic freak who was getting off on her fear and helplessness.

You had to know they weren't going to let you escape. You had to know that.

She was trapped. She was at the mercy of her captor as she had been all along. She did not fight. She did not try to throw him off the box. It felt as if the air had been let out of her. There was no fight left. She did not want to die, but she felt hopeless. Afraid? Yes, but more so without a chance of living through this.

I'll just close my eyes, pray it ends quickly.

But something in her was not satisfied with that. It did not want to give up, it did not want to give in. She rolled it all through her mind and all she could come up with was that maybe she was doing the right thing. Just lying there, playing dead. Maybe that was the best thing under the circumstances.

If they want to get to you, make 'em work for it.

Now the weight on the lid shifted as if her captor was getting bored. Something tapped on the lid. *Tap, tap, tap-tap-tap.* She laid there, waiting. The tapping came again, followed by silence. And then again. It was as if the weirdo was trying to send her Morse code messages. The tapping, for some odd reason, was more terrifying then who or what might have been making it. If they just showed themselves and quit playing games, it would have been easier somehow. The fear of the unknown was devastating.

Now the tapping stopped.

It was replaced by what sounded like knife blades drawn the length of the box lid.

Emma was not given to theatrics—that was solely Chloe's department—but the terror she felt filled her stomach with ice. She shook. Her lips trembled. Hot tears spilled down her cheeks.

Now the clawing stopped.

The lid began to rise.

No more games. The lid was pulled up four and then five inches. In the light she saw a hand. It was reaching for her, not in a threatening way necessarily, but the way you would reach out to take a hand in your own to help or guide someone.

Emma cringed from it.

She feared, more than anything, that she'd see a face. A face she would recognize.

Her guts rolled over like a hedgehog. She could smell her tormentor—a gamey, high stink of rotting pelts and old meat and entombed things, the way she imagined the breath of a corpse-eating jackal might smell. That was bad, but what trumped it was the hand itself. It was gray and seamed, the knuckles knobby and the fingers unnaturally long. Fine hairs grew from them, the nails splintered, dark earth packed under them as if they'd been digging in the soil.

"NO!" she screamed without even thinking, a knee-jerk reaction. "GET AWAY FROM ME! GET THE HELL AWAY FROM ME!"

The hand pulled back as if she had startled its owner. The lid snapped shut. She heard the sound of retreating feet crunching through the leaves. Still mainlining on fear and dread, she hit the lid and popped it open, athletically jumping out at the same moment, rolling in the grass and wet leaves. She saw a shape disappear into the forest and she nearly cried out. It ran low to the ground, wearing the flapping hides of an animal. What bothered her most was what was under them.

She didn't think it was even human.

NINE

The shack.

The goddamned shack.

That's where they're hiding.

Steph, still supercharged with rage, eyed it. It sat on a little weedy knoll. It was not much bigger than an outhouse, thrown together out of knotholed boards and scraps. Leaning precariously to one side, it looked like a good kick could knock it over.

She needed a weapon, a stick or a rock, something she could hit with. Something hard. She found nothing and her impatience got the better of her; she charged the shack, shouting obscenities. Even though a voice in her head told her she should run as fast and far away as she could, she ignored it. Her anger demanded vengeance and she was going to get it, one way or another.

She grabbed the flimsy door, noticing that its hinges were not even metal but leather, and as she did so she heard a voice from inside call her name.

She threw the door open.

It was Chloe.

She was on the dirt floor, trying to untie knots that roped her left hand behind her and to her ankles.

"Steph!" she said.

Steph was glad to see her, yet part of her was unsatisfied. It wanted the shithead that pissed on her. She wanted to beat his face and kick his head until his brains spilled out in warm gray jelly. She breathed in and out, slowly calming.

"They got you, too," she said, dropping to her knees and fumbling with the knots. It didn't take her long.

"What is this?" Chloe wanted to know. "How did we get here?"

"We were taken here."

"By who?"

"I don't know and we don't have time to fuck about figuring it out. C'mon."

Steph pulled her to her feet and Chloe collapsed against her. After being tied so long she had trouble getting her feet beneath her. Finally, unsteadily, she stood there. She was gasping, complaining about the pins-and-needles in her feet.

"Just let me get some blood into them."

"We don't have time," Steph said a bit more harshly than she'd intended. "We weren't brought here for no reason. Someone out there is fucking with us and when they've had their fill, they're going to kill us."

"Oh God," Chloe said, sobbing, wiping tears from her face and leaving dirty streaks across her cheeks.

"We have to go," Steph said. "We don't have time for this."

"I'm scared! I can't help it!"

She was shaking and moaning and Steph wanted to slap her. She guessed she'd always wanted to slap Chloe but it wasn't something civilized people did. All these years she'd held back, now the urge was getting the better of her. She knew damn well that if she was going to survive this ordeal, she'd need to channel every bit of anger inside her. And what she couldn't have was this little pink princess slowing her down.

"Where are the others? Where are Emma and Yvonne?" Chloe asked in a teary voice. "Are they dead? Did someone hurt them? Are they going to do the same to us? Will we—"

Crack.

Steph slapped her across the face and she couldn't remember the last time anything had felt that good.

"You hit me!"

"Yeah, I did. And I'll hit you again if you don't straighten up. We don't have time for your little girl drama. I'm not here to hug you and hold your fucking hand and make it all better. We're in the shit. This is a survival situation so act like a big fucking girl already."

Chloe glared at her, her eyes darting from her head. Beneath the grime of her face, her cheeks went hot and red. "You…you fucking cunt," she snapped.

"That's it. Get mad. Get really mad."

Chloe came at her, swinging, trying to slap her and landing a couple good ones before Steph shoved her down.

"Now you're pissed-off," Steph said. "Stay good and pissed-off and maybe we'll survive this nightmare."

Chloe climbed slowly to her feet. If her cramped legs and feet were bothering her now, you wouldn't have known it. Her eyes were hot and intense, her lips pulled into a cruel bloodless line. With the dirt streaked on her face, she looked like a Cheyenne warrior ready for battle, ready to take blood and die on her own if necessary.

Steph nodded, looking out the door. "Let's go," she said.

TEN

Yvonne ran wildly through the woods for a long time, completely out of her head with not only terror but an escalating sense of unreality. She'd watched horror movies like anyone else, but you didn't live one. They weren't real. They just couldn't be real. Still she ran, crashing through the brush, feeling that she was being hunted as branches whipped across her face and hands, laying her raw, making her blood run.

Finally, she tripped over a log and went face-first into some wet leaves, her knees finding mud that soaked through her jeans.

Then she began to sob.

She was not a crier. She could fold up just as fast as the next person, but it took some doing. She had never felt so small, so inconsequential, so totally helpless before. Regardless of what life threw at you, there were always options. Society existed as a support system to help you through the rough spots. But this…this was beyond accepted norms, beyond rationale.

"I'm dead," she whimpered under her breath. "I'm fucking dead."

Now, now, dear, she heard her mother's voice say. *You've come to a very nasty crossroads in your life, haven't you? A place where no one can help you. You must stand up and face the horror of this situation. Above all, you must not be a victim. If you act like a victim, you'll have a victim's mindset and you will die. You don't want to die, do you?*

Yvonne lifted her head up by precious inches. No, she did not want to die. But she also didn't think she was strong enough to fight what she sensed all around her—a vicious, sadistic enemy that would keep toying with her, tormenting her until she had nothing left. Then it would come in for the kill.

Better reason to get moving, isn't it?

Yes, it was the best of all reasons. Yvonne stood, slowly rising to her feet. Her back protested, her muscles ached. She felt like she had been beaten down and then kicked into submission. She had never been a physical sort of person, in that she was the last to volunteer for any sort of hard work or anything that involved the least amount of effort. Yet, for all her laziness and sloth, she breezed through gym in high school and discovered to her surprise that when she had to take mandatory PT classes at the U—she'd taken Aquatics because swimming always came easy to her and fencing because it was offbeat—she was naturally athletic and graceful. Nobody was more amazed than she.

She tried to keep that in mind now. If she was to make it through this, it would mean a lot of running and a lot of stamina.

Move.

She gave herself a good stretch as she'd been trained in Aquatics and began. She cut through a close-packed thicket, burst through the other side, jogged down a hill, slipping and sliding, crossed a boggy hollow of sucking mud, leapfrogging from fallen tree to fallen tree, then climbed back up into the forest again.

This was better. She was moving. It made her feel stronger, capable. She came to a stream, following it as it twisted and turned through the woods, glad that it was September and not July or the mosquitoes would have sucked her dry. Circling around a large, mossy oak, she stopped, smelling something nasty. Cautiously, she cut across a meadow, the yellow grasses coming up to her hips, and into a dark stand of trees beyond.

The smell had not dissipated, it had increased.

She was not moving away from the smell as she had hoped; she was getting closer to it. The trees around her—big elms and maples, she thought—had choked off the undergrowth. The ground was hilly with lots of sudden dips and cuts, a carpet of dead leaves several inches thick going to mulch. The air was damp, yet fresh, slowly being canceled out by the stink of decay.

Moving through the trees, going from trunk to trunk, touching them as if she needed to be convinced of their physical reality, the stench grew stronger and stronger until it was practically gagging. Another twenty feet and her guts were squirming, feeling as if they were filled with greasy, gray water.

There's something dead just ahead, her mom's voice told her. *If you keep moving in this direction, you're going to see exactly what it is.*

Yvonne didn't want that. She would circle back, made a wide swath around this area. She began backing away, ears attuned and body tense. Then she heard the worst possible sound coming from a shadowy tangle off to her left: a low, terrible growling. The sound of a mad dog whose jaws were white with foam. It paralyzed her. She stood there, trembling, not sure if she should move at all.

Swallowing, she moved back again and the growling got louder. It was not just off to the left now, but behind her from three or four different locations.

A pack, she thought with rising horror. *A pack of animals hunting me.*

She was frozen in place again. They would attack at any second. Sweat ran down her spine, her entire body bunched like a straining muscle. She did not dare move. She would do nothing to incite them. She waited as her respiration grew faster and faster, her heart pumping madly with the realization that she was about to become prey. Childhood and instinctual terrors ran riot in her. The former filled her mind with images of fanged monsters that crouched in the dark like terrible, grinning goblins; the latter told her she must run, she must flee, make for the highest tree she could find and climb up it.

She took two steps back and the growling increased, echoing through the woods. A rising clamor of snarling and yapping and something like the braying laughter of hyenas.

She moved forward two, then three steps in the direction she had originally been going and the noise became a steady murmur. She was being directed forward. The beasts wanted her to go toward that wet, putrid stink. They demanded it.

Yvonne did as they wanted. There was nothing she could do. *They're driving you like prey, pushing you into a killing zone.* Yes, she was certain of it. The farther she went, the more the growling sounds faded away. She knew they were still there. They were patient, inhumanly patient. She was frightened, yet she did not feel as helpless as she had earlier. She was oddly attuned to her environment, channeling eons of ancestral memory.

She moved between a couple trees and there was a clearing. The stink of death and putrescence was revolting now. Bile inched up the back of her throat. She had found the source of that hot, rank smell.

The carcass of deer.

It was splayed in the leaves, torn open, flies rising in clouds from it like cartoon balloons. Its meaty, repulsive fetor filling her nostrils, she could plainly see long white maggots writhing happily in its flesh.

But that wasn't all she saw.

Gathered around it like piglets crowding their mother's offered teats were a group of children. They were filthy things. All of them naked and dirt-caked, their matted hair hanging in their long faces. They were the children from the cages set loose to hunt and kill. As she watched, they tore strips and globs of meat from the carcass, shoving it into their grease-stained mouths. Some of them had their faces right inside the deer, others snapping and barking at each other like scavengers feasting on the remains of a lion's kill.

Yvonne stood there, shaking from head to toe. In her mind, she could hear the voice of the woman that had been nailed to the tree. *Run! For Godsake run!* The children kept feeding, stuffing themselves with carrion. One of them—a girl, she thought, or something like one—raised her gore-streaked face from her meal, ripping out a red shank of fly-flecked meat and holding it out to Yvonne, willing to share her bounty.

Yvonne took a step back, swooning with terror.

The girl made a guttural growling noise in her throat. Her ears were pointed, laid against her skull, her eyes red as fresh arterial blood. Her mouth was pushing out into a vulpine snout, lips pulling back from yellow teeth that had grown long and sharp in this terrible, primeval wilderness.

Yvonne screamed because the horror inside her needed to be vented. It came out in a high, shrilling noise that reverberated through the woods, working up the pack that trailed her into a cacophony of roaring and howling.

Yvonne, nearly out of her mind, broke into a run, seeking the trees and the shelter they offered.

ELEVEN

Emma followed a stream that meandered like a crawling snake. It was only about four feet across, less than three feet deep in most places with a bottom of loose stones. Now and again it disappeared beneath hanging foliage, gathering in deep shadowy pools. Ten minutes after she'd run from the place where she'd been trapped in the box, she came across it. She washed the dirt from her face and sipped from it, regardless of what toxins might be in it.

Now she followed it.

She had no idea where she was, but she now remembered how she had gotten there.

It was a set-up. Right from the beginning it was a set-up.

There was no doubt of that. The four of them had been at Cut Creek Campground, a place Steph had picked at random. It was twenty miles from the main highway, reached via a snaking collection of gravel and dirt roads.

"Now we're in the boonies," she had said, taking in the primal forests pushing in from all sides. "We can raise all the hell we want."

That's how it had started. The thing that had been purged (or blocked) from her memories was the guy who'd come literally out of nowhere, walking out of the woods with a green jug. It was like something from a fantasy. He was tall and good-looking, a hot woodsman from the cover of an erotic romance paperback—tanned and cut, wearing tight jeans and a loose red-and-black checked flannel shirt, a shaggy mane of black hair falling to his shoulders, his eyes so dark, so intense, he melted anything he looked at...particularly four lonely college girls.

"Hey, girls, how's it going? I'm from just up the road," he told them. "Saw you guys pull in, thought I'd bring you a little something." He hefted the green jug. "Dandelion wine. I make it myself."

"Um...I don't know," Chloe had said, displaying natural, healthy paranoia.

The others had had no such hesitation. Had their guest been some bucktoothed shitkicker it might have been different, but, good God, this guy looked like he'd stepped from a magazine ad. They took the wine. He told them to enjoy it. Then he was gone. The wine was sweet and fruity with a slightly sour, but not unpleasant aftertaste. It was good. Unusual. And spiked, obviously. The last thing Emma remembered was passing around the jug.

She had always prided herself on being smart, on making good choices, but she'd been taken in just as easily as the others by a pretty face. The level of her naiveté disgusted her.

Screw it. No time for recriminations; that would be for later in a safer environment. She kept following the stream. She was a city girl. What she knew about wilderness survival she'd gleaned from TV shows and books. She'd grown up downstate in Livonia. Down there, the only woods you saw were in city parks, carefully cultivated and landscaped. Nothing like this, nothing so...primeval. That was the word that kept occurring to her, because nothing else so perfectly encapsulated what she was seeing and worse, what she was feeling. Following the stream seemed like the logical course to her because sooner or later she would find a bridge and road which would lead her out of there.

Or deeper into it, a pessimistic voice taunted her.

She moved uneasily through thick underbrush, stepping in muddy holes and squeezing through stands of saplings. She circled a low, boggy area, found the high ground and then found the man.

He was sitting on a stump, a grizzled old guy with a heavy beard, a time-weathered face, eyes that were distant yet kind. He looked up at her, not with surprise, but almost a sort of sadness. He wore an olive drab army coat. There was a shotgun across his knees, a pack at his feet, a pile of dead birds nearby.

"Heard you coming," he said, chewing on what looked like a stick of jerky. "I suppose anyone within five miles would have."

Emma ran over to him. "I need help. My friends…oh God, I don't even know if they're alive! We were camping…we were drugged…I woke up in a box. Please, please, just get me out of here!"

He motioned to the dead birds. "I was grouse hunting. Season don't open for a few weeks, but, hell, I grew up in these woods. I've lived in them my entire life. I take the liberty."

"I need to get out of here! Please…you must have a car or a truck. Something. Just get me the hell out of here! We need to get the police, we need…"

Emma's voice trailed off because she realized that nothing she had said was even sinking in. He was oblivious, completely oblivious.

"All these years, all these many years," he said in a morose tone as he studied the poplars and their yellow leaves. Now and again, one of them would drift earthward. "Been going on a long time, that's for sure. I always stay out of it. My old man knew about it as I suspect his father did. But we always keep out of it. Healthier that way."

Emma stood there, feeling very weak in her knees. Hope drained from her. She did not go into theatrics or make any demands of one human being to another. It was not her way.

"So you're going to let them hunt me down and kill me?"

He sighed, running a hand across his face. There was a shine to his nose as if he did this a lot. "They're only active this one night. All these woods and you have stumbled onto me, leaving your blood trail for them to follow."

Emma didn't understand until she looked at the cuts on her hands, felt the others on her face. From sticks and poking branches. Yes, she had bled. Not a lot, but enough for her enemies to follow.

"They'll sniff it out like dogs," the old man said. "Better 'n dogs, I hear."

"You're not going to help me, are you?"

He studied the ground, his face drawn long, his gray eyes filled with tragedy. "I can't. If I do, they'll hunt me down. They'll take me, make an example of me. And what they'll do to my old woman all alone there in the cabin by Copper Springs…no, I can't let that happen. They know I'm here. But they leave me alone and I stay out of their business."

"I'm twenty-one years old," Emma said, as if that would make a difference. "Remember that. Because you killed me and I hope to God you see my face everyday of your miserable fucking life. I hope it haunts you...*murderer.*"

"I'm sorry," he said.

"You're a coward. That's all you are."

"Yes, you're probably right," he admitted, taking up the shotgun and leveling it at her. "Now get...they'll be coming and I don't want your scent mingling with mine. Not tonight. Not on Blooding Night."

Her eyes filled with tears, her overall impression of the human race deeper in the cellar than usual, she ran flat out into the trees. The old man said they'd be coming, but she knew that. She could feel it as easily as she felt her oncoming death.

TWELVE

"It was the wine," Steph said as she walked at Chloe's side. "It was drugged. That guy put something in it. He's part of this. We were doped up so we could be brought out here and used for sport. He probably took our phones, too."

"I told you guys there was something funny about all that," Chloe said, vindicated in her appraisal of a hot woodsman bearing gifts. "But you took the bottle. You didn't even ask any questions."

She was right, Steph knew. She wanted to argue the point, but Chloe was definitely right. She was the only one who'd been outwardly suspicious. Maybe they all were, at their core, but they never admitted it.

"He was a hottie," Steph said as if that explained it all and excused their lack of discretion.

"So what? What does that matter?"

"If you don't know the answer to that, I can't help you."

Chloe rolled her eyes, convinced, Steph knew, that they were all idiots by being taken in by looks. As it turned out, she was right. Yet, it aggravated Steph. Earlier, she had slapped Chloe to cancel out the drama and give her an edge. And it felt good. Too good. She'd wanted to keep slapping her. But violent behavior like that was negative and she knew it. Nothing good could come of it. You had to accept that, make it part of your internal wiring. Responding aggressively was natural to her but anger management training through the years had taught her to be assertive yet diplomatic. You needed to suppress your anger, convert it, redirect it positively.

She knew this. She knew it very well and yet...and yet, out here it seemed perfectly natural to externalize your aggression. Nature understood violence because nature was basically violent: kill or be killed.

Steph was trying hard to cultivate her hostility and somehow temper it with rational thinking. But Chloe pushed her to the limit. She wanted to beat her down and leave her.

Leave her for the wolves.

She didn't know why she should have thought that...but it felt right. Being out here in this primitive wilderness was beginning to feel right, too. As if she belonged here. Her entire life she'd felt like something was missing and she'd searched for what it was...and now she feared she had found it.

The call of the wild, she thought.

That was also the name of the Jack London book that she read six times in high school. The others were good, *White Fang* especially, but *The Call of the Wild* summed it up for her, how you could only deny your true nature for so long.

"What are you doing?" Chloe asked, standing under a spruce. "We have to go!"

Steph hadn't realized she'd stopped. She stood there feeling the afternoon sunlight in her face, smelling the fresh air, the pine boughs overhead and the humus underfoot. It was wonderful. The former made her want to climb high into the trees and the latter made her think of the black earth beneath her feet, the decomposing leaves and plant material becoming rich, dark soil that would nourish seedlings and saplings until they grew into dense bushes and high trees beneath which prey animals would forage as the eyes of predators watched from forest deeps.

Chloe came over and shook her. "Would you please knock it off? We need to get out of these woods. Find a road, something, anything."

Steph nodded. There was simply no way to explain to someone like Chloe what she was feeling. How vital the forest made her feel, how she breathed deeper and her heart beat stronger and her blood flowed purer. How clear her eyesight was, how focused was her mind, and how attuned her senses were to everything around her. There was no way to put it into words.

Chloe was looking afraid. She studied Steph. She studied the encroaching thickets. She studied the heavy green undergrowth filling the hollows. She looked disturbed. More so, she looked like some weak, soft-bodied prey animal waiting for a blood baptismal of teeth and pain as its carcass was rent by claws.

Steph giggled, picturing Chloe's body at her feet sinking in a pool of blood, disemboweled, split, skinned, the good white meat at her throat and thighs gnawed away in gaping cavities.

"I think something's out there," Chloe said, her nerves humming like telephone wires. So loudly that Steph could almost hear them.

"Yes, I think you're right," Steph admitted.

Eyes, she thought, knowing it was true. *Eyes are watching us the way a leopard watches a herd of gazelle, seeking the straggler, the weak one, the easy kill. But that won't be me. It'll never be me.*

What was out there could have attacked at any time, but there was no thrill in that, no sport. The stalking was a big part of the sheer joy of running your prey to ground. For as you stalked, you studied and as you studied you learned so that you knew your prey's strengths and limitations, how it would react in a given situation. And when you sprang upon them, you could do it in the most efficient manner, wasting no unnecessary effort and taking no true risks.

Chloe was hugging herself and Steph nearly laughed because she'd never met anyone who was so clearly out of their element. "What are we gonna do?" she asked with the petulant voice of a little girl frightened of the dark. "C'mon, Steph, what can we do?"

"We keep moving," Steph told her and bravely—at least in Chloe's mind—moved off into the forest as if she was perfectly at ease with it and what it contained.

Chloe came after her, walking at her side, so close they were practically conjoined. She pressed herself tightly to Steph, reaching out and taking her hand. Steph nearly shoved her away...then thought better of it. Chloe was such a weak, helpless little thing, her soft white underbelly always exposed, always made ready for the big bad wolves of this world. She gripped her hand tightly, realizing for not the first time that there were so many things she despised about her and so little she actually liked.

But I'll keep her with me and when the shit hits the fan, I'll throw her to the wolves and make my escape.

She couldn't believe she was thinking that way or why she was making so many allusions to wolves. There was something unsettling to that and enormously exciting.

Still feeling eyes on them, Steph found what appeared to be an old game trail. It cut through the spruce and oaks, zigzagging down a forested hill and through a stand of mossy hemlock trees. She led Chloe on, crunching through yellow leaves as spears of misty sunlight pierced the interwoven canopy of branches high overhead, bathing the woods in a yellow, fey light like something from a fairy tale. The boles around them seemed to glow like golden pillars. The path meandered around them, back and forth, back and forth, cutting through small clearings and thickets where the shadows grew long and deadly.

Chloe was holding her hand tighter than ever and Steph was lost in the primitive beauty of the wilderness, feeling as if she really was in a fairy tale, following a path to grandmother's house, evil wolves watching her progress, slavering for the bundle she carried which was Chloe.

She nearly giggled, sensing the voracious appetites of the creatures that stalked them so patiently. And it was at that moment that something shifted in her, changed, realigned itself and she thought, *You're out of your mind. This is hell. Why are you acting like this is a good thing? Something you want, not a tragedy but an opportunity?* But she didn't know. She really didn't know. All her life she'd had to keep the beast within at bay, stifling her natural aggression and competitiveness, but out here, it all seemed not only unnecessary but a hindrance—

Chloe gasped as a low howling came from somewhere behind them. It started in one location and then soon, it seemed to be coming from everywhere, an echoing primordial baying that filled the world and made it shudder. It sounded enraged, hysterical even, before settling down into a low, rumbling cacophony of growling and yapping and squealing, the sound of beasts fighting and nipping at one another…or things that were almost beasts.

Steph began to feel threatened, then scared, and the more scared she became, the more angry she got. But even her inborn rage could not cancel out what she was feeling in her belly or make the flesh at her spine stop creeping. She expected that at any moment, yellow-eyed shaggy shapes would leap from behind the trees and tear them apart.

And if she was frightened by the sound of the pack—and, yes, she knew *pack* was the proper word here—then Chloe was petrified. She had stopped moving. Her hand in Steph's own was suddenly ice-cold, her breathing coming in short, sharp rasps, her eyes glassy and fixed. She was stiff as a post and Steph had to exert herself to get her hand free of Chloe's iron grip.

"Chloe," Steph said with alarm in her voice. "Chloe…Chloe! Look at me!" But she was incapable of focusing on anything; she stared off into dead-end space. Steph snapped her fingers in her face. "Chloe, goddamnit! You can't do this now! We don't have time for it!"

Since nothing else seemed to work and Steph was getting agitated, she did what came naturally—she slapped Chloe across the face and then slapped her again. It was the second one that did it. Chloe began screaming with incredible volume, her head whipping back and forth. She shivered. She jerked. Gouts of white foam gushed between her lips.

"Chloe!" Steph cried.

She took hold of her and Chloe went wild in her arms, convulsing with rapid muscular contractions, limbs flopping, head lashing from shoulder to shoulder, teeth clenched, an oily warm perspiration making her shirt cling to her like a damp rag.

She was out of it.

She was having some weird fear-induced seizure, some sort of scary neurological episode. Suddenly overcome with something she did not know she possessed (maternal instinct), Steph clutched Chloe to her and held her tightly with all her strength as she screamed and screamed. Gradually, they subsided as did the convulsions and Chloe went limp in her arms, her breathing rapid but shallow, her mouth opening and closing but no words coming out.

Steph held her for some time and it was like clutching a rag doll. After a time, her eyes opened and she blinked a few times.

"Did I lose it?" she asked.

Steph nearly burst out laughing as dire as the situation was. "Yeah, you did."

Chloe pulled away from her, shaking her head. "Of all times." She looked around. "Have you seen them yet?"

"Who?"

"The wolves."

Steph shook her head. She wasn't going to put into words what she was thinking. *No, I haven't seen them, Chloe, but I've felt them inside me, getting bolder and…hungry.*

THIRTEEN

When Yvonne blundered out of the woods and saw the cabin sitting there in the open, grassy field, she was certain she was hallucinating. Blinking her eyes, she leaned against a birch tree, her fingers nervously picking at a strip of loose bark.

"A cabin," she said as if the idea of such a thing out in the woods had never occurred to her.

Though she saw no vehicles around, it didn't look abandoned. Wood was carefully chopped and piled against one side. The logs looked freshly varnished. A finger of smoke rose from the stacked chimney, painting a gray smear against the late afternoon sky.

She saw no danger or threat (for the first time in her life that was an imperative), so she walked down there and knocked at the door as if she was selling Girl Scout cookies...something she'd done when she was nine and failed miserably at.

She kept knocking, wondering in the back of her mind if an old witch would invite her inside for cakes and candy. The door was opened nearly immediately by a stout little middle-aged woman with beautiful gray eyes and a kind face.

"Hello," she said, more than a little surprised. "I didn't expect anyone way out here...good God, what happened to you?"

Ah, now there was the question and Yvonne didn't even know if she had the strength to tell her tale. The woman took her arm and led her inside where it was cozy and comfortable, a fire burning in a fieldstone hearth. The floor was gleaming hardwood, wildlife prints on the walls, a stuffed twelve-point buck mounted over the fireplace.

This is exactly what I'd expect a cabin in the woods to look like, Yvonne thought.

The furniture was rustic and looked homemade, pine log tables and chairs, a sofa upholstered in some sort of downy fur. It was unbelievably comfortable. She felt her eyes growing heavy as she sank into it. The only thing that made them open back up was a sudden rank, invasive animal stink that was there and then gone. It went so fast, she was not sure if she had smelled it at all.

Probably not.

The kindly woman said her name was Elizabeth and brought Yvonne a steaming cup of tea. "Now tell me what happened to you," she said.

The thing was, Yvonne found that she just didn't have the strength. As she rolled it all over in her mind again and again, sorting through the lurid and impossible bits, she began to wonder if she was out of her head. Yet, for all that, she began to talk, sipping her tea, and telling Elizabeth all there was to tell, from the campground and the dude with the dandelion wine to waking up in the bag, the eye she stabbed and the children in cages, and, ultimately, the pack that had hunted her and the creatures eating the dead deer.

She finished by saying, "I need to get out of here. I need to leave. I need to get to the police so they can look for my friends." She realized she was sobbing and tried to stop, but that only made it worse. A few minutes later, she had gotten it under control. "I know how all this sounds, how crazy it seems…but it happened, it really happened."

"Of course it did," Elizabeth said. "I can see by your state that you've been through hell."

There was something condescending in her tone that Yvonne did not like. Elizabeth was humoring her. Yvonne knew the tone well because it was the very one her mother had used so often. It grated on her nerves, it irritated her. It was the tone you reserved for children.

"I don't know what those things were," she said, "but they weren't children."

"Definitely not children as you know them," Elizabeth said in that same patronizing tone.

That was one way of putting it. Far in the back of her mind, Yvonne knew, there was a name for what she had seen and it had been the first thing she had thought of. An old name for an old superstition, one that she would have laughed at a week ago but did not find funny in the least now. She kept pushing it back farther in her mind, but it was still there in red lettering, fluttering like a banner: *Werewolves.* Nobody believed in such things anymore, of course, unless they were delusional or taking mass amounts of medication. It was a silly seam of folklore that had been reinvented and often watered down by movie producers and writers chasing a cheap buck. It was full moons and silver bullets and Lon Chaney, shitty paranormal romances and laughable TV series about beast men with perfect six-packs. If there had been any fear associated with the genre, mass exploitation had turned it into a bad joke.

Now Yvonne wasn't above believing in weird shit. Maybe it was the drugs and maybe it was her own fertile imagination working overtime, but she'd been crazy obsessed with more than one fringe subject. UFOs had occupied more than a little of her teenage years after she was certain she saw a triangular-shaped object in the sky on her 15th birthday. After that little episode, she'd read every UFO book she could get her hands on, haunted UFO chat rooms, and became convinced that alien entities were harvesting human genetic material. Finally, her mother had asked what it was all about. Yvonne told her and in great detail. *Listen, my dear,* Mom said in that patient and very condescending tone of hers. *What if they are harvesting us? What are we going to do about it? I don't know anyone that's been abducted and neither do you. If such things are real, we're probably better off not knowing about them, don't you think?* But Yvonne didn't think that at all. She didn't lose her passion for extraterrestrial visitation until she'd posted her story about the triangular-shaped object on a UFO board and was told that it was only a military reconnaissance drone. *Amateur, unless you've been anally-probed, you know nothing.* So she'd moved on. Government conspiracies. Chemtrails. Bigfoot. In the end, even her excitable imagination had to admit there was really no hard evidence, just a lot of twice-told tales and crappy video.

But werewolves...that was something else. That was even hard for a conspiracist to swallow.

"There are stories about such things," Elizabeth told her.

"Yeah, I've seen the movies," Yvonne admitted, leaving out the fact that she'd seen *Ginger Snaps* like a dozen times when she was fourteen, certain the movie had been made specifically for her and was trying to tell her something.

Elizabeth smiled. "I'm sure you have. But you don't really believe in such things, do you?"

"Of course not."

"Good. Glad to hear it."

"I just want to get out of here."

"Of course you do and I can point you in the right direction." Elizabeth nodded her head. "Yes, I most certainly can do that, you poor thing. I can show you the path to follow, the proper path, the one that will bring you to your ultimate destiny."

"I…um, okay, what do you mean?"

Elizabeth laughed. "I think you know exactly what I mean."

Yvonne smelled that rank odor again; this time it was sharp and nauseating. It brought tears to her eyes.

"It's a wild smell, isn't it?" Elizabeth said. "The smell of the hunt, the kill, the spilling of blood. It's the most natural smell in our world. Don't pretend it doesn't excite you. It's in all of us, buried deep down in our animal brains—the lust to kill, to run wild with the pack, to roam through moonlit glens as we hunt down our chosen prey."

Yvonne realized, of course, the mistake she had made because sweet, kindly Elizabeth was in reality a fucked-up, deranged monster herself.

There was a sudden scratching at the door as if a favored dog wanted to come in.

"It's open," Elizabeth said, her teeth grown long. They gleamed like icicles in the firelight.

Yvonne was trembling. A voice in the back of her mind wanted to beg, *please, please oh dear God please don't let it in.* But it was too late, far too late. The door swung open and a child stepped through the door. It was a girl. The very one that had offered Yvonne the rancid meat of the deer. She stood there, a feral and monstrous thing, her naked body filthy with ingrained dirt, stained with blood. Greasy strands of hair hung in her face. Her eyes were bright and silvery, reflective like those of a beast in a cave. She grinned with sharp teeth, her wolfish hunger on full display. Drool ran down her chin.

"She's here," Elizabeth said, her voice dropping several octaves until it was nearly the bark of a dog. "The one you seek. The one you've chosen."

Yvonne was dizzy, her mind spinning like a top. She squeezed her eyes shut before she fell over and when she opened them, the cozy cabin was gone.

It was replaced by something like the den of a beast.

There was urine-smelling hay on the dirt floor, beds of dried grasses, ribs and bones and stripped joints scattered about.

Elizabeth was there, but she was a low, awful thing that picked at a rent animal carcass. Surrounding her were wild children, their vulpine faces smeared with grease, bodies caked with dried blood. Globs of yellow marrow dripped from their lips. They watched Yvonne with narrowed glassy eyes, snouts wrinkling back to expose sharp upper and lower canines stained pink.

Yvonne knew there was no way out. She was the fly in the spider's web. It was only a matter of milking her dry now or, dividing her amongst the hungry, saliva-juicing mouths around her.

"Yvonne," Elizabeth said, now a horror from a fairy story, something that sharpened its teeth on the delicate bones of children, "you need to run. You must learn to hide, to cover your scent, to fight when needed and flee whenever possible. This is the only way you'll survive this night and reach your goal. Do you understand me, child? Tonight is Blooding Night and only the smartest and strongest can survive."

Yvonne sprinted out the door and into the warm sunlight and fresh air. She saw the tree line and made for it, her instinct telling her that she had a chance there. She could hear the wolves in the cabin howling and yipping with excitement.

When she reached the cover of the trees, she looked back. Though she could still hear the baying of the pack, the cabin was gone. There was only a pile of rubble and green-rotted timbers. The chimney still stood, moss-grown and ready to fall.

And from the forest, she heard the howling of the pack.

FOURTEEN

Emma was young. Her entire life lay open before her like a book with blank pages waiting to be written on. And, yet, she was going to die. For reasons that were unclear and a logic that was insane and convoluted, her life was going to end. That was the reality of her situation.

She had not really lived, certainly never really loved. There had been Ryan Glass in high school whom she had convinced herself was her one true love. But that was just a crush. Now that she was several years removed from it, she knew it had been nothing but teenage melodrama—despite the fact that when he'd broken up with her, she refused to eat for nearly a week and cried her eyes out every day. There had been guys at the U. Some of them meant something to her; most didn't. But she had never truly been in love. The kind of love she'd always wanted to be in where you could see nothing else but your lover's face and your heart beat with theirs and you lived together inside the same skin. Real fairy tale, Harlequin romance, movie love.

She would never know that and all because Steph wanted to go camping and chose that awful spot at Cut Creek where they had been seduced by the hot guy with the dandelion wine. And it had been a seduction. He knew exactly what he was doing and how to do it—they were girls enamored by his looks and it was easy to play and exploit stupid girls.

And if I ever see you again, Pretty Boy, I'll cut your fucking liver out, she thought because it made her feel better.

This was where Emma found herself twenty minutes after she left the old man with the shotgun, that pathetic piss-poor excuse that would not help her.

He knows. He knows all about this and what it is, what it means, but he's too afraid to intervene and put a stop to it.

Emma stumbled along, running and leaping, walking and often tripping over her own feet. She had lost the stream. There was only the repetitious landscape of green hills and thickets and trees, trees, trees. How could there be so many goddamn trees? There seemed to be no end to them.

In her mind, she kept hearing the old man's voice. *I don't want your scent mingling with mine. Not tonight. Not on Blooding Night.*

Blooding night. What did that mean? What was it? And maybe she was better off not knowing. She would find out soon enough because Blooding Night would be tonight and already the shadows were growing long.

She badly wanted to stop and rest but she didn't dare because someone was following her. They were making no attempt at stealth, perhaps following her blood trail as the old man warned.

Several times she'd found herself slowing, her limbs tired and achy, her throat dry, her head pounding. She wanted to sit down. But she couldn't. She had to keep moving. That was the imperative that pushed her along: move or die. So she kept moving and as she moved, she pictured her own death again and again, how her corpse would look splayed on the ground— gutted, crushed, and broken, gore leaking out of her eyes and mouth, her insides scattered in the leaves. It was a disturbing image and it kept her moving.

She moved up a knoll, pulling herself to the top with the aid of saplings. When she was up there, she paused, breathing, every inch of exposed skin cut and bruised and abraded. She peered behind her. She thought for a moment she could see a gray form back there darting in and out of the shadows of the big trees. Maybe. Maybe not.

Think, she told herself. *Not about Blooding Night or what any of this is about but of how you can use your brain. If a stalker is indeed following your blood trail, scenting you, then you need to do something about it.*

Yes, that made perfect sense.

So she ran.

She plunged down the hill and entered the tree line, moving in circles and darting about in a circuitous route, not truly sure if that would do the trick of confusing her stalker or simply confusing herself all the more. She came to a swamp. Normally she would have went around it, but now she plunged straight through, the black stagnant water above her knees. Then she climbed out halfway across, leapfrogging from one log to the next. Several times there was dry ground, but she avoided it because that's exactly what they would expect her to do. In her panic, like any hunted animal, she would take the most direct, easiest course.

There were fallen trees everywhere. She climbed up one, leaped onto another and then another, jumped up and grabbed the limb of a standing cedar and swung herself over the water and into the grass.

Follow that, motherfucker.

Again she ran until the woods became very thick with secondary growth and knotted underbrush. Instead of trying to fight her way through it, she crawled on her belly beneath it and made better time. In the process, she became covered in black mud.

After a time she found the stream again. She stepped into it and stood there, despite how freezing the water was. She followed it, stepping on large loose stones in its bed. Several times, she stepped out, walked a dozen feet into the woods, then backtracked into the stream and kept going. It would take an expert to follow a trail like that. Finally, when her feet and lower legs were so damn numb she could no longer feel them, she pulled herself up onto a large rock whose surface was warm from the sun.

She climbed a short, easily-navigable cliff face until she was up high enough to see what was behind and below her. For five minutes she stood like that, unmoving, clinging to a scraggly beech tree.

She saw nothing, she heard nothing.

There was a depression filled with rainwater. She caught a glimpse of herself, a distorted reflection. Streaked with mud, wet leaves clinging to her, she was nicely camouflaged. It was like wearing a dirty crust. She found a birch limb that had fallen from above, maybe in a storm. It was four feet long, stout as a baseball bat. It felt good in her hands. She knew she could crack a skull with it.

Now you're getting it, a voice said from some dark, secret place in her mind. *Now you're learning. Now you know what this is about: survival.*

She moved on, feeling more confident but growing tense as the shadows lengthened. It was bad enough out here in the daylight, let alone the night.

Her thirst had been slaked by drinking from the stream, but she was hungry. When was the last time she had eaten? Oh, that hot dog while they sat around the fire at the Cut Creek campsite, getting more and more fucked up as they passed the jug of dandelion wine around and around.

Shelter. Food.

Her instinct and her rational mind agreed on this. She needed both. She couldn't keep on going hour after hour. Her stamina was impressive, but years of cross-country running will do that for you.

As she jogged up a dry stream bed, she saw something in the woods off to her right. There was so much underbrush she could not be sure what it was. A shape. Not a tree. Something else. Something hanging there as if it wanted her to find it.

And that's a reason to stay away.

But she was not going to stay away. Her curiosity demanded that she investigate it. It was insane and she knew it. She was being stalked, hunted, yet something in her demanded that she see what this was. It didn't seem to be a choice but an imperative.

Getting to it, meant fighting through a stand of leafless saplings whose intertwined twigs scraped and scratched at her. When she got through, she stopped. It was some sort of animal hanging five feet off the ground from a stout tree limb by a length of rope. She wasn't sure what it was—it was simply hairy and large. It had four dangling limbs and a massive head.

Not an animal, but the pelt of an animal.

Maybe it had been hung there to dry. Was that what people did? Dried them in the sun? An odor came off it that was sharp and foul, almost savage. It made something inside her clench like a fist. It was disturbing. But what disturbed her even more, as she got closer, studying the thick dark fur, was that it appeared to be the pelt of some gigantic wolf or wild dog. In life, she believed that it would have stood taller than she on its hind legs. The pads of which were huge, much larger and broader than her hands, ending in curled yellow claws that must have been three inches long.

The musky, pungent smell of the thing nearly drove her off, but then she saw its forepaws…except they were not paws at all, but something like hands. The fingers were skeletal and knobby, longer than human fingers with long black claws.

Emma shook her head because such a thing just wasn't possible—wolves didn't have human-like paws. It was insane. It was storybook shit. This pelt was some kind of fake, a scarecrow left to mess with her head. But that smell, that awful gamey wild stink—

So they sprayed it with mink piss or something.

But she did not believe that. She circled around so she could see its head. It was huge and shaggy, large pointed ears rising from it like horns. The jaws were agape, the teeth impossibly sharp, the upper and lower canines looked as if they could have opened her throat with a single slash.

She stood there, shaking. A small and frightened voice whispered in her skull. *Not the pelt of an ordinary wolf, no, no, no, this is from a—*

But she refused to let the thought run its course because she did not want to hear that word, that terrible word that teased at the shadowy edges of her mind. Part of her wanted to scream and another wanted to laugh.

Her instinct, which was very alive and very close to the surface, told her that this was no fake, no sideshow mermaid. Its smell gave it away. Nothing faked smelled like that. It was an old, old odor, a scent her instinct recognized from antiquity and cringed at.

Yet, her reasoning brain refused to accept what she was thinking. The hide could not possibly be real. Summoning up her courage, she reached out shaking fingers and touched it. The hair was not soft, but spiky and sharp like the bristles of a hog. The feel of it sickened her, yet some perverse urge wanted her to touch it again. She pressed her hand against it and jerked it away quickly. It was warm.

Alive, it's still alive.

No, no, no, such a thing was impossible. It could no more be in the real world than the creature itself. She pressed her hand against it again, her stomach heaving at the feel of it. Yes, it was warm, the hairs prickly and rough. The grotesque head seemed to grin at her, grim and mirthless. She was certain that if she put her hand in its jaws, it would bite her.

She yanked her hand back.

Now it was swaying back and forth and a perfectly hysterical terror rolled through her, her mind spinning on its axis. It was alive and it wanted her to touch it, to pet it, to run her fingers through its fur which was something she would not do. But even as she thought that, she found she was doing it and not with just one hand but both. They seemed to sink into the pelt, luxuriating in its feel, the amazing tactile sensations it offered which made her hands feel not just warm but incredibly strong. Her flesh tingled up to her elbows. And as much as she did not want to touch it, did not like the feel of it and warned herself against it; she wanted it … she wanted to push her entire body into it. She wanted every inch of her to feel as good as her hands did, tingling with desire.

Now the gaping eye sockets seemed to be watching her and she imagined her own eyes looking out of them and seeing the world as she had never seen it before—not something to be feared, but something to be tamed, something to be brought under her claws and teeth and mastered.

"Stop this," she told herself in the weakest of voices.

I don't want this! I don't want any of this!

But now her entire upper body was in contact with the pelt, magnetized to it, drawn into it, her cheek pressed against the bristling blood-smelling fur. She was drowning in horror, the blood being squeezed out of her heart, and she wanted to pull herself away from the evil, living hide before it engulfed her the way a corpuscle engulfs a disease germ, taking her and converting her, making her part of it.

The desire to pull it over herself and run wild was overwhelming. As terrified as she was, she wanted to wear it, to feel it against her naked skin, to answer the primordial song that called her into a misty never-never land of black forests and blood rituals.

Yes, she must wear it.

No, it must wear *her.* That was it, that was the key, that was what it wanted. *Put me on so I can wear you and cover your flesh with my pelt. Dance in my skin. It is a joining, a communion, a rite whose origins are primeval, much older than the church you knew as a child. We shall become one with nature.* Emma screamed and pulled herself away, the vacancy in her brain exploding suddenly with burning red light and planting her on her ass as sweat ran from every pore and she shivered and convulsed, the shadow of the wolf pelt covering her like the dark wing of some immense predatory bird.

She crawled away, frightened and sobbing as the world danced around her with phantasmagorical shapes that reached out for her with claws and grinned with bloodstained mouths, growling and panting.

When she was able to stand again, she ran, fearing the pelt was coming for her, to claim her as its own.

FIFTEEN

Yvonne was a wounded deer that ran swiftly if not exactly silently. The pack was closing in from several directions, running her to ground, running her to death. They pushed her this way and that with their ferocity, confusing her, mixing her up.

It was a game to them.

Sport.

Like red-coated British aristocrats of yore driving foxes to their deaths, they were going to run her until she was exhausted, until there was no fight left in her, then they would kill her. That's it. That's all there was now. She was in an utterly hopeless situation and there was nothing she could do about it. And there was no time to think her way out of it.

So she ran and ran and ran.

There was no way to throw them. They were following her scent and possibly her blood trail. Her face and hands and arms were slashed open and she was probably leaving blood on leaves and twigs and tree trunks. Every time she paused to catch her breath or think, they got more excited, their howls echoing through the forest, rising higher and higher into squeals of joy.

She moved through thick undergrowth, climbing rocks and scaling deadfalls, forever moving forward (or back and around for all she knew). She burst through a barrier of nettles that scratched her cheeks and knuckles. She found a clearing and raced across it, up a hill and into the trees again, the same trees she was certain she'd seen a dozen times. She tripped on a root and rolled back down the other side, through dried leaves and wet humus beneath. Pulling herself up, she ran again until she came to a weird forest of black, denuded trees. They were like pillars and posts, rising up straight and fallen over and leaning against one another, their branches interweaved and woven together, blocking out the sunlight. The forest floor was hilly, covered in mounds of leaves with soft mud beneath.

As she clung to the bole of a tree, wiping sweat from her eyes, she could hear her mother's voice again. *So this is your plan, dear? To let those beasts run you until you're dead? Hmm. Doesn't seem like much of a plan to me. Even off the top of my head I can come up with something better. But you're a big girl and I know how you hate my interference.* Listening to the pack and their shrilling cries, Yvonne began to sob.

"Please tell me," she whimpered. "Oh God, please somebody help me."

My God, Yvonne, think! Think! What's chasing you are basically dogs, wolves. They'll find you and they'll tear you to pieces. So get off the ground. Climb a tree. It's a start, isn't it?

It was.

Yvonne chastised herself for not thinking of it. Her instinct had been trying to lead her in that direction for some time but she just wouldn't pay attention. It was the first thing a primate did when it was threatened—it climbed trees. And it was the first thing she needed to do. Get up somewhere high.

She ran again, stumbling through the black forest, noticing with unease that there were no trees she could climb. They were all tall, the lowest branches on them ten and fifteen feet off the ground. There was no way she could snake her way up them.

The pack was louder; they definitely had her scent. They were barking like bloodhounds now, getting excited, yipping and squealing and making a sort of staccato woofing that sounded very much like human laughter. They would have her soon and they knew it. The very idea was thrilling to them. She could hear them crawling through the underbrush, not silently stalking but making plenty of noise—tearing through bushes, clawing through the leaves, sticks cracking beneath their feet—and it was all part of the game.

They had her.

They knew it.

Now they would drive her mad with terror, force her lips to the teat of primal fear and make her suck, make her drink the milk of atavistic horror and fill herself with it, driving her insane, tenderizing her meat with glandular secretions of adrenaline and hormones as her neurotransmitters jacked up.

They could smell her fright and it excited them. This was the climax to the stalking, the hunt, the foreplay right before the orgasm of blood ritual.

And Yvonne was playing right into their hands as they knew she would. The behavior of prey was predictable but that made it no less satisfying to the pack.

Out of fear and anger and frustration for being in that situation, she screamed with everything she had. It was loud. It filled the forest. It echoed through hollows and dark glens. It was terror, yes, and anguish, but it was also fury and aggression. It stopped the pack, made them hesitate, quieted them down momentarily as something in her knew it would.

Then she ran, breaking free of the black forest and climbing one wooded hill after another, charging forward with incredible speed and agility. She splashed through a stream, wading up to her hips until she found a clear opening on the other side. Drenched and shivering, she was up and out. She stumbled through a stand of picker bushes and darted through a field of high yellow grass. Into the tree line again, she stopped behind a dead oak that was gnarled and lightning blasted. She panted, gripping the tree so she did not go right over.

The pack were on the hunt again, howling and barking. The stream would throw them for a time until they caught her scent. She breathed. Her throat was so dry it felt like it might crack. The amazing thing was she did not feel nearly as freaked out as she should have. In fact, she felt emotionless. She was scared, her senses heightened, everything activated and aware to a startling degree, but she was not losing it.

Of course not, dear, her mother said. *You are running on pure instinct now. There is nothing else in your tank.*

Time to move.

She wiped the sweat off her face and her hand came away with dirt and blood. This would have offended her yesterday or the day before, but now it seemed to mean nothing. Her feet were soaking wet, leaves stuck to her, grime and grit clinging to her, and she stank like a drained swamp, but it seemed to mean nothing.

Off she went, through the trees. For five, maybe ten minutes, then there was a small clearing surrounded by tangled thickets. And a body. It was the body of a man. He was hanging upside down from a tree limb, rope around his ankles, his head three feet off the ground. He was naked, blood-crusted, bruised as if he had been beaten into submission and maybe he had.

Yvonne moved closer to him, the sound of the pack distant now. She did not know what to do. He was dead, he must be dead. In the back of her mind, real world logic and response was still active—*get the police, get someone, this has to be reported*—but it faded away quickly enough. There was nothing she could do. Her plotting, scheming animal mind told her that maybe the body would give the pack something to do while she got away. She began to back away from it, then she heard Mom's voice again.

You need to be practical now, Yvonne. Beyond practical. If you want to survive, you need to use every trick in the book that your ancestors used and perfected. Listen to your instinct. It knows.

The imaginary voice was there, then gone.

Yvonne cocked her head, thinking, feeling, trying to get in touch with the race memory in her genes. Impulses. Yes, it came as impulses. The impulse told her to touch the corpse. Not just touch it, but handle it. Get its scent on her. That would confuse the hell out of the pack. If their sense of smell was so powerful, so canine, then turn it against them because every strength belies a weakness.

She stepped up to the corpse, feeling sick in her gut. She would have nightmares of this the rest of her life. Just days ago, she was a different person living a different life. Her biggest concerns were whether she could afford pizza on Friday night or she would be eating Ramen noodles and Campbell's soup all week again like all the other starving students at the U. She worried that people would find out she blew her chemistry professor for a passing grade or they would learn about that night Steph and she had been wasted on Vodka and out of their heads on Spice and had got it on. And she worried about Chloe finding out that she had been raiding her stash of Effexor and Paxil because the world just made sense when you were mellowed on antidepressants.

Now that was gone. All the weak-kneed, fear-induced, lazy, devious shit she'd did on a daily basis no longer seemed to matter.

There was only here.

There was only now.

So she went over to the hanging corpse and placed her hands against the cool skin of his back. The first touch was revolting, then not so bad. He wasn't rotting or anything, just cool to the touch. And he was muscular, very toned. That somehow made it easier.

She ran her hands up and down his back, gathering his scent and brushing it over her body. He had a tattoo of a bulldog on his shoulder, underneath it there were four letters: USMC. A Marine. Dude was a Marine. Yes, yes, of course, he was. She saw that he wore a single hiking boot. He was the boyfriend or the husband of that woman that was nailed to the tree. Out hiking. Enjoying the day. She kept touching him, then rubbing herself. Particularly her breasts. She was excited and she knew it. It was wrong and it was sick, but she was turned on. She kept doing it even though she knew there was a nasty word for getting your kicks with corpses.

Like that time you got laid in the cemetery by Tony Shields. Remember how excited you were because it was like you were being watched, you were performing for the dead? Tony wasn't much, but like they said location, location, location, that's what made you cum your brains out again and again.

It was hard to say what might have happened next, but as she touched him and then touched herself, her nipples standing hard against her T-shirt, her breath coming fast, he opened his eyes.

SIXTEEN

In seconds, the beast would have them. Chloe could not only hear it growling in the spreading darkness of the forest as sundown edged ever closer, but she could smell it—the primal, blood-smell of its hide and the hot meat-smell of its breath. It had been getting closer for some time, shadowing them, inching in the way a lion will as it separates stragglers from the herd and targets them for death. They were prey. That's what it came down to. In a civilized world, they were human beings, lords and masters of nature, but out here just meat walking on two legs, seasoned sweetly by the rich food they ate on a daily basis.

Steph had picked up a stick and brandished it in one hand as they walked side by side, Chloe clinging to her like a little girl on a spooky Halloween night walk with her father. It was a stout oak limb. Maybe it made her feel better but Chloe doubted it would do much against what was coming for them.

You can't fight these things, she thought as she began to feel wobbly and disconnected as she often did right before a major panic attack. *Not with sticks. Maybe guns, but not sticks. All you'll do is piss it off.*

"Steph—"

"Quiet," Steph said. "Just keep quiet."

The beast was closer, its stink pungent in the air, musky and offensive. The smell of not only its hide and breath, but its glandular secretions.

Chloe knew she was going to fold up. It was a given. In many ways, this whole awful business had made her stronger, stronger than she had been before, but she still wasn't strong enough to stand up to the beast. Her stomach felt like it was full of wet leaves, her guts hanging in loose writhing coils. Sweat ran down her face and a debilitating headache began to squeeze her brain. White dots popped before her eyes. She was dizzy, the world wavering around her. It took great concentration to keep walking, to place one foot in front of the other and get her muscles to move, to flex, to carry her forward. And each time they did, her head spun as if the oxygen-rich blood was being leeched from it.

Steph could feel it happening to her and she tightened her grip on her hand until she was practically crushing it. "Don't you dare," she whispered with an angry tone. "Don't you even think of fucking falling apart on me. You do and I'll leave you for that fucking thing."

Chloe wanted to cry. She wanted to curl up into a soft white blob of dough and sob. She needed Steph as she'd never needed anyone before and that bitch was threatening to abandon her.

Are you surprised? There's always been something cold and hard about her.

No, Chloe was not surprised. She had read once that if you really wanted to know someone in depth, get to know them under desperate circumstances, get to know them in a survival situation. Then you'll know what makes them tick. The strong became weak and the weak become valiant.

She was weak. She knew she was weak. It took every ounce of strength and resilience she had to keep walking on spongy legs when all she wanted to do was fold up and cover her head as the world threatened to squash her with its weight.

Now there was a growling noise off to their left behind a row of bushes. The beast was that close. God, its smell was sickening and getting stronger all the time. Did it really smell that bad, Chloe wondered, or was it some biochemical thing, a weapon it used to reduce its prey to shriveling, beaten dogs?

She couldn't take it anymore.

She fell to the ground, weak and dizzy, vomit spraying out of her mouth that was mostly just sour-smelling bile because she had not eaten anything in many, many hours now.

Steph swore at her.

And the beast jumped out of the brush not ten feet away.

Chloe screamed.

Steph just stared at it, gape-mouthed as if in awe of its size and its savagery. It was huge, monstrous, a shaggy child-eating horror from a storybook. It was hunched over, but stood at least six or seven feet in height. Thick, tangled steel-gray hair grew over its body, its chest massive, its hind paws very much like those of a dog, but its forepaws like huge hands, the fingers long, the nails like surgical scalpels. It breathed with a low rumbling that was somewhere between growling and ordinary respiration.

It was a killer.

It was a werewolf.

That was self-evident, of course, but it kept running through the reels of Chloe's mind, *it's a werewolf, a werewolf, a werewolf,* as the sight and smell of it awakened misty atavistic memories whose associations made her cringe in terror and shake uncontrollably.

Steph had her oak club in both fists now and her stance was much like that of a batter waiting for a pitch.

"Well, c'mon then, you sonofabitch," she said in a pissed-off voice. "Come and get me."

And for not the first time, Chloe was amazed at her bravado and her stupidity. You did not dare a thing like this to kill you anymore than you dared a shark to bite you or a rattlesnake to sink its fangs into you. It reveled in death. It fed upon human flesh. It ripped people open, gored and gashed them, then rolled in their blood and entrails. It was an ogre that hung the skins of men in its den and fed on the soft white meat of infants. You did not taunt such a thing.

It cocked its massive head, as if it was trying to understand the stupid, stupid woman that challenged it with a stick of wood. It made garbled noises that were not growls but nearly human words. It watched Steph with cruel yellow eyes, its gaping fangs on full threat display. Its claws scraped against the palms of its hands as it clenched and unclenched its fists. The fur of its snout was frozen in spikes and barbs, stiff with dried blood and curds of animal fat.

Chloe screamed again because it seemed there was little else she could do. She let go with a high-pitched, screeching wail that was horror movie perfect. It was practically hypersonic. So loud, so sharp, that the werewolf flinched, its ears twitching. It did not like the sound or perhaps the pitch of it. Either way, it angered it and maybe even hurt it.

It growled.

Then roared with enormous volume, its jaws wide, the inside of its mouth pink as bubble gum.

"GET OUT OF HERE!" Steph shouted. "GET OUT OF HERE OR I'LL SPLIT YOUR FUCKING HEAD OPEN!"

As she said this, advancing a foot or two, the werewolf seemed confused. It cocked its head again, its jutting triangular ears twitching rapidly. It made that garbled imitation of speech again and a stabbing motion with one extended finger.

Chloe found that she was perplexed. Was it trying to communicate with her? Is that what this was about? But, no, it wasn't trying to communicate with her…it was giving an order.

Now another beast, not nearly so large, charged from the brush, closing the space between it and Steph in two or three bounds, snarling, claws extended for the kill. It moved so fast, it was nearly a blur. Chloe saw the yellow claws, the yawning red mouth and canine fangs streaking at her.

It was fast, but Steph was ready for it.

As it jumped at her, she swung her club and connected with its head as its claws slashed her across the cheek. The club landed with devastating impact. The creature yelped as it was knocked aside and down.

But no more had it been incapacitated when another beast charged. Steph brought the club around, but not fast enough. It hit her, knocking her down, its claws laying open her scalp. She let out a cry and punched its muzzle repeatedly as its red maw opened inches above her face, ready for the kill.

Again, that bravado. Blood running down her forehead and cheeks, she grabbed the beast by the throat, holding it with everything she had. "Run!" she cried. *"Chloe! Get the hell out of here!"*

Chloe found her feet and raced away, behind her the beast—the one that seemed to be in charge, the alpha male—brayed with guttural laughter that echoed through the woods.

SEVENTEEN

The wilderness turned against her.

Emma did not know the precise moment it happened because it was gradual, but it was almost as if nature had decided she did not belong there and it was going to make an example of her. It was going to punish her for turning against the natural order of things, the way it wanted to punish all her kind who had left the forest and fields for the cities then thought (in their arrogance) that they had some right to return for amusement and recreation on the weekends.

She had been doing so good, too.

Things had been working for her and she had entertained some silly notion that she just might survive this.

Then it went to shit.

It started with little things—tripping over roots, sinking up to her knees in muck holes—and then it got progressively worse as she slipped on wet leaves and tumbled down a hill, smacking her head on a shelf of rock and seeing stars. She tried vainly to climb a wooded ridge, slipping and sliding, finally making it to the top only to grab hold of a dead tree for leverage and bringing the entire thing down with a mighty crash that must have been heard for miles.

If the pack didn't know where she was by that point, then they just weren't listening.

After her experience with the wolf pelt (she preferred to think of it this way), she had fled in terror, wondering if she had imagined it all and knowing that she hadn't. That thing that made her keep going, faster and faster.

Slow down, she told herself. *Think. Reason this out.*

But there was no reason and no logic that would explain the pelt. It was unnatural and—she gasped inwardly—possibly even supernatural, a word she despised because it made her feel like some ignorant peasant.

She started moving again, studying the terrain ahead and the position of the sun in the sky, knowing it would be dark in an hour or so and worrying what she would do then. She made sure of every step, avoiding logs and sticks that might crack loudly and give away her location. There was another stream, maybe just the same one, and when she tried to cross it, she sank up to her knees in the muck and had to fight her way out.

No good, no good.

She followed it, hoping it might spill into a river, but it kept going on and on as the shadows grew longer. Another hill ahead, green and grassy, a plateau atop with high trees. A vantage point. She moved up it as quickly as possible. When she reached the top, she hid amongst the trees and watched below for any sign of movement, any hint that her stalker or stalkers were still out there, closing in.

After ten minutes, she was convinced she was alone. She was not entirely sure if that made her feel better or worse.

She moved along the ridge line, studying the landscape around her, desperately seeking a road and finding none. Nothing. Not a cabin. Not a trail. Nothing but forest, green hills and scrub, thickets and heavy timber, a few finger-like projections of bare rock, a small clearing or two.

She thought: *And to think my ancestors lived in places like this. Forests without end, primeval wildernesses unbroken by cities, fighting, struggling day by day, year by year, ages upon ages. No wonder people like to clear-cut forests and kill animals and carry guns—it's the inborn fear of having to return to that godawful existence they left behind. It must be broken, all ties cut, kept at bay at all costs.*

It was a bad thing and it must be kept in the past.

All bad things must be kept in the past.

She was daydreaming now, the exhaustion getting the better of her. Hunger. Deprivation. The knowledge that she was being hunted. Not a human being. Just a prey animal. A bag of meat and blood, a side of beef ready for rendering and carving.

Wanting to cry and knowing she didn't dare weaken, she shook uncontrollably.

There was no sign whatsoever of who or what was after her, but that did not mean they weren't there. Things like them would be very good at stealth, at camouflage, at sneaking up on their kills. Even though she could not see them or hear them, she was still unnerved. The forest itself was unsettling, scary, a hunting ground of primal terror. She wanted to call for help, to bring someone to her. Someone who could get her out of there. But there was no help save that which she gave herself. She had been independent most of her life, even as a child, and she had prided herself on the fact, but she no longer wanted that. She wanted someone to take care of her, to watch over her, to lead her out of this place.

God, if I only had my phone.

But it had been taken from her. And there was probably no service out here anyway.

Probably? She nearly laughed out loud at that.

"Get moving," she whispered to herself. "Keep going until you find a road. There has to be one somewhere."

Standing atop the plateau, she plotted her course. No sense in rushing headlong in flight. No, she needed to have some idea of where she was going, an objective, otherwise she might wander in circles for days.

There were a series of hollows below and beyond them another ridge capped by birch trees. That was her objective. And when she got there, she would choose another. Line-of-sight navigation: it kept you moving in a fairly straight line.

Okay.

She moved down the face of the hill, careful of loose stones that would put her on her ass and rotting logs that would trip her up. A hawk cried out overhead and a rabbit broke for cover. At the bottom there was a huge blowdown of dead trees tangled in a rampart of trunks and limbs and upended roots.

Now she had to be careful, very careful.

She began climbing over the trees, placing her feet very carefully so they did not slip on loose bark. She did not need a twisted ankle now or to get impaled by a sharp branch. It took her about twenty minutes to get through it all. She had done very well and was impressed with herself. She came to the first hollow and stepped down the grassy slope into it.

And promptly went on her ass.

There was slick clay beneath the leaves and her foot skidded. For about five seconds, she surfed on one foot, then down she went, rolling and bashing into stumps and saplings, nearly knocking herself out. But the final indignity was when she came to a rest and what she came to a rest *in.*

She let out a cry of disgust when she fell into the carcass of what appeared to be a wild pig. It was soft and spongy, her arms sinking right into it and releasing a mucid, green stench of decomposition. She rolled away, gagging and vomiting out a thin, watery bile until her throat ached as if it had been scraped by forks.

She tried to wipe the gore off in the leaves but they only stuck to her along with dirt and pine twigs. The carcass had literally exploded with decay when she hit it, casting rotten meat and bones in all directions. She crawled through it, still gagging, still convulsing with dry heaves.

The stink of it was now her smell: it was not only on her arms, but soaked through her jeans, the putrescent juice saturating her hoodie and splashed into her face and hair.

Whimpering, revolted to her core, she crawled away, trembling and stinking like carrion.

There she paused.

Its smell is on you. It's all over you.

The idea was repugnant, but at the same time good in that she was no longer hungry and her own scent was now masked by the smell of the pig.

She climbed to her feet, crossing the hollows and making for the birch trees on the ridge, leaving a perfectly ghastly trail of stink behind her.

EIGHTEEN

Out of the fog of delirium there came a moment of clarity for Yvonne. When the hanging man opened his eyes, she suddenly became aware of what she was doing—standing there, under a tree, stroking a body and stroking herself—and the revulsion that rose up in her nearly put her on her knees. She had been channeling the voice of instinct and somehow she had gotten lost in it. Lost? Hell, she had submerged, sunk with a trace.

"Help me," the man said.

Yvonne, shocked, disgusted, her stomach rising up and filling her throat, backed away.

"Please…"

Yvonne uttered a weak sound in her throat that was somewhere between a laugh and a moan. The man had been dead and now he was not dead. She shook her head from side to side. Everything was confused, unreal.

"Help me."

Yes, he had only been unconscious, but still her flesh crawled. She did not think she could touch him again without feeling repulsed right to her core…by him *and* by herself. The very idea made her stomach rise, filling her throat.

"Please," the man said. "Please…cut me down…please…"

Yvonne didn't know what to do. The right thing, of course, was to help him, but her instinct (which did not understand ethics and morals), didn't care about such things. It was alive inside her head, whispering in her ears.

What is it you think you're doing? it asked her. *Why are you standing here? Why are you hesitating? The pack is moving in! You picked up his scent, you've gotten it all over you, now use that to good effect—run, run, run! Save your skin!*

She waited for some rebuttal from the calm, practical voice of her mother, but there was nothing but a low hum between her ears: her reasoning brain on low idle.

The man kept saying something, but she was miles away, oblivious to his words. What she *did* hear was the enthusiastic yelping of the pack as they closed in. It was at once harsh and bestial, the sound of savagery and appetite…yet, there was something nearly musical about it, a choir from hell singing its primeval ballad of the hunt.

In her mind, she began to picture them like twisted little elves with long gray teeth that hopped merrily through the underbrush.

"Please!" the man cried. *"They're getting closer! Untie me! Cut me free! For god's sake, woman, don't let me die like this!"*

But it was too late.

The window for helping him had closed. She heard movement in the thicket off to the left. There was something in there, something hiding in the shadows of the brush. She wondered with a hot jolt of terror how long it had been there. It was shaggy and streaked with mud, leaves clinging to it. It brought a wild, evil smell with it.

"Oh God," the man whimpered, swinging from side to side as he tried to wriggle free.

The creature in the thicket let out a low growl and now she could see its sharp, glistening teeth.

You could have helped him, Yvonne heard her mother say. *Just for once in your dreary, selfish little life, you could have done the right thing without me kicking you in the pants to get you moving in the right direction. But it's too late now. They're going to eat him and they're going to make you watch. And by the time it's over, they might even eat you.*

The pack had gone silent now and that's because they were surrounding the clearing, pushing silently through the underbrush. Yvonne began to sob and she did not seem to be able to help herself—it was as if she had been lost in a dream, a self-deluding dream of escape, and now she was awake.

They were stepping from the thickets now, not just one or two but seven then eight, finally at least a dozen. None of them were adults; they were feral children like the ones in the cages. They watched her with bright yellow eyes set in blood-red sockets, their naked bodies covered with a fuzzy down of fur. They gnashed their teeth and scratched playfully at the earth with their claws.

One stepped forward, a shaggy girl with a full mane of yellow fur down her back, a blunt snout pulling back to reveal exaggerated canines. Gouts of drool hung from her jaws. She made a growling, garbled sort of sound that was nearly speech.

Yvonne was ringed in by them and at any moment, she would die. She stood there defiantly, not daring to enrage them. Horror spiraled inside of her and she wondered if they could smell it. They watched her, yipping and woofing to one another, their faces changing quickly from children to those of beasts, most caught somewhere in-between. Several of them were spattered with blood, another had what looked like a strip of pink meat hanging from its jaws.

It was a nightmare, an absolute nightmare.

And then it got worse.

There was a sound of underbrush being knocked aside and Yvonne felt a shadow fall over her that was freezing and black. Whatever it was stood just behind her breathing hot, rancid breath down the back of her neck. She refused to turn. Let it kill her. Let it scatter her guts to the four winds. She would not turn. She did not want to look upon it.

Then something hit her in the back of the head, planting her face-first to the ground. Trembling, her breath coming in short, sharp gasps, she still did not look. The very idea made her eyeballs seem to crawl in their sockets. She dragged herself a few feet like a road-struck dog, but there was nowhere to go; they were all around her. Another had come and they wanted her to see it, to drink in its form. Her terror was delicious to them—they wanted to savor it.

They would not be denied.

"Please…oh, please, just let me go," she heard her voice say, knowing they never would. The note of pleading in her voice was very much like that of the hanging man, fueled by stark, hopeless dread.

Raising her head slowly from the ground, dirt on her lips and pine needles stuck to her face, Yvonne looked up at what had stepped from the covert of the dark and secret woods. Dear God. It was a monster. That was it. There was no getting around that word—this creature was giant, muscles rippling beneath its shaggy pelt—a great wolf in the upright form of a man. It grinned down at her with huge teeth bursting from a lupine snout, its eyes yellow as urine, bright and demonic and filled with a hunger that could never be satisfied.

She whimpered at the sight of it, her belly filled with slimy, warm mud.

The beast stepped forward until one of its hairy, broad hind pads was nearly touching her nose. She could smell its feral stink, feel the heat of what dangled between its legs.

It threw back its grotesque head and shook with snarling, triumphant laughter. Its human-like hands opened and closed, the claws scraping against the palms like ten penny nails.

The arrival of the beast had the wolf children worked up into an absolute froth. They snapped at each other, nipped and clawed and growled. They hopped about on all fours, rubbing their asses against each other in some primal display of good cheer. One of them jumped onto Yvonne's back and bit playfully at her left ear. When she twitched, it licked the back of her neck as if it was trying to calm her.

But she was beyond calming, light years and galaxies away from such a thing. The muscles in her body trembled, her mind whirling around in her head with a cold, mindless horror.

Hot drool dripped onto her neck.

She did not whimper now; something in her had shut down, overwhelmed and broken from a deadly dose of terror. She felt like a frightened rabbit trapped in a cage of bone. She could not escape. The very idea was ludicrous. She was going to die and something in her accepted the fact that she was meat offered at the feet of this dark, rapacious lord of the aboriginal forest.

The beast let out a horrendous, rattling roar and she waited for it to tear her into pieces, but its hunger was not directed at her but at the hanging man. She saw teeth flash like knife blades. So many of them.

The hanging man screamed as the beast hit him like a shark striking a slab of meat, its claws flensing him open and its slavering jaws gutting him in a spray of blood. The beast pulled back, its snout red and dripping.

This was not for him—the hanging man was a pretty gewgaw for the wolf children to amuse themselves with. A diversion. A new tasty toy to get their blood up.

Howling with unbridled excitement, they raced in a circle around him, leaping over each other, jumping and rolling…then they attacked. Their playfulness turned to ferocity as they batted the hanging man with their claws, making him swing back and forth and round and around. His blood gushed and splattered, becoming a fine mist like perfume from an atomizer. Writhing in agony, he made a screaming noise that became a wet gurgling as his mouth filled with hot red wine.

Yvonne tried to block out his cries by pressing her hands over her ears. She squeezed her eyes shut. It did no good—the beast seized her by the back of the neck in one hot, oily paw and yanked her to her feet. He held her like a limp Raggedy Ann doll, making her watch. This was entertainment, high theater.

She must see this.

She must witness this.

She must understand how quickly man becomes meat.

Suspended a foot off the ground, she fought with a momentary, foolish surge of bravado, kicking and squirming. She tore at the gnarled fist that gripped her throat, trying to free herself from the knobby, leather-skinned, blood-blistered fingers that squeezed so tightly that she nearly blacked out. No good. They held her that much tighter. And, worse, the beast reached down with another clawed hand and clutched her between the legs, one long scabby finger pressing up between her thighs and exerting an unpleasant pressure as if to tell her that, yes, if she did not cooperate, there were other ways to discipline her.

The wolf children leaped and vaulted, their claws slashing the hanging man and their teeth puncturing him, ripping out his flesh in globs and strips and bloody shanks until he was a writhing, red-dripping thing divorced of skin, well-bitten and well-chewed, a beef carcass hanging in a slaughterhouse that had been worked with knives and meat saws.

Yvonne did not move.

The beast wanted her to watch, so she watched, her mind sucked into itself, a black and shriveled prune. It did not function as such and neither did she. She was dead, she was empty, she was a sack of laundry and nothing more.

Meanwhile, the children kept at the man. He was a human piñata swinging back and forth, challenging them with his motion as a bell on a string challenges a kitten. So they went after him with fury, shearing him open and yanking his stuffing out, pulling loops of entrails in opposite directions in a grisly game of tug-of-war until all his goodies spilled to the ground for hungry mouths.

By then, he was nearly dead. Nothing but hanging meat—inert, juicy, well-marbled and succulent, as incapable of fighting back against their attention as a steak was against the knife and fork that cut it.

The children bit into his head, one of them finally getting his or her jaws around it and cracking it open to get at the warm, chewy gray matter within.

Yvonne, her face wet with a splash of the dying man's blood, sobbed and shuddered, her heart pounding wildly as the beast gripped her throat tighter and tighter, her pulse pounding at her temples. Then the blackness came, her mind fizzing one last time, then going flat.

NINETEEN

It's getting dark. It's getting dark.

These words kept echoing through Chloe's head as she stumbled along through sucking black swamp mud, pushing cattails aside. The forest was black and encroaching, the long shadows stretching out, forming even pools of darkness.

And she was alone.

In many ways, more alone than she'd ever been in her life. That was the most terrifying thing of all—there was no one to guide her, help her, no hand to hold or shoulder to lean on. All her life she'd been afraid of the dark. Therapy had told her that there was nothing to be afraid of, but that wasn't true. There *were* things to be afraid of. The dark was filled with monsters. She'd known that as a child and now she knew it again.

"Steph," she said under her breath. *"Steph."*

Whether she thought this would make her stronger or make Steph reappear, she wasn't sure. The sound of her name gave her strength because Steph was tough and nothing scared her. And now—

Now she's probably dead.

Which Chloe did not want to be thinking because it filled her belly with fluttering moths. *Steph, Steph, Steph.* As she waited there, uncertain which way to go or what to do, she thought about Steph and how she had never really liked her that much. And it wasn't so much a matter of like but of respect. Chloe did not respect impulsive, reactionary people like her. They were wild, out of control. Dangerous. Yes, that was it: *dangerous.* People like that always ended up in ugly situations because of lack of forethought and careful planning and very often they took you down with them.

Conflicted, anguished, Chloe did not know what to think or what to do. Everything inside her head was flying apart.

She thought of the other girls. Did she like them? Had she ever really liked them? Yvonne was okay. Essentially harmless, just completely lacking in ethics. Always living for the moment, the next thrill, the next high. Absolutely no rudder. She was actually quite sweet and kind, as long as you didn't turn your back on her. Because given the opportunity, she would rob you blind.

And Emma? Emma was complex. She was strong in many ways and weak in others. She never dated and could get more than a little pissy if a guy showed any attention to her. They all suspected there was something traumatic behind this, but no one dared ask. She would not discuss her past and they all assumed her family life had been shit. Chloe was always jealous of her dark good looks, her olive skin and shiny black hair. And her brain. Emma was smart, but there was something damaged about her and you could see it there in her eyes. A disconnect between who she was now and who she might have been before.

Listen.

Yes, they were coming again. Chloe bit her lower lip so she did not start whimpering. The wolves were closing in. They could have had her before, but they had let her run away. Now why was that? Purely for sport? She didn't know. And there was no time to think it out because she could hear them yipping and barking with what sounded like joy.

Now they were growing excited.

They knew they had her.

Whimpering, Chloe moved forward out of the muck and into tangled yellow grasses that crunched under her step. The ground beneath them was soft and spongy. She was easy to track because she made so much noise, but she knew that it really didn't matter. They were wolves. Maybe they walked upright like men, but they were still wolves and they would scent her wherever she went.

She climbed a hill into a thicket, pushing through saplings and skirting dead trees. Branches scratched her face and hands. Burrs got stuck on her pant legs and when she tripped over a stump, they got in her hair, too.

Frantic, beaten, but unwilling to give in, she crawled on her hands and knees, tears rolling down her face, the taste of blood on her lips.

Give in, she thought. *Just give in. Maybe they'll make it quick.*

But that only made her crawl faster and faster until she vaulted to her feet and started running, bursting from the tag alder thicket into the real woods where the trees were larger and widely-spaced. She picked up speed, not even sure what was pushing her on by that point. Whatever it was, it refused to stop. It kept filling her head with graphic images of what the wolves would do to her when they caught her.

Why was there nothing out here?

Shouldn't she have come across a road or even a trail by now? Surely there had to be a cabin out here somewhere, some sign of encroaching civilization. But if there was, she had missed it entirely.

She could feel night coming on and this scared her more than just about anything else. The wolves were barking and yipping behind her, not getting any closer but surely not any farther away either.

She paused to catch her breath and she could hear them moving through the alder thicket. Sometimes they made the sounds of animals and sometimes she could hear them laughing with low, evil sounds as if they were enjoying themselves immensely. And they probably were. Sooner or later, they knew, she would tire and then they'd have her.

Looking behind her, she could see their eyes gleaming from the shadows, smell the wild pungent odor of them that riled her guts and brought her stomach up into her throat.

She ran faster now, putting everything into it.

They were closing in.

They were howling and snapping their jaws. She could hear them running full out. They were going to take her down now. Maybe they had tired of the game and wanted to stuff themselves with her meat and maybe—

Road!

Right there in front of her: a dirt road that wound through the trees. She got on it and really started pouring on the speed. It had to lead somewhere and she was going to get there, oh yes, she certainly was. The slavering, braying wolves did not want that to happen and she could almost sense their desperation, read their primal thoughts in her head—

stop her! Stop her! Stop the prey before it escapes or our bellies go empty tonight! Whether imaginary or real, it was like an injection of fuel into her tank, high-octane fucking rocket fuel, and she ran faster and still faster, feeding on it, letting it fill her and power her in her flight.

Oh, they won't get me! Not now and they damn well know it!

And then she skidded to a halt, going to her knees and rolling through a mud puddle. Then she was up, brushing mud and dirty water from her face, a perfectly organic sort of terror rushing through her, making her breath rasp in her throat and her heart pound and her nerve ending positively ring out with a foreboding of danger.

The bushes shook off to the left.

There was a horrible stench of bones and blood and maggoty hides. She heard a ragged snarling, then the bushes parted and the alpha male stepped out to meet her. Somehow, as the others chased her, he got ahead of her, and now he was coming for her.

TWENTY

Chloe shriveled with fear. It felt like everything inside her (particularly her exhilaration and optimism) had shrunken.

The beast growled at her.

It got no closer, but it certainly did not back away. It was a massive creature, bristling with spiky fur, blood-matted and tangled with leaves and small sticks. Its eyes were a brilliant yellow, gleaming like wet chrome, thin lips pulling back to reveal gaping jaws and bloodstained fangs. It made a snuffing noise like a dog, its nostrils flaring visibly. It smelled her. It wanted her. It dreamed ensanguined dreams of splitting her open and lapping at the hot red juice that splashed forth rich and salty. She could hear its belly rumbling with hunger like a great, smoldering cauldron that needed to be filled with human meat, blood, and bones.

Yet, for all that, it did not close on her.

It simply stood there as if waiting for an order from its master.

Chloe sensed something, an undercurrent to it all. Something she did not know and could not know. Yet, she was certain of one thing—the beast would not attack her. Killing her here and now was not part of the game. It was too easy. Too simple. The beast was a horror, but it was not a dumb animal. It had a mind, cruel and depraved and violent, but still a thinking brain and whatever the history of its kind was, it obeyed the call of ancient traditions. There were sacraments to be observed, age-old practices whose origins were lost to time that were ritualistic by nature.

Breathing hard, her life hanging by a single tenuous thread, Chloe stepped forward and walked past the beast on shaking legs. It growled low and hungry in its throat. She could feel the heat coming off it and the hatred it felt for her. The very idea that she could walk past it freely made it tremble with rage.

When she was ten feet away, she turned and ran. She expected at any moment that the beast would take her down with claws and teeth, that maybe all this was some colossal mind-fuck intended to put her at ease… but it didn't happen.

She sprinted down the road like a gazelle that had outwitted a lion. The road moved left to right and right to left, serpentine, forever turning. Black, gnarled trees pushed in from both sides. She had never seen trees like them before, their boles huge and mossed-green, their spidery branches reaching skyward like twisted fingers piercing the mold of a grave. They reminded her of trees from a book of fairy tales she had as a child. This was how the artist had painted them—exaggerated, looping and grotesque.

Then, as the wind in her lungs was nearly played out, the black and malevolent forest opened and she saw a village in the distance. Even from her vantage point, she could see that there was something strange about it…but there were lights which meant there were people which meant she was finally safe.

Yet, as she followed the road, she began to feel tense inside. Her stomach felt like a screw that was slowly, inexorably being tightened. As the sun set in a lagoon of orange-red blood splattered at the horizon, she felt tense. Her skin crawled. A chill ran up her spine.

The road leading in was a two-rut dirt track like something made for antique carriages and gigs. The banks to either side rose high and grassy. It was as if the ruts had been worn deep through decades of wagon traffic and, perhaps, even centuries. The idea of this, though patently fantastic, disturbed her in ways she could not understand.

As the road meandered gradually up a low hill, she saw that the trees off to the left had thinned, pushed back by a wide, weedy field of narrow, headboard-shaped tombstones that looked old and weathered. In the reaching shadows of dusk, they phosphoresced whitely like the shades that must rest uneasily beneath them. The graveyard was somehow menacing with its leaning stones, frost-heaved markers, and fallen monuments. It looked like something out of medieval Europe, out of an old movie.

To the right there was a cornfield and it had been a good growing year for the stalks were above her head. The breeze made the leaves rustle and whisper secretively. She sensed that something hidden in their dry, crisping depths watched her progress with saturnine eyes.

Wishing that Steph was still with her, because she would know how to make sense of all this, Chloe concentrated on the village ahead. Her imagination was already at full rev and she knew she couldn't feed it anymore fuel. She made herself focus. There was light there which meant people. They would help her. They would protect her and maybe even give her something to eat, to drink.

That's all there is now, she told herself. *There is nothing more. If you want to survive this night, then you had better believe it.*

That was rational. She had to quit worrying about all this feeling terribly wrong. There were probably lots of reasons why a village like this—out of place, out of time—existed. A perfectly rational explanation and she would find it, given time.

Yet, the closer she got to the outskirts, the less she believed this because she could see the village now with its jagged rooftops and it was all wrong. The buildings and houses were crowded together, rising up high and crooked, stepped gables hanging out over the streets, tall attenuated chimneys looking ready to fall. Everything was made of the same dark, splintered wood, the windows tall and narrow, multi-paned, and oddly set askew. The doorways were warped, too, sinister shadows bunching in entries and crawling like snakes from claustrophobic alleyways which were so tight you'd have to squeeze down them sideways.

The two-rut road had given way to a brick street now that wound amongst the buildings. Chloe followed it, part of her even more afraid of the village than the woods. There was a smell of age in the air, the odor of mossy wells and crumbling foundations, wood-rot and the fusty guano of bats roosting in walls. It was a sickening, ancient stench that crawled inside her, making her nauseous.

Amidst it all, she stood there, visibly trembling, thinking, *This village does not belong here and you know it. It's like something out of Central Europe in the 15th century, a woodcut brought to life. It can't be here. There are no cars. There's no evidence of the modern world. It's like a movie set.*

Again, it was like an illustration from that book of fairy tales she had as a child. A romanticized version of a medieval village, all the weird angles and impossible architecture like something out of a German Expressionist film like *The Cabinet of Dr. Caligari* that they studied in her 20th Century Film class. The village, the way it was designed and presented, seemed to be expressing anxiety and paranoia, nightmares and subconscious fears.

And that was it exactly, she realized with a shudder of fear, because hadn't it been in her mind the entire time? This place? Hadn't she imagined something like it as the wolves closed in? That if she found a town it would be as grotesque as the creatures that hunted her?

She moved forward up the brick road, trying to push such thoughts from her head. If she kept thinking that way, she was going to get even more freaked out and begin to panic. And she couldn't have that now. She was on her own. There was no one to protect her or hold her hand and this scared the hell out of her.

Ahead, she saw a large building, perhaps the biggest in the village. Lights glowed in mullioned windows and she could hear voices and laughter and good cheer. This was where everyone was. Having some sort of party. Her first instinct was to go in there, but common sense told her, again, that this was all wrong and she'd better run, find a ditch to hide in until daybreak. A third voice told her that it was far, far too late for such theatrics—they knew she was here because the wolves directed her to this place.

Played, she thought. *I was played the entire time. Manipulated. Herded like a stray cow by a sheepdog, brought here into the pen and—*

"Well, look who's here, Patience," a voice said.

Chloe turned around, white panic exploding in her chest. Two women stood there, both elderly. In keeping with the apparent age of the village, they both wore long gray skirts and button-up bodices, lace collars and cuffs, simple linen bonnets on their heads.

"Is it her indeed?" asked the second woman. "Why, I believe it is, Sarah. And here we had given you up for lost!"

Chloe looked from one to the other, her throat so dry she could not swallow. Terror incubated in her belly. What sort of fucking nightmare was this? When they tried to take hold of her arms, she jerked free.

"Oh, the poor child is frightened!" said Sarah. "And no wonder! Out in those damnable woods by night! She's lucky she's still got her skin!"

"And such fine skin!" said Patience. She reached out and brushed Chloe's cheek with a leathery finger. "Soft and smooth as a baby." She moved in and clutched Chloe's hand in her own. "Lucky that you made it to us! You'll be fine now and everything will be a joy."

Sarah's wrinkled face grinned sardonically. "Oh, if them out there had caught you…*uh!* The things they would have done to you! Tearing your flesh from your bones would be the least of their indiscretions." She moved in even closer until her wizened countenance was but inches from Chloe's, her teeth like long yellow pegs. "When they find a maiden like you…well, you know what comes first, don't you, child?"

"That is supposing she's still a maiden," Patience said.

Sarah sniffed at her. "Oh, her field is unplowed, her secrets unseeded. I can smell it on her." She sniffed again. "Oh, the sweet joy of what she conceals!"

Chloe let out a cry and tried to fight free, but they held onto her now, both surprisingly strong for their age. Yes, they had her and they would hold her. She squirmed and wriggled, but they gripped her the way a hawk grips a rabbit and there was no escape.

"Please! Please just let me go!" Chloe cried. "I haven't done anything! Do you hear me? *I haven't done a fucking thing!*"

Sarah slapped her. "You'll want to watch such language! It's unbecoming for a lady, a special maiden like you with a special destiny!"

They dragged her off toward the building and as they approached, the oaken double doors opened to greet them. Chloe could see people mulling about in there in period dress, drinking from earthenware jugs and pewter steins. The smell of roasting meat reached her along with the smell of something far worse.

"Come, child," Patience said. "This night only comes rarely and there are many anxious to make your acquaintance."

TWENTY ONE

Steph crawled through the woods, pulling herself forward with animal drive and little else. She was bruised. She was cut. She was clawed. The pack had made sport of her after Chloe ran off. They used their claws and teeth, nipping and biting and slashing. It was like play to them. None of the wounds they inflicted were intended to kill, just to torment. The alpha male had seen to that. At some point in the festivities, he had taken her away from them and tossed her down into a gully.

Kept alive, she thought again and again. *Kept alive because the night was young and they were far from done with her. And a living animal provides sport, a dead one only meat.*

It took her some time to crawl free of the gully. Through the mud and cattails, brambles and dead leaves.

It was night now.

She was lost worse than she had been before. Everything was black. A sliver of moon hung in the sky.

After a time, she got to her feet, but it wasn't easy. Her head was spinning, maybe from the loss of blood and maybe from the beating she had taken. But she wasn't dead and she didn't think she was dying. Holding onto trees for support, she began walking, moving slowly so she did not trip over stumps or break an ankle in a sudden dip. As she moved, she listened for signs of the pack but heard nothing. They would come for her eventually. She was sure of that.

And I'll kill them!

I'll kill every last fucking one of them!

I'll do it with my bare hands! I'll tear them apart!

The anger was back and it made her feel real again somehow, renewed, invigorated. Fighting against them was highly impractical and probably even impossible, but the rage in her that she had fought for so long would accept nothing less. They had used and abused her and somehow they would pay for it.

Just keep going.

She came to a ridge, climbed it, and saw something down in the hollow below. A cabin? Yes, but that was a little gracious for what she was looking at. More like a shack. Quietly, she moved down the hillside toward it. She could see light coming from under the door. Flickering light. Firelight.

I need to get by that fire. I need to bask in it.

Swallowing down her fear and trepidation in one large mass, she went right up to the door, which looked like it had been hammered together out of splintered planks and scraps.

She knocked.

Silence. Then someone moving in there.

"Who's there? What do you want?" a woman's voice asked.

Steph swallowed again. "I'm lost. I need help."

Silence again for a few moments as if whoever was in there thought it over. There was some fumbling and the door was opened. In the firelight, Steph saw a young woman with tangled black hair standing there. Her eyes were huge and dark. She wore a simple dress that looked like it had been made from sackcloth.

"Come in then," she said.

Steph stepped in, cringing from the smell which was like that of a kennel. The stink of dogs living in their own waste and scraps. It was a bad smell and she knew it. Yet, she was drawn to the fire and the warmth it provided. She kneeled before it, letting the heat warm her hands and unlock her aching muscles.

"You're hurt," the woman said.

"Yes."

"They're hunting you, aren't they?"

Steph looked at her. "You know about it?"

"Everyone in this forest knows about Blooding Night."

Blooding Night. Just the sound of it made Steph tense. "What is that?"

The woman cocked her head. "Why it's…it's the all and everything. You have to be very cunning to survive. I survived it, many years ago and here I am still."

"I don't understand."

She nodded. "Of course not. Not yet. But you will. I am Alice. I will be your friend. What are you called?"

"Stephanie."

"I like that name."

Steph had a strong feeling that her host was not exactly in her right mind. *And can you blame her? She's been here for years. She was you once.* Steph looked around. The cabin was dirt-floored with a flagstone hearth and what looked like a couple willow-framed beds shoved in the corner. She saw some pots and pans, several buckets.

And eyes.

Several pairs shining from the darkness where the firelight did not reach. They belonged to a pair of small, dark forms that made no sound whatsoever.

"Don't mind the children," Alice said, stirring the fire into a high blaze with an iron poker. "They're afraid of you. They won't hurt you."

But Steph wasn't so sure of that. There was something unsaid in her words—*unless I tell them to.* She poured some water in a bucket and came back. She had a rag and she began swabbing Steph's wounds with it.

"Easy," she said. "I won't hurt you."

She cleaned her wounds the best she could, taking special care with the bites and cuts, the laceration at Steph's scalp.

"If you know about this," Steph finally said, "then you can help me get out of here."

"Yes, I could. But they wouldn't like it. I would be punished." She poured something from a jug into a steel cup. "Here. Drink this."

Staring into the fire, Steph did. It was wine. It had a fruity taste to it, like plums. It was sweet and strong. She drank it down and Alice poured her some more. She produced a plate of greasy meat.

"Pheasant. Eat it."

Steph wolfed it down, tearing the carcass apart and delighting in its savory saltiness. She washed it down with more wine. She was beginning to feel delightfully buzzed. She drank some more, her fingers and mouth greasy from the pheasant.

"You're better now," Alice said.

"Yes."

And she was. The food, the wine. She felt human again, warm inside and out. She knew her primary goal should be getting out of there and getting the woman to help her if she would, but she felt warm and mellow, easy with everything. The wine was so good. It made her want to lay down and dream. Rest. Truly rest for the first time in what seemed days. Alice seemed to understand that. She stroked Steph's hair lovingly as if she were a child. She let her drink more wine.

"It's so good," Steph said. "It makes me…it makes me…"

"Feel like you can fly? Out of your head and up into the sky?" Alice said, seeming to read her mind. "Up over the treetops and over the hills, through the clouds and beyond."

Doped, Steph thought. *I've been doped.*

It should have angered her, but it didn't. It should have made her angry at herself for letting her guard down and exposing her soft white underbelly…yet, she found it nearly impossible to be anything but smooth and relaxed. With heavy-lidded eyes, she noticed that Alice was naked now. She had a good body, firm and well-muscled, breasts small and pert. She had a small wooden bucket in her lap. She dug her fingers in it and they came out oily and glistening. With gentle, seductive motions, she greased herself. Her breasts, her belly, her legs, even her face and neck.

"The salve," she said in a low, throaty voice, "it unlocks what's inside. It teaches us how to leap from our skins and run through the forest."

Steph nodded, because somehow it made perfect sense. *The Call of the Wild.* Yes, yes, yes. The very idea of the book and its central theme had been in her mind all night and she had felt the call building in her, crying out from the primal night in the ebon depths of her soul. Now here was salve that would bring it out, make it so, make her into something that could run wild and free.

And even though she knew there was something terribly wrong about all this, she went with it like a leaf being carried by the current of a rushing stream. It not only felt good to go with it, it felt *right.* When Alice unbuttoned her shirt and began massaging her breasts with the salve, she wanted to object but she didn't. The salve was warm, more than warm. It made her breasts feel hot, burning to be touched. When Alice began kissing her, she went with it, sliding her tongue in her mouth as hands cupped her breasts and fingers worked her nipples.

"Yes," she heard herself say. "Like this…just like this."

Alice sucked Steph's left nipple into her mouth, licking it and pulling it gently between her teeth. Her hand was between Steph's legs, rubbing her. It hadn't felt this good since that night she spent with Yvonne.

As Alice continued sucking on her, she saw one of the children step from the darkness. Except it wasn't a child but a wolf that stood on its hind legs, hunched over but clearly bipedal. Its hands were human hands, its hide shaggy. The firelight winked off its long teeth and bright yellow eyes. A pang of fear erupted in Steph. And as she tensed, Alice sucked on her with more ferocity, squeezing and kneading her breasts violently.

Steph tried to push her away, but she felt so weak. She was putty that Alice worked, clay that she sculpted. Steph made a moaning sound that was half pleasure and half terror.

The wolf-child was tearing itself open.

It was gutting itself.

No…it was peeling itself from the wolfskin as if it was a costume. But it was no costume because it fought independently of the child, writhing and bristling, moving with muscular contractions as it was pulled free of the small, blood-matted form beneath with red straining fingers. Threads of rubbery connective tissue snapped one by one, blood and globs of yellow fat dropping to the floor. When the head was pulled back and away from that of the child, it made a low baying sound, its huge teeth snapping together out of pain or anger. And then it was dropped to the floor where it continued to move, throbbing and bleeding like a living heart. Its claws scraped in the dirt and its jaws snarled, its hide jumping with spasms.

The very sight of it made dozens of sensations war in Steph's head. What she should have been feeling was repulsion and pure terror, but that wasn't it at all. It felt like her spine was red-hot, burning into her back. Like her veins were pumping with hot oil that flowed through every quivering inch of her. Fires burned inside her, rising up into a central blaze and she began to melt under its delicious cremating heat. For the first time in her life, it felt like every inch of her was alive, every cell energized and awake. Her vision was clear. She could see into the shadows of the cabin. She could smell the night outside. She could hear dew dripping from leaves and pine needles falling and rodents scampering and spiders spinning their webs. She could smell the hot marrow-fat stink of the salve, taste the wine on her tongue like the juices of a thousand plump ripe plums. A piece of pheasant meat was caught in her teeth and her taste buds exploded with the pure rapture of its meaty, salty juice. Everything suddenly seemed so simple it was liberating. You were hungry, you ate. You were horny, you fucked. You were frightened, you ran. You were tired, you slept. You were thirsty, you sipped from cool streams and secret night pools. Her muscles bunched. Her breath rasped in her throat. She dreamed of wild things and stalking shaggy things, moonlight streaming down into the forest and the joy of the kill: hot blood flowing down her throat and flesh torn in her teeth.

The blood-smeared child stood there, wiping protoplasmic jelly from itself…or *him*self, for it was clearly a boy. He seemed to understand exactly what she was experiencing. He grinned with malice and hunger. And Steph could almost hear what he was thinking—*Now you'll be with us, as us.* And isn't that what she wanted all along? Deep inside where her primeval motivations cowered in the darkness of her subconscious? Hadn't she, on some level, *always* wanted this? To be free and wild, unrestrained, her innate penchant for rage and wrath and violence totally unfettered?

It's why you drank the wine when you knew you shouldn't. Why you let the salve be rubbed over you and the woman's hands touch you in ways you've always wanted to be touched…you wanted this!

"NO!" she cried, pushing Alice away.

Alice snarled at her, her teeth grown long and sharp, pointed ears laid back against her skull. Drool dangled from her mouth in white ribbons. She was salivating. Hungry. Horny. Maybe both at the same time.

When she came forward, Steph punched her in the face and it was pure release. She punched her again and again. She yelped like a kicked dog. Now the children were coming. One of them was a wolf-child, the other the feral little boy that had just shed its skin. With his triangular ears and mouth of fine, sharp teeth he looked like a goblin that snatched infants in the dead of night.

Alice reached out for her.

"GET AWAY FROM ME!" Steph shouted. "STAY THE FUCK AWAY FROM ME, YOU CRAZY BITCH!"

But that wasn't going to happen and she knew it. Alice crept toward her, no hostility whatsoever at being struck repeatedly. No, she was not angry—she was visibly excited. Her obsidian eyes glistened blackly, unblinking like those of a snake. Slow, reptilian muscular contractions ran down her back and up her belly, making her quiver with what looked like lust.

Her tongue painted her lips with saliva.

She made a husky sound in her throat that was part growl and part orgasmic moan.

Like a dog in heat, she lowered her head in submission, looking up with dark shining eyes and a lurid carnal grin of teeth. She raised her ass in the air, wiggling it as if to tempt.

Steph began to edge her way in the direction of the door, wondering with rising horror if she would be able to make it before the children leaped on her and brought her down like a stag.

"Now, Stephanie," Alice said in a hissing tone of voice. "There's no need to fight...no need to run. I can show you things. I can teach you the way and make it that much easier for you. With my help, you can survive the Blooding. You can be the one. You can be the chosen. *You can be the bride of Blooding Night! The adored one! The Daughter of the Horned Moon! Let me rub you with the Wild Salve, the ointment of the hunt! You'll wear the skin of the primal beast! The incorruptible wolf girdle! Then you'll know! Then you'll see with the eyes of the forest! They'll come to worship at your feet as is just and right!*"

And in Steph's confused, convoluted, dreaming brain, she could see it, she really could see it. The tribute paid to her as Bride, the offerings made in Her name in moonlit glens, the hilltop sacrifices of little ones laid at her feet...their fire-blackened bones and tanned hides, tender meat and organs braised to delicate sweetness like soft roasted apples. She would wear a shawl of their scalps and sit upon a throne of human bones, howling madly into the night as the innocents impaled on stakes writhed and bled and screamed for mercy that would forever be denied them.

It was all too vivid and too real, corrupting her, the imagery owning her mind, the wildness creeping into her soul and making contact with the ancient beast that had waited for countless millennia with gnarled teeth and ensanguined claws to be released from its cage.

It was there.

It was hers for the taking.

All she had to do was accept it.

But she would not accept it. The idea was repugnant to the human being within her. It terrified her. And with terror came anger, because with Steph one usually followed the other like spring follows winter. Alice sensed it. No longer submissive, no longer playing a game of sex and ancient salves, she darted in at Steph, slashing at her with her fingers. Her nails cut Steph's face open in bleeding ruts. Steph shoved her back. She lost balance and fell back and Steph kicked her, driving her right into the fire.

Alice screamed as her hair lit up and one arm went into the hot coals.

The children attacked.

The feral boy dove on Steph's back, riding her viciously, tearing at her back and sinking his teeth into the nape of her neck. Steph shrieked, spinning in circles as the wild child seized her legs and bit into her calf with sharp fangs. She managed to throw the boy who crashed into his screaming mother. The wolf child bit down deeper and Steph could feel blood running down her leg. The pain was excruciating. Seeing red, she reached down and grabbed handfuls of the wolf child's hair, pulling its teeth from her leg. It snarled and thrashed in her grip and she tossed it aside.

The feral boy launched himself at her and she flattened him with a fist to the face. The wolf child rolled over, its fur standing on end, eyes burning a malevolent yellow. Its snout wrinkled back from huge teeth. It would take out her throat this time and she knew it. As she tried to get away, her leg went out from under her. She fell to the floor, her hand reaching out for something to grasp and it found the iron poker. Alice had knocked its end into the flames when she fell.

As the wolf child leaped with pure animal ferocity, Steph jabbed it with the poker. The red-hot tip sizzled as it pierced the creature's throat. It let out a shrill cry. The smell of burnt hair was nauseating.

By then, Steph got back to her feet, unsteady, but braced for action. The feral boy came at her again and she brought the hooked end of the poker down on his head with everything she had. There was a satisfying cracking noise as his skull split open, a gout of blood shooting up and splattering against the hearth. He went down, making a strangled noise in his throat. When he tried to rise again, she hit him two more times and finally he went down, trembling, blood and brains leaking from his head.

"The children! Not my children!" Alice cried and attacked, more gruesome than ever with half the hair burned from her head.

She jumped at Steph and Steph swung again; the hook caught her in the face, tearing across her left eye. She went down to her knees, her eye welling with blood and dripping slime. Steph pivoted and smashed the poker into the wolf child, driving it back.

She stumbled to the door, pulled the heavy bolt aside and threw the door open. And framed in it, stood a monster, this one a man, the father of the brood. He was huge and shaggy, his fur encrusted with dried blood and grease. His eyes glowed with evil sentience, his slavering jaws widening to tear out her throat.

The Big Bad Wolf had come home.

TWENTY TWO

When Yvonne woke, she was alone. Her hearing came back to her first and described a world of silence broken only by an occasional puff of breeze or a leaf falling from a high branch and skittering over the ground. She opened her irritated, bloodshot eyes and it was true: they had left, the beast and his pack of merry bloodsuckers and gut-rippers were gone.

But why?

Why would they leave her?

Why didn't they tear her apart? A ruse. It must be a rusc. Thcy wanted to give her a false sense of security so that she would rise up and think she was free and then they would charge out of the woods to claim her.

So she didn't move.

She lay there, numb and mindless, her limbs sprawled around her. She knew there were things she needed to be doing. Things that would safeguard her life, if such a thing was even possible by that point. But her body did not obey. It ached. It hurt. Every time she moved, pain shot through her aching muscles. So she just laid there and as she did so, she remembered what the beast and his pack did to the hanging man. A scream filled her throat and she needed to give it vent…but she pressed her lips tight and choked it off.

Screaming would do no good.

What was the point of a scream? To draw attention to your plight and that was the last thing she wanted. The very idea inspired a deep dread within her. So she did nothing. It had always been her way. When faced with what seemed insurmountable obstacles, she did nothing, hoping that the wheels of fate would turn in her direction. Sometimes they did and—

Often they don't, dear, her mother's voice said in her head. *This situation is not like others. You're not waiting to hear the results of a pregnancy test or whether you passed a class or if that inappropriate video you made with so-and-so will end up on the web. This is a little bit different, isn't it? Waiting means death and I think you know that. And if you really think that the pack will forget where it left you, then you are a little fool that deserves to die.*

Yvonne began sobbing, bemoaning in her mind how unfair all this was and how unprepared she was as a human being for what survival entailed.

Pissing and whining will get you nowhere. It'll only end with the meat stripped from your bones, don't you see that?

She did. She really did. She knew she had to move…but to where? It was dark now and the woods were even more unfathomable than they had been in the light. At least to her. The pack would be able to navigate it easily, of course, and they would be able to find her scent trail and find her wherever she went.

So you're just giving up?

"Yes," she said under her breath. "I've had enough."

That silenced the mother voice in her head. There was nothing now, just the forest pressing in, the whooshing breeze in the high branches. The sound of skittering animals and leaves falling. And then something more…footsteps moving in her direction, but not the many of the pack, but only one set. They crunched through the leaves and loam.

She could hear a ragged breathing.

A low muttering voice.

A wild smell of animal dens and bone-strewn burrows, dark spaces and wet fur. It was *their* smell and she knew it. The footsteps were closer now. They paused four or five feet away.

"Hiding there, eh?" said the wizened, straw-dry voice of a woman. "If you're quiet, no one hears you and if they don't hear you, you are not there. *Bosh!* Mother Streega hears and she knows. You need a place to hide and lay your head, my child, and Mother Streega shall provide."

Yvonne, of course, could not see the old woman—or what she assumed to be an old woman—just a dark shape that now squatted next to her, but she certainly could smell the wet-dog stink of her and it filled her with horror.

The old lady reached out and touched her face with a hand that was rough, almost scaly like the belly of a lizard. She stroked her cheek, humming some off-key dirge of a melody. Her breath was sour and rancid.

"My poor, poor child," she said, stroking her, then cooing at her like she was a baby. "What they've done to you, my girl. What they've put you through." She made a smacking sound with her lips. "But no more! Mother Streega has you now and she'll protect you. She'll take you to a special place they don't know about."

Yvonne, despite herself, made a pained moaning under her breath.

"Ssshh, my darling, ssshh. No more of that. I'll take you home and care for you, my Nabby. Oh yes, I certainly will." She took hold of her, lifting her up with a surprising strength and clutching her tightly. "I haven't forgotten what they did to you, my child. The horrors they inflicted upon you. But I'll make it right now. I'll protect and keep you and there's nothing they can do about that."

Yvonne was shaking. The old woman was insane, completely insane. She thought she was someone else. A daughter? A sister? Who could say? She held her like a child, rocking her back and forth as she made that perfectly profane cooing noise that made Yvonne's skin crawl. It was too much. It was just too much. Yvonne cried out, trying to fight free but the old lady held her that much more tightly.

"You mustn't fight against Mother Streega, my child. She only wants to help you and hold you, care for her poor lost baby. *There. There. Ssshh,* my child. We must be quiet or they'll hear us."

But Yvonne could not be quiet. She fought. She squirmed. And when that did nothing to free her from the old lady's iron grip, she let out a shrill, cutting scream that echoed through the forest.

Immediately, the old lady clamped a hand over her mouth. *"No! You do not do that! You will bring them! They will take you from me again!"* Her hand, which was cold and tasted of dirt, was pressed tighter and tighter, her forefinger and thumb squeezing Yvonne's nostrils shut until she could not draw a single breath. Again, she fought, but it was no good. *"See? See, how Mother Streega handles bad girls like you, Nabby! Once again, she does right by you and you reject her!"*

Yvonne was shaking, fighting with everything she had to break free of the old woman's deathly embrace. She hit her, slapped her, tore at her hair, but her strength was diminishing. Black dots popped in her head. The world spun and she felt herself falling into darkness.

"Ssshh, ssshh, my Nabby," the old lady whispered. *"Now to sleep with you… when you wake, Mother Streega will have you in a far better place. That's it…quiet, quiet now…go to sleep…to sleep…"*

When Yvonne passed out, the old lady waited to see if she was playing possum. Satisfied that all was well, she stood and gripped Yvonne by the ankles and dragged her off into the shadows, humming happily and unpleasantly.

TWENTY THREE

It was dark and Emma was still moving, still intent on finding that mythical road that did not seem to exist. Maybe it was a fool's quest, but she needed to keep going. Forward momentum was everything. It was only this that kept her mind intact, kept the seams of her sanity from splitting completely open.

The others are dead by now, she kept thinking. *I'm probably the only one left.*

She did not know it to be true, of course, but she feared it was so. She kept thinking of the wolf pelt. How the skin wanted to cover her and make her part of it. It was insane. And what was even crazier was that there was only one sort of creature it could possibly have come from, a monster out of folklore. The word was in her mind, but she would not think it, not let herself be drawn down into that abyss of superstitious terror, because once she fell, there would be no getting out. She would have to accept the fact that what was hunting her was no ordinary human being.

Just stop it. Don't go there, don't you dare go there. You know there are no such things. There can't be. There just can't be.

Yet, as she walked deeper into the woods, going completely in circles for all she knew, she kept scanning the forest for watching eyes. Luminous eyes. She was certain they would glow in the dark. Every time a stray shaft of moonlight winked off a dewy leaf or a glistening stump, she thought they were coming for her.

She picked her way carefully amongst the tall, leaning trees, stepping over logs and avoiding mucky holes and rotting logs, skirting blowdowns and places that were especially dark, woven blackly with shadows. Places like that might be good to hide in, but *they* might spring an ambush from them.

Wait.

Goddamn…wait.

She stood atop a hill, leaning against the trunk of a pine and right before her, just below the hill, was a road. She could see it in the scant moonlight. A dirt road that wound away into the night.

If her energy had been flagging, it was now recharged, rekindled. Her belly was full of hot coals and there was fire in her veins. Maybe, just maybe, she would get out of this yet.

She stormed down the hill, vaulting through the grass with long-legged jumps. The road. Oh, the dear sweet road.

But there was no time to admire it.

She set off at a jog, moving quickly but setting a reasonable pace so she would not tire out. She ran like that for ten minutes until she saw a farmhouse just off the road. When she saw it, she skidded to a halt.

Am I really seeing this?

She knew she should have been overjoyed (and, God knew, she wanted to be), but as she stood there, she found that she doubted the reality of it. It was a mirage. Her mind was easing her pain and fear, giving her the very thing she needed to see, the way the minds of dying people showed them a light at the end of the tunnel and family members waiting to embrace them.

These were the things that went through her mind in a hot rush, but the house did not fade.

It waited there for her, a light burning in the window as if to welcome her. Tall, ancient trees surrounded it. Dead leaves blew through the yard.

And although something in her warned her to just keep running, she was drawn to it. It was a typical Midwestern farmhouse with a low wraparound porch, spindle-like newel posts, a dark upper story, the entire affair whitewashed some time in the past, but now weathered and peeling.

Emma stepped up onto the porch. She stood before the door, wondering if she should knock or just get as far away from it as fast as she could. For so many hours now she had been living by her instincts, trusting in them, but now they were failing her. She was conflicted.

Without even really thinking of it, she raised her fist and knocked on the door. A face appeared briefly in a window and then the door was opened.

"Yes? May I help you?" It was a woman, middle-aged, with steel-gray tresses falling to her shoulders and a smiling, kindly face.

Emma swallowed. "I need help. I'm lost."

"Well…I don't know."

"Please."

Dressed in a red-and-black checked flannel shirt that seemed to float on her, she was incredibly thin. Her bones seemed to swim inside her, surfacing violently and only being held in check by a rubbery membrane of skin. Her eyes were gentle, though sunken in their sockets, her cheekbones jutting, her jaw sharp like the claw of a hammer.

"I'm on in years," she said, "and I'm alone. I have to be careful."

"Please," Emma said, so entirely wrung-out that she was willing to get on her knees and beg if that's what it took.

"Well, come in then."

Emma followed her into the farmhouse. It was pleasantly warm in there. There was a wonderful aroma of something like hot chicken soup that invaded her stomach and made it growl. In fact, it roared like a starving beast. She was led into a kitchen where the wonderful hungry smells were amplified, making her mouth water.

"I'm sorry if I seemed a little hesitant," the woman said, "but…well, way out here, I don't get too many callers. And not at night."

Emma sat at an oak table. Everything was so neat and cozy that she wanted to cry. Her hands on the table shook violently. She realized suddenly how dirty she was, an animal brought into this fine, tidy home, dragging her filth in with her. There were leaves in her hair. Her face was scratched from branches, smeared with dried blood. Her hands were grubby. There was a rank odor of decay wafting off her from the rotting pig carcass she fell into. Her hoodie was stained with bits of gore from it.

Why would she even let me in? she wondered as the woman busied herself at the stove. *I must look like some foul, wild thing. And I stink like death.*

The woman appraised her with sad eyes. "My name is Meg. And you?"

Emma rubbed her eyes. They felt crusty. "I'm sorry. Emma. I'm Emma."

"Oh, that's a nice traditional name. No Brittany or Kaitlyn for you, but a nice solid functional Emma. It's a good name. A solid name. A strong name." She smiled and her eyes seemed to twinkle like stars. "You'll forgive me. Here you are, in a real state, and I'm going on about names. Foolish old woman, I am. Now tell me, what happened to you? If you don't mind me saying, you look simply awful."

Emma smiled at that, brushing a tear away that rolled down her cheek. *That's the understatement of the year.* She cleared her throat. "Do you have a phone? I need help. I have friends that are lost out there. We became separated…we…"

She found that she couldn't go on. She could not tell the awful tale that needed telling. It was all insane. Being here in this normal house only intensified that feeling. Meg would throw her out. The way she looked. The way she smelled. The crazy story. She would think Emma was a walk away from a state institution.

"I need a phone," Emma said. It was the only thing she *could* say. Everything else was a jumble in her head.

"There's no phones out here, dove," Meg told her. "No lines, you see. And I don't have a cell phone. Wouldn't know how to use it if I had one. I have no car. At my age, well, they don't like people like me driving about and endangering others." She sighed. "You're in a real spot, I'm afraid."

Emma put her hands to her face. The tears were coming and she could not stop them. Her body hitched as she sobbed.

"Oh, it's not bad as all that. You can spend the night here. Clean up, get a rest. Mailman comes by every morning around ten. You can catch a ride with him back to town. He'll help you."

Emma knew she didn't have much of a choice. She kept thinking about that road out there. If she got on it and jogged it, she would get somewhere. It had to lead to something.

Meg directed her to the bathroom and once the door was locked, she showered the filth off herself. There was no way she was climbing into her rank clothes after that, but Meg provided her with a flannel shirt and a pair of jeans. They fit surprisingly well. They smelled like mothballs and probably were retrieved from an old cedar chest, but the smell was negligible compared with what her things stank like.

There was a bowl of soup waiting for her when she came back. It smelled wonderful. Realistically, it smelled far beyond wonderful. The hot broth rising into her face and seeping up her nostrils made her feel more human. It was better than good. It warmed her up down deep. It gave her strength and focus. The soup became her. She seemed to live in it. There was nothing but the soup and its aroma and its heat on her tongue, the pleasing yellow broth and the tender meat in her mouth.

How long? she thought. *How long since I woke up in that fucking box? Ten hours? Twelve?*

She couldn't be sure of anything. All she knew was that she was exhausted. The soup seemed to make her aware of that. Every bone and muscle and strand of tendon begged for rest. She didn't think she'd ever been this tired before. At least, not in a long, long time and she didn't want to remember when that was.

"You've suffered, haven't you?"

Emma looked up and Meg was watching her. There was tenderness in her eyes, something like pity. It was as if she knew everything and maybe she did at that, because there hadn't been many questions.

"Yes. But I'm okay. Really, I am."

Meg shook her head slowly. "Not tonight, dove. Not tonight." She licked her lips and continued watching. "I mean, in the past. There's been bad things. Things that have taken hold of you and never let go."

Emma felt her face flush and then drain of blood. She went hot, then cold. The spoon slid from her hand. She shook visibly. It was as if there were fingers inside her snapping her bones one after the other. That's exactly how she felt—like a bag of fragile sticks cracking and breaking.

"It's in your eyes, dear," Meg said. "It's just behind them. I can almost hear your memories screaming."

Emma's mind went in and out of focus. At night, half-memories and distortions of the same rose from the dead and haunted her dreams. That was, on the nights when she could sleep. Insomnia kept her rigid and awake several nights a week and she dragged through her days, studying and going to school and working and pretending none of it was happening. Sometimes she would be so tired she'd hallucinate, hearing popping sounds in her ears and thumping noises like moths at the window. She'd see shapes out of the corners of her eyes or feel fingers touching her when no one was there. All of it had a common origin that terrified her because she did not know what it was.

Tell her, a voice in her head taunted her, one she suspected was from the distant past. *Tell her the kind of girl you are. One that doesn't have parents or a family or any memory of her childhood. Tell her about that. Tell her what we did to you…and what you did to us.*

"You don't have to talk about it if you don't want to," Meg said. "Your pain is obvious to me. You were damaged as a child, poorly-treated."

"Yes."

"And even now you feel it."

"Yes."

"Tell me."

Emma tried to. Words floated in her head, but she could not string them together. Memories flooded her brain and none of them were good.

Go ahead, the voice from her past said. *Tell her all about it. You've never told a soul. Tell her what it's like when you have no mom or dad, when you grow up in a foster home and the older girls are all damaged, minds twisted out of shape, how mean they were. How they pinched you and scratched you, beat you up. How they burned you with cigarettes and cut you. Tell Meg all about it. Then tell her how the nuns let you go to the mall once a month and how you ran away when you were twelve. But you didn't run far. Mrs. Cupp found you in the parking lot. Women like her could spot a little lost girl instinctively. She took you to the van. She didn't force you to get in—you did it willingly. Anything to be away from those terrible girls and oblivious nuns who turned a blind eye to the abuse. Tell Meg about Mr. and Mrs. Cupp. How they locked you in that room. How you were their angel by day and a plaything by night. How Mrs. Cupp giggled when Mr. Cupp did terrible things to you. Go ahead, Emma, dish out the dirt. And don't forget to tell her what you did after a solid year of being treated like an animal, a pet, a slave, a whore. Tell her how you got out of your room, found Mr. Cupp's sledgehammer and beat their brains out while they lay in a drunken stupor. Tell Meg about the blood and brains splashed over their pillows, how you kept swinging that sledge until their heads were pulped. Go ahead, tell her. Tell her how you ran off into the night, how you lived in the streets, how they found you and brought you back to the orphanage where you gained a reputation as the meanest girl of all.*

And while you're at it, tell her about the nuns. How they didn't seem to want to know where you'd been or what happened to you. How every time you tried to tell them about the Cupps, they gave you that look, that terrible withering look, and changed the subject because they didn't want to know about the van and the house at the edge of town and how the Cupps were kind and understanding during the daytime, but at night became werewolves—slavering, degenerate beasts. Tell her all about it. How when the sun went down, they were either drunk and perverted or reading the bible in shrieking voices and slapping you around or how Mrs. Cupp masturbated when her husband was on top of you. Because you did not talk about such things or how you exacted your revenge or the brutal monster you became when you got back to the orphanage. The one that bit and clawed the other girls and when they were bigger than you, how you jabbed your thumbs into their eyes.

"You need to rest," Meg said.

Yes, yes, that's exactly what she needed. Her body was tired, yes, but it was far beyond simple physical exhaustion. She needed to close her eyes and turn her brain off. She needed to stop thinking. Stop trying to remember things that did not want to be remembered, the sort of things that you never dared talk about. It was imperative.

Meg took her by the hand and towed her away down the hallway and to a room. "Lay there and sleep. You won't be bothered. In the morning, everything will look differently." With that, Meg offered her a large, toothy grin.

The room was small and the lamp was dim. Everything from the bed to the nightstand to the chest of drawers was rustic, slapped together out of pine and oak. The walls were log and she could still smell the sap despite the apparent age of the place.

It was nice and it should have been relaxing, especially after what she had been through, but it made her skin crawl. She felt imprisoned. The room was like a cage, the walls hemming her in. It reminded her of the room the Cupps kept her in. She lay there, terror close under her skin, fearing she would never, ever escape. Not only what hunted her in the dark woods, but who she was and who she would never be again.

TWENTY FOUR

Chloe was lost in a grand, wild, impossible celebration that seemed to be in her honor, even though such a thing seemed absurd and impossible. She sat at an immense table that had to be thirty feet long, Patience to one side of her and Sarah to the other, each whispering different things in her ear, weaving some hallucinogenic web in her head that she was trapped in like a fly caught between two spiders. Sometimes she could understand what they were saying, at other times it made little to no sense.

"You'll be such a lovely bride," Sarah told her.

"Yes, and a fruitful wife," said Patience.

They each held onto her, never letting go. She was a prize they had won and would never part from. It was all crazy and Chloe was certain she was dreaming or dead or both at the same time. Nothing seemed real. It was as if she was tripping her brains out.

There were easily thirty people in the great room, all drinking and raising glasses, toasting her with goblet after goblet of wine. Shouting. Singing. Laughing. It was like a drinking hall from a fantasy or a hunting lodge. There were mounted deer antlers on the walls, dozens of sets of them along with the accoutrements of the hunt itself: pelts and hunting horns, pikes and arrows and longbows. She was nearly certain she had seen such a place in a movie or read about it in a book.

Twice now, she had fought free of Patience and Sarah, gotten to her feet only to be pulled back down again. And each time she did so, the gathered revelers let out such a resounding cheer that it shook the building. *Such spirit!* voices cried. *A true bride in every way! The beast hungers beneath her skin! See how it writhes! See how it hungers!* And with that, more wine made the rounds. Chloe didn't want any; she had never been a big drinker. Not that it mattered, for all here must drink to excess. Wine was poured down her throat. It was sweet, but strong, and she felt herself getting buzzed and becoming part of the celebration even though she knew she should have been rejecting it all.

Don't be frightened of your destiny! Patience told her. *Embrace that which you will become!* Sarah said. Their voices were in her ears and in her head and with all the noise it seemed impossible that she could hear them at all.

The wine made her giddy. It made her forget how absolutely impossible all this was. There could be no such place as this out in the woods of the Midwest. These people were from a fairy tale. Whatever common sense the wine had not dulled told her she must get away, but she didn't think they would let her. She was a prisoner even though they treated her like an honored guest, everyone hugging her and kissing her, all of them seeming to want to touch her at the same time.

A huge bear of a man stood up and everyone fell silent. He wore the skins of animals, a massive shaggy gray beard trailing to his chest. His eyes were bright green like emeralds. *"What can one say of the Beast?"* he called out to the faithful. *"What can one say of his or her ways? The Beast is here among us! It snarls and howls and hungers! It hides beneath our skins and bays in our brains! We worship the Beast beneath the horned moon as our ancestors did! As the Beast, we walk by moonlight and hunt the dark woods and give praise to the Lord of the Forest and the Mother of all things here on Blooding Night! Let us sing and chant—by tooth and by claw! Bleed the pig in the straw! Let it run and hide! Through the sky she shall ride! Let it end and begin! We shall dance in its skin!"*

They all sang it together and the perfectly crazy thing was that Chloe did, too. She had never heard the ditty before, yet it seemed to be in her head and all she had to do was open her mouth and give it breath. Once she began singing, she couldn't seem to stop. She sang louder and louder, keeping tempo with the others.

And the song seemed to mesmerize everyone. They swayed in time with the music, side to side, eyes glazed and mouths shrieking as they gave praise to the moon and the woods and the wildness of the Beast. Now brass pots appeared. Steam rose from some sharp-smelling unguent in them. Men and women began pulling off their clothes and rubbing their bodies with it until they were greasy and shining, all of them linked together and dancing widdershins, around and around and around. And somewhere during the festivities, Chloe realized that her shirt was open, her pert breasts on display. It should have made her gasp with embarrassment, but it didn't. She thrust out her chest and the men howled and the women, most of them completely naked now, imitated what she did.

The hands of Sarah and Patience were busy, dipping fingers into one of the pots and salving Chloe with the ointment inside. By God, it should have been a horror having those old women massaging the salve onto her breasts and belly, but it was wonderful. The salve was hot as it covered her, exciting her, stripping away a lifetime of inhibitions and anxieties and body issues. It honestly felt as if her skin was just a costume she had been wearing her entire life and she could disrobe at any time and let the real Chloe out, the one that had been hiding in the shadows of her mind for ages. It wanted to be free and she wanted to open its cage. Her mind seemed to jump from her head and her body burned pleasantly, carnally, every cell filled with a ravenous appetite.

She jabbed her fingers into the pot and stirred the jelly within, scooping out great globs of it and covering her chest and belly and face with it. She used it to slick back her hair as she cried out with animal fury at the feel of it seeping into her, deeper and deeper.

And then the food was brought—huge pigs that had been roasted brown. They dripped with grease and the savory odor of them was unbelievable. Everyone began rending the carcasses and Chloe was there with them, tearing out great oily slabs of meat and shoving them gluttonously into her mouth, chewing and tearing. It was wonderfully salty and sweet and pleasingly rich. Her face was greasy with it. Globs of fat dripped from her mouth as she ate and ate and ate and then, and then—

Everyone pulled away, stuffed and sated, grinning happily and something in her brain sharpened and her eyes focused and she saw what was on the table. She shook her head violently, rejecting it, as cold sweat burst from her pores.

Those gathered were quiet now, eyes closed, enjoying their repast, full and sleepy, most dozing, some snoring loudly

On the table were the remains of two human beings that had been rendered to bone—shanks of rib glistening, vertebrae well-gnawed, metacarpals sucked free of flesh and chewy ligament, skulls shattered, teeth scattered like dice.

Chloe fell back out of her chair with a scream, still shaking her head, reeling with disgust. *Pigs, they were pigs! We ate pigs! I know we ate pigs!*

Hands gripped her and pulled her to her feet. It was a young guy around her age that had helped to carry in the pigs.

"Ssshh," he said. "I'll get you away, but you must not wake them."

Chloe found that she could not speak. She fell to her knees and vomited. When it was over, he helped her up again and took her away. He dragged her up a flight of stairs, down a corridor, then down another. He pushed her into a room and closed the door.

"You're safe here," he said, lighting a candle. "If you just hide until the sun comes up, all of this will be over with."

Chloe was sobbing, fighting against a panic attack. "But…but what is this? What's it all about?"

"Blooding Night," he said. "Now be quiet or they'll come for you and for me."

"I don't understand. Why are you helping me?"

"Because they took me, too. One night years ago. I've been little better than a slave since."

Chloe sat there on the bed, staring at the candle, feeling that she was more like them and less like who she had been before. Self-conscious finally, she buttoned up her shirt and the guy smiled at her.

TWENTY FIVE

The Big Bad Wolf that filled the doorway was closer to seven feet than six—a towering, shaggy mass of muscle and ferocity and plain bad attitude. Its splayed hands dangled nearly to its knees, each finger tipped by a gray-black claw like the talon of an owl. From its throat to its belly, its pelt was stiff with dried blood, standing out in spikes and needles. Its eyes—just as yellow as rising harvest moons—appraised the situation in the cabin and it growled low in its throat with a terrible rumbling sound.

Steph, as tough and instinctive and world-weary as she was, felt a stream of piss run hotly down her leg. This was it. This was the endgame. This was Death standing there like a man on huge wolf pads, its teeth stained pink from feeding, its black-spotted tongue coiling in its mouth like a cobra in a basket, ribbons of saliva dangling from its huge jaws.

She backed slowly away, waiting for the monster to jump on her and split her wide open with its claws. There was intelligence in its eyes—sly, evil, and coldly calculating—and it knew what she had done. That she had invaded its lair and brought harm to its pack. So as it looked at her, it was not just with savage hunger, but with anger like boiling magma rising up the cone of a volcano.

It approached her slowly, though visibly trembling with rage. Its head was cocked to the side, lupine jaws opening and closing. She could smell its hide which was rancid from the dead things it had been rolling in to mask its predatory scent. That was bad enough, but its breath which blew out hot and sickening was not like carrion exactly, but the stink of something that *feeds* on carrion. And in her mind, she saw the wolf opening graves and tearing apart soft, mucid corpses with its huge teeth.

She still had the fire poker in her hands, but it felt puny, like a pathetic little stick in the face of the true primeval aggression that was the werewolf. In the back of her mind, she wondered if her ancestors felt as she did when they faced down a giant cave bear.

Alice cowered near the fire, making a hissing sound deep in her throat. Slowly, she climbed to her hands and knees, ready to spring. The wolf child, emboldened now by the appearance of the male, moved in closer as well.

The fight-or-flight response in Steph kicked into high gear. Since there could be none of the latter, it was all the former. Adrenaline was spiking inside her. Muscles tensing, tendons straining. Blood flow had decreased to her frontal lobe which was responsible for logic and planning. The deep-set animalistic parts of her brain had taken over now. She knew she was going to die, so she went into full battle mode.

"Come on then," she said in a low but resolute voice. "Get it fucking over with."

Yet, the Big Bad Wolf hesitated. Whether it was out of confusion or even fear, it was hard to say. If Steph had been thinking clearly, she would have realized it was out of admiration. The beast did not see her as prey, but as an adversary that did not cower but stood ready to fight and kill.

The waiting was over.

Battle was engaged.

The beast growled and strode forward and Steph stood her ground, holding the poker in both hands like a baseball bat, ready to swing it with everything she had. It would kill her, she knew, but she would exact blood and pain from it before it did so. And in her savage state of mind, there was satisfaction in that.

As the Big Bad Wolf came for her, Alice rose up to fight with her mate, but he batted her aside. He did the same with the wolf child. This was his fight, his kill. He charged, ears laid flat against his skull, and swiped at Steph with his claws. She darted out of the way and brought the hooked end of the poker down on his skull with brutal, amazing force. There was a loud, very satisfying cracking noise as his skull fractured and the hook tore out a three inch strip of fur and meat from the top of his head.

As it did so, he made a pained yelping sound and slashed at her. His nails tore open her jean jacket from the shoulder to the left elbow, slicing trenches in her arm that spurted blood instantly.

She swung again and missed. He slashed out and laid her chest open. Threaded with pain, her brain wanting to black out, Steph did not give in. When the wolf made a groggy lunge at her, disoriented from his head wound, she brought the poker up in a perfect devastating arc. The hook caught the beast's upper lips and ripped its snout open in a spray of blood.

It lunged.

Steph swung again and the poker bounced off its well-muscled shoulder. It took hold of her with irresistible strength and threw her against the wall. She flew four feet and the impact against the log wall knocked the wind out of her. She landed in a bloody, broken heap.

She was in agony, bleeding profusely, but she still would not give in. She played possum as the Big Bad Wolf stepped over to her. Its gait was shambling, uneven. It stood over her and she could see lice jumping in its pelt. It was breathing heavily, shaking, its fur wet with blood. Its head wound was bleeding heavily. But for all that, it was excited: its penis stood erect and if it got her, Steph knew that it would rape her as she died.

It brought its clawed hand back to split her head open and she moved, striking like a snake, jabbing the sharp end of the poker right into its balls. It made a shrill barking sound that was nearly a scream and stumbled back. Like any man whose genitals had been gored, it went to its knees, cupping them in its great gnarled hands.

She got to her feet.

She was unsteady from the loss of blood and trauma, but she jumped forward and swung the poker. The beast brought up a hand to defend itself and the poker smashed into its fingers with a snapping sound. It yelped again, fighting to get to its feet. And Steph brought the poker down on its head twice in rapid succession, screaming as she did so.

The beast was badly wounded, but it would not submit. It dragged itself to its feet and as she swung the poker, it batted it aside with its bad hand and slashed at her with the other. Her abdomen was sliced cleanly open, her entrails bulging out.

It would not die, but neither would she.

As it closed in on her, moving with a loping seesawing motion like a drunken man, she swung the poker with her last reserve of strength and tore its snout open again. Then the beast seized her arm in its jaws, bearing down with primal strength. Steph screamed as the ulna and radius of her forearm snapped and blood sprayed in her face.

The beast, still gripping her arm, lifted her off her feet and swung her side to side with what remained of its strength, then tossed her to the floor. It took two steps toward her and collapsed.

Clutching her guts with her good hand, drenched red with her own blood, she hobbled past it and out of the door. She was dying and she knew it, but something in her would not stop. It kept going until she was in the trees, fighting, ever fighting, then the wind went out of her and she fell into a ditch filled with leaves.

Her eyes stared up at the stars high above, slowly closing.

And in the distance, the Big Bad Wolf let out a resounding howl. It was far from dead, probably only stunned, and now it was coming to finish her off.

TWENTY SIX

Consciousness returned slowly to Yvonne. Many times, it seemed, her eyes opened only to shut again, as if her brain was trying desperately to keep her in the darkness where there was no pain, no horror, no raging mania to cloud her thoughts and her sanity. There was peace in the darkness. The nightmares that played out in her mind were trifling in comparison to what the real, physical world served up to her, and this not in small bites, but on platters.

Wake up, wake up already! she told herself. *You need to wake the hell up...*

The first thing she realized was that she was lying on something soft and furry like a heap of pelts. Another was thrown over her and her fingers were stroking the nap, petting it like the fur of a kitten. The second thing she realized was that she was in what looked like a cave. A fire was burning maybe ten feet away in a central pit and the light it threw was flickering and orange, smoke hanging in its beams.

There was an awful smell, one of decay and rotting hides, burnt fat and yellow marrow. A smoky, hot stink of it that was perfectly sickening.

And at that moment, she remembered it all—the crazy old woman in the dark, the awful things she said.

Now to sleep with you...when you wake, Mother Streega will have you in a far better place.

This was it then. She had brought Yvonne to this awful lair where she hid from the others. Even by their standards, the old lady was probably crazy. A hermit. A recluse. She existed on the edge of their loose tribal society, but was not part of it. She called herself Mother Streega and hadn't she warned Yvonne to keep quiet or the others would come and take her?

Oh, Christ.

Yvonne realized she was in a bigger fix than she had been before. The wolves wanted to kill her, true, but Mother Streega wanted to *keep* her like a pet, thinking she was some long lost daughter or sister or God only knew what. If she cooperated, the old lady probably wouldn't hurt her. She would care for her like an injured baby bird.

And somehow, that was even worse.

Yvonne choked back the scream that was born in her throat. It trembled on her tongue. It wanted to be vented, but to do so would bring trouble because the old lady was just over there by the fire. And no doubt, she was listening.

As Yvonne looked around, she saw there were bones strewn over the floor. Some of them looked to be human. There were a couple shattered skulls amongst them that were definitely human. There were scraps and animal pelts, all manner of debris. Mother Streega lived in squalor and filth like a buzzard, surrounded by the scraps of her meals.

It was disgusting.

Horrifying.

And what was even worse was hanging not five feet away, slowly moving from side to side. Yvonne had to bite down on her lip so she didn't cry out. The carcass was human, a well-stripped husk that looked like it had been crudely fileted. The head and limbs were missing, the abdomen opened and emptied. She was certain it was the guy she had found hanging that the wolves tore apart, but how she could know that when it had been skinned like a rabbit, was anyone's guess.

Well, it looks like you're in more trouble than ever, Yvonne, she heard her mother's voice say. *It's always been your way, hasn't it? From the frying pan into the fire. You always seem to dig yourself a deeper hole and get into more trouble.*

Even though she knew it was true, the last thing she wanted to be listening to now was some crazy voice in her head. She was living a nightmare and she was pretty sure that not even her mother's practical wisdom could get her out of this one.

Mother Streega was working on something by the fire, hands busy and head nodding. Her voice echoed off into the cave with an off-key musical cadence. *"Stitch and sew, stitch and sew, that's what we do when the sun gets low..."*

Yvonne lay there, trying not to shake and trying even harder not to lose her mind in this terrible vault. If she lost it, she was done for. That was it. Plain and simple. She had to keep her wits and be ready to exploit any opportunity. No one was going to help her. No one was going to rescue her. Whatever happened now would be because of what she did or what she failed to do.

She could not be afraid.

She could not be weak.

If the old lady thought she was some long lost relative, then she needed to play that card for all it was worth. If the old lady saw her as an adversary, it would get ugly. She was ancient and frail as a bag of sticks... *but,* she had been strong enough to drag Yvonne to this place and that must not only have taken some doing and determination, but strength. So she wasn't as feeble as she appeared. She was insane or senile, possibly both, but capable of violence if she was crossed or her delusions were questioned.

Yvonne's grandmother had been like that.

She spent her last five years in a dementia ward at an elderly care facility. Whenever they went to see her, Mom always told Yvonne to agree with whatever Gramma said, never to contradict her. And Yvonne hadn't. Then one day, Gramma was going on about something that had happened thirty years before and Yvonne, not thinking, had pointed out that that was many years ago and Gramma had lost it. She screamed and raged, tossing her dinner tray aside, accusing Yvonne of being some stranger, some delinquent that had been stealing all the Diet Coke from the pop machine. In retrospect, it sounded almost comical, but it wasn't. It was weird and frightening. Gramma had to be restrained and given an injection. Despite her years—she was well into her eighties—she fought with amazing vigor.

Yvonne thought of that now and knew she had to proceed with caution because Mother Streega was no doubt much more dangerous than Gramma had been.

And what is it you plan to do? her mother's voice asked her. *What's your plan?*

But Yvonne already knew: she would be nice to Mother Streega and when she had the chance, she would bash her brains out.

TWENTY SEVEN

There was no sleep, so Emma listened to the house breathing around her like a living thing. That it lived, that it had a soul and a presence, she did not doubt. Like her, she sensed that it had a past that it was inexorably connected to, that informed and influenced what it was today and at this very moment. So she listened, trying to hear what it had to say because she knew she was in terrible danger and that Meg was not her friend, despite what she had said.

You can see it in her eyes, Emma thought. *And you can feel it just behind her face like it's a mask she can't wait to take off.*

So, with these thoughts and feelings, there was no sleep. She listened to the house and while she did that, she knew what she was really listening for was Meg herself, creeping about in the night, plotting and scheming dreadful things.

Like Mrs. Cupp. She had awful insomnia and she wandered the house from dusk till dawn if she didn't drink herself into a stupor. She—

"No," Emma said under her breath. "No more of that."

After about an hour of it, she just couldn't take it anymore. The walls of that tiny room were closing in and the house was uneasy. She got out of bed and looked out the window at the night, the encroaching forest. But that did her no good; it made her feel even more disturbed, darker to her core. She went to the door. For some reason, she placed her hands flat against it as if she expected it to feel hot like there was blaze in the corridor.

She listened.

She could hear Meg's voice. She was chatting it up with someone or just talking to herself. Emma couldn't hear what was being said, but she had the very worst feeling that it was about her. There was no way she could know that, yet the certainty remained.

She unlocked the door and stepped out into the corridor. Shadows crawled over the walls like spiders. Was it her imagination or did she smell a wild, musky odor like stale urine? It was very strong for a moment, then it tapered off and she wasn't sure if she had smelled it at all.

She followed the sound of Meg's droning voice and it led to the kitchen. Emma stood there in the archway, feeling a dozen different emotions at once, listening to Meg's whispering voice as she set the table, putting out six tin plates. No glasses or silverware, just the plates. They gleamed like newly-minted nickels.

She placed each one quite carefully, stepping back, admiring them, moving this one an inch to the left, that one a bit to the right. Their placement seemed to be of the utmost importance. Proper, equal distance had to be maintained between them. She was so fastidious about it, it was as if chaos would result if one was off just a fraction. She puttered about like that for a few moments, then stepped back.

"Well," she said, clasping her hands together, "all is in order here. All is made ready." And though her back was to Emma, obviously she was aware of her presence. "That was a quick nap, dear."

Emma took one faltering step forward. "What are you doing?"

"Why I'm setting a table, of course. Even a silly little girl like you should recognize that."

There was bitterness to her words now, and, perhaps, even a certain degree of loathing beneath that. It wasn't there before. Now, much like her teeth that seemed to have grown long in her mouth and the silvery glaze to her eyes, it was on full display. Meg's grandmotherly demeanor had slid down a few inches like a mask she was tired of wearing.

She's going to change all the way, Emma thought with a white-hot bolt of panic in her chest. *She's going to show you what she really is.*

Meg sighed with great contentment. "When the children return from the fields, they'll be hungry. I like to have a little something ready for them. They have such fierce appetites, you know."

Emma just stood there. It seemed there was little else she *could* do as the air grew heavy with menace around her. It thickened, congealed like a scum of fat on a kettle of stew. She began to wonder what was real and what was not. If maybe Meg had slipped something into her soup and she was hallucinating wildly. Her bowl of soup was still at the head of the table. It no longer looked warm and inviting or deliciously golden. No, now it was gray like drainage from a septic tank, bits of dark meat floating on its surface. One of them looked like the knuckle of a finger.

"Wolves," she said, barely able to keep the revulsion from her voice. "Your children are nothing but wolves. Animals. *Dirty fucking animals.*"

"And with your past, who are you to judge?"

Emma was shaking all over. "You don't...you know nothing about me."

"I know everything about you."

Outside, a wolf howled in the distance. "One of your children," Emma said with distaste. If she could have spit out the words, she would have.

Meg giggled. "And what makes you think you're above them? Because you're from the city? Because you have others slaughter the food you eat?" She shook her head. "No, my dear. You and the rest of your generation are out of touch, your brains are addled by drugs and technology and poor lifestyle choices. You live a synthetic existence. You—and generations before you—have disassociated yourself from nature, from the good earth and the soil, from the sweet joy of the hunt and the kill. And it's destroying you, bit by bit."

"You're insane," Emma said, though secretly, deep inside, she had to wonder if she wasn't right or nearly right on some level.

"Hardly, dove, hardly. Those who are in sync with the natural world as we are, rarely suffer from mental aberrations. Madness is a symptom of your kind and the drab, utilitarian boxes they've forced themselves into."

"Wolves. That's all you are: wolves," Emma said, because she could think of nothing else to say.

Meg sighed. "Oh, come now, dear, that's not the word in your mind, now is it? You're not thinking *wolves,* you're thinking *werewolves.*" She cackled at that, shaking her head again, and returning to the stove, stirring what she had in a kettle there. "Where I come from, we had a different name for them—*vulkodlak*, they were called. But that was ages and ages ago when I was a child. Which was long before your great-great-great grandmother was even born. So very long ago."

She carefully began ladling out sauce and meat on the plates and the stench was awful, like boiled blood and flesh moldering with decay. The sauce was thin and pink, shining with grease. The meat dripped with fat and was nearly gelatinous.

Emma nearly swooned at the stink of it.

Now Meg turned and looked at her. Her eyes were terrible, blood-veined and sickly yellow, her face gray and seamed with deep-set lines and cracks. Her lips were split open and shriveled back from liver-brown gums and their attendant yellow teeth. "Now, Little Miss, let me tell you how you fucked up," she said and her voice was low and throaty like the bark of a dog. "You came into my house. With everything you've experienced this night and all you've gone through in the past, you should have known better than to trust me. Yet, you silly little bitch, in you came. I offered you food, you accepted. And the greatest fuck-up of all? I offered you a shower and you took it, washing the animal stink off you and getting rid of your filthy clothes. How stupid are you? The smell on them and on *you* confused the pack. You could have hid from them all night and they would have been scenting you in fifty different directions. So sad, really. And we had such high hopes for you."

The spit had dried up in Emma's mouth. "For me? What the hell are you talking about?"

"I'm talking about what this is all about, you simple little idiot. Only one can survive. The most cunning one. Only she can be the bride of Blooding Night..."

Emma began edging her way to the other side of the room. If she made it, she could get out the front door. But Meg shook her head and blocked her path.

"There's no point now, is there? They're outside. I can smell them. Your race is run."

The thing was, Emma could smell them, too. But it was nothing definable exactly, just the smell of the wilderness that lay cheek to jowl with the cabin in an intimate, timeless embrace—it had grown stronger, more primeval, more...*earthy*. It was inside her, trickling down into her bones, creating a pure burning seam of atavistic dread that bubbled closer and closer to the surface. It was as if something at her core had woken up and acquired a voice: *That smell, that smell, that terrible smell...it means they're coming...it means you must run!*

Meg approached her slowly as a predator will approach prey paralyzed with terror. She got closer and closer. Emma knew she had to run, but she could not think, she could not speak, she could not even move. It was like her body was filled with wet cement. It had become a lumbering, heavy mass.

Outside, she heard a growling noise.

It was like the sound of a very large dog, a gigantic dog mad with rabies, its red eyes bulging from their sockets, white foam slathering from its jaws.

Fear, real fear, was pure kinetic energy—overwhelming and irresistible and completely unstoppable like a missile fired from a silo. It exploded with a wild, irrational, animalistic kill-or-be-killed fury inside of her and she ran toward Meg who leaped forward to stop her. Emma hit her like a battering ram and laid her flat. She kept right on going, jumping over her, nearly colliding with the icebox, and heading toward the back door which she reached through a small vestibule.

Immediately, she saw two things: a shotgun leaning in the corner and skins hanging on the walls. Wolfskins. Just like the one she saw in the forest. And like them, they were horribly, impossibly alive, writhing on their hooks, pads and claws scraping the wall, hides moving with muscular spasms, jaws opening and closing.

They sensed the hunt.

They wanted to be worn.

No...they wanted someone to *wear*.

Emma screamed at the sight of them, fumbling the back door open and she vaulted out into the night. She landed in the grass, sensing dark shapes moving about her. Before they could take her down, she was running into the forest, leaving them far behind.

Once again, the chase was on.

TWENTY EIGHT

Steph was dying and she knew it. Everyone wondered from time to time with macabre curiosity how their end would come, but she no longer wondered. She was bleeding and broken and stitched with agony. Though she had very little left to fight with, she kept crawling because there was nothing else she could do. Even a dying animal will keep moving until there's nothing left to move *with.*

Twice now, she tried to get to her feet, but each time the pain forced her face down into the loam which smelled so delightful—black earth, rotting needles and leaves and organic decay of all sorts. Her body was done. Nothing seemed to work. Everything from her muscles to her nerves to her dwindling blood supply seemed to be at odds with one another. When she was whole and healthy, there was unity; now she was a collection of disparate parts, a crude anatomy stitched together out of scraps.

Her mind, though gradually narrowing in perception, still worked well enough to tell her that she was leaving a perfect blood trail behind her. Her smell in addition to the disturbed leaves and broken fronds and bent saplings would lead them right to her.

Blood was caked in the wounds at the back of her neck and at her calf. It had coagulated in these places, but it still flowed freely from the ruts in her chest and her open abdomen. Her bitten, fractured arm barely bled now. As a limb, it was next to useless. She could no longer feel it save for occasional spikes of pain. She dragged it along with her like a broken stick.

She couldn't seem to remember her name or why she was in the woods. She never liked the outdoors, particularly wild, inaccessible places like this. Maybe the call of them was too strong and her animal instinct was simply too close to the surface.

If she paused and breathed deeply—something which, too, was painful—her head cleared enough so that she could remember it all.

Yes, them. This place. My friends. The werewolves.

She moved mainly by pushing with her knees and hips. Her good hand was at her belly, holding her guts in place, keeping her entrails tucked in. They were warm and greasy under her fingers. Even though she was dying inch by inch, she knew they were valuable and she couldn't let them go. Already, her open belly was packed with brown leaves and dirt and dry pine needles.

With great, nearly superhuman effort, she got to her knees, but the agony was crushing. Her head spun. Her eyes seemed to swim in their sockets. Down she went. She was looking for a good, safe place to die now like a dog struck by a car. She wanted to crawl in somewhere dark and sheltered where she could close her eyes.

The pack was after her again. They were excited, worked up into a snarling, yipping froth. They no longer bothered with stealth, with the fine subtleties of the hunt as it had been taught to them and passed down their ancient bloodlines. They had her and they knew it. They were like cats, cruel and vicious and sadistically patient; she was the mouse, already gored by its claws, injured, bleeding out, making a last desperate and futile crawl for freedom. There was no need for subterfuge, so they were loud and brash, confident that she was nearly played out and their teeth would soon strip her flesh to bone.

It made her angry.

There wasn't much fight left in her, but she didn't want to die, not without throwing the pack a curve and denying them what they were so certain was theirs.

She kept crawling, dragging herself really, through tall wet grass and over soft spongy moss and cool loam, fighting through a ditch filled with leaves and across a mudflat that she nearly sank in like movie quicksand. There was a hill before her. It canted at about 45°, which wasn't much had she been healthy, but now it was like Mount Everest and Kilimanjaro.

Behind her, the pack was getting louder and louder. Soon they would have her. The idea of this made something in her soul positively ache. She could hear them clearly and she knew they were children out for a bit of sport.

That's all she was in her final hour—a bit of sport. A rabbit to be run to death or a rubber squeak toy to be mauled by anxious jaws.

She wished for a weapon so she could take a few of them with her like a battle-scarred, blood-spattered hero in an old war movie. But there were no guns, no knives, no swords of valor to fall on. Nothing but sticks and a few loose stones.

With a last reserve of strength, she pulled her body up the hillside. The pain of her injuries nearly made her pass out, but she made it. And then—

Was she completely delusional or was she seeing lights through the trees? Flickering lights of the sort that might be thrown by a bonfire? She tried to blink it away, but its reality was unimpeachable. There was indeed a fire ahead. If she could reach it, she could die warm.

The pack closing in, she crawled faster and faster, the will to live (or at least to face death on her own terms) was not quite extinguished. Over grassy mounds and down into leaf-choked gullies. Over rocks and fallen, rotting trees. Finally through brambles that tore at her ragged clothes and what bits of skin that were not already bruised or cut.

The fire.

It was real.

It sat in a little bowl dug into the earth, stones heaped around its perimeter as sort of a fire break. It was hardly a bonfire, just a small blaze fed by a few logs. The heat it threw, though, was pure joy, like warm fingers reaching deep inside her and unlocking her muscles. *It's all in your head. You're dead or near to it and your mind is showing you what you need to see. That's all it is. Dying people see all kinds of things that aren't really there—angels and fucking spirits, their mother and the dog they had in third grade that got pulped beneath a delivery truck.* She crawled within two feet of it and the heat increased. She reached out a hand and the flames burned her fingers. If it was a fantasy, then it was the finest she'd ever had. The flickering blaze threw tongues of yellow and orange light against the surrounding forest and its tangled deadfalls. It crackled and popped, snapping from time to time and sending up sparks and plumes of smoke.

What the hell is that?

Set back about fifteen feet was a sort of lean-to that was so perfectly camouflaged by the woods she didn't see it at first. It was like an extension of the forest itself, which, essentially, it was. A huge elm had fallen in a storm years past, but was held up by the limbs of a mighty pine, about six feet high. Someone had leaned thick evergreen boughs against it, creating an A-frame sort of structure.

This was a place to rest, to wait for the end.

Steph crawled over to it, away from the warm embrace of the fire. The inside of the lean-to was dark and secret. Anything could have been hiding in there. She backtracked, pulling a flaming stick from the fire and advanced on the lean-to, creeping on her side like a crushed worm. The floor of the lean-to was covered in compressed leaves and dried grasses. She wanted to lay on them and go to sleep listening to the crackling of the fire.

But there was a shape in there, too. Something crouched in the back where the shadows were heavy and enclosing. *Furs.* A heap of furs. Whoever lived in the lean-to must have used them as blankets. Yes, she would cover herself in them and die in peace before the pack found her.

As she approached them, she saw something else, something familiar. Something terrible but exciting and invigorating at the same time. There was a steaming pot near the furs and from the smell of it, she knew it was the salve. The same stuff Alice had rubbed her belly and breasts with.

You can be the bride of Blooding Night! The adored one! The Daughter of the Horned Moon! Let me rub you with the Wild Salve, Alice had said. *The ointment of the hunt! You'll wear the skin of the primal beast! The incorruptible wolf girdle! Then you'll know! Then you'll see with the eyes of the forest! They'll come to worship at your feet as is just and right!*

It was left here for Steph to find and she knew it. Here was her choice—she died now in the straw and prayed that her life faded before the pack tore her into pieces...or she ascended to the next level as Alice wanted her to, casting aside all that she knew and running wild and free, living by tooth and claw, hunting her prey beneath a blood-red moon of sacrifice. She died proud or lived feral.

There was no thinking.

There was only acceptance.

Ignoring the agony of her broken, nearly bloodless body, her limbs stiff and unyielding, her eyesight dimming, she tore off the remains of her coat and shirt, pulling off her boots, and wiggling from her jeans. She was naked, naked as she had never been before in her life. Shivering, wracked with pain, her mind whirling, she dipped her fingers into the pot and the touch of the ointment was warm. It made her fingertips tingle. She scooped up handfuls of the slimy, rancid-smelling goo and rubbed it over her arms and legs, up between her thighs, over the edges of her sheared open belly, the jagged trenches at her breasts. The more she rubbed on her skin, the more she wanted. She covered her face with it, greased her blood-stiffened hair back. The smell of it was high, sweet, nauseating yet ambrosial.

She was engulfed in heat. It burned in every cell of her body. It was healing her, changing her, reconfiguring her. Her eyesight sharpened. She could hear the forest—leaves falling, twigs snapping beneath the feet of the pack. She could smell the hot meat-stink of their breath, the secretions of their glands, their asses and armpits, and the hides they wore. She could sense their hunger and instinctual drives, hear the grinding of their teeth, and taste the scraps of meat wedged in their teeth. Burning, shaking, now convulsing and crying out with pain and the succulent orgasmic joy of release, she squirmed in the dried grasses and leaves with millipedal gyrations, her hips bucking, her hands pressed between her legs. Galaxies exploded in her mind and her thoughts rode the moonlit skies in psychic trains like Walter de la Mare's Ride-by-Nights, scattered across the Milky Way like stardust.

She laid there, gasping, trembling, fingers reaching out for the luxurious furs which were not furs at all but the single hide of an immense wolf. It rippled beneath her touch, hairs rising into spikes, musculature pulsating. The wolf's head was huge, triangular ears jutting from the skull, jaws opening and closing. They exhaled hot breath into her face, gouts of bubbling white saliva dripping from them. The limbs twitched, clawed pads scratching in the dry grasses. The forward pads were not pads at all, but human hands that gripped her, claws emerging, glistening and black.

Wear me, my tender sweet little one, and I shall wear you, the guttural, growling voice of the shaggy hide whispered in her mind like a wolf in a fairy tale that seduced budding virgins in red hoods in dark, secret glens. *Together we'll join and become one, commune into a glorious night thing of wildness and primal hungers. We'll share the same bones and wear the skin of the beast like a cloak, and make a wicked, wicked merriment in the darkest part of the woods as we howl at the glowing moon high above.*

Accept the malediction of the primal dark forest.

The wolfskin was moving onto her now and something faraway in her soul screamed at its touch while something else welcomed it. The limbs of the wolf covered her own and while she expected the communing to be violent and ugly like rape, it was gentle and soft, almost loving. The hide covered her, grew into her, its roots digging deep within her. Immediately the pain of her wounds ceased as she was healed and reborn. There was a galvanic crackling at her ears and a sweet, syrupy warmth engulfed her mind as Steph, the old dying Steph, disappeared completely, sinking without a trace in a black mire.

The hide was a mantle that absorbed her completely, not just covering her but *becoming* her as she and it became one, a polymorphic thing that writhed with the mystical joy of one another.

Steph opened her eyes and new dimensions unfolded around her. She lifted her hand and it was the hand of the beast. The world of the night and the forest were no longer threatening, but welcoming. Everything seemed more real than it had ever been before. In fact, *she* seemed more real than she had ever been before. The woods were alive in a million ways and she was part of it, not separate from it. Her senses were focused, acute, from hearing to taste to smell to touch, amplified, sharpened to a lethal cutting edge. Stimuli came from every direction and she instantly processed it, understood it, and used it, rising up on her hind feet and howling into the night.

The first of the pack appeared, charging from the tree line on all fours. She was upwind from the wolf, so it did not smell her. It came at her and she stepped from the shadows. It looked up at her with bright, terror-filled eyes, making a brief squealing noise right before she decapitated it with a mighty blow from her claws. By the time the others arrived, she had stripped away its hide and was devouring the soft, warm meat beneath, stuffing herself with tender, succulent child-flesh.

TWENTY NINE

Chloe never learned the boy's name. Who he was before they took him and how long ago that was remained a mystery that would never be solved. Everything moved so fast. She was downstairs with those *people* and now she was up here with this boy who couldn't stop staring at her. He was younger than her, but not by much. He saw her breasts and she had the feeling that he wanted to see them again.

Like he didn't see enough of that downstairs, she thought with distaste, though the idea was somehow more than a little exciting.

She chastised herself for thinking such a thing, but she couldn't help it because he was good-looking. She liked his broad shoulders, his muscular forearms, the sweep of his long blonde hair, the way his blue eyes flashed at her when he put them on her. It had to be the wine. She was still giddy with it, still buzzed. And that stuff the old ladies rubbed on her. She did not know what it was, only that she was inebriated with it and it had an effect on her, stripping away her inhibitions and filling her brain with crazy thoughts and dangerous impulses and desires.

But, Jesus, you must have been tripping your brains out or something. Letting those old ladies touch you like that, oil you with that stuff.

Yes, it was horrible, absolutely horrible. This was what the easily offended, uppity princess in her pretended, but the reality was that she liked it. She *really* liked it. Just as she liked all the men and women stripping down and rubbing that salve all over each other. God help her, she'd gotten off on it. And when Sarah—was it Sarah?—began to slide oily fingers down the waistband of her jeans, her intent all too obvious, Chloe had liked that, too. If the food hadn't arrived, she would have pulled them down to make it easier for those glistening fingers to slide into her.

The memories made her shudder, the breath catch in her throat, and though she told herself it was with revulsion, it was anything but. She could still feel their hands on her and it made a pleasant warmth invade her loins. She could smell the rich, pungent, foul salve. It was all over her arms and chest, slicked into her hair. She had a mad, throbbing desire to pull her clothes off and let the boy mount her right there on the bed and from the look in his eyes, he seemed to know it, too.

But the food…think of what you ate, what you put into your mouth and…and…

Enjoyed. Because that was it, wasn't it? She *had* enjoyed it. The sweet, delicate flavor of the meat seasoned in its own steaming juices, savory and well-marbled. Its flavor was not so much tasted, but experienced, erupting in her mouth and making her taste buds explode like cluster bombs and filling her belly with teeth. Every inch of her wanted to taste it. To crawl through it. To lick it and roll in it and cover herself with its aroma.

Again, she wanted to feel revulsion, but what she felt was anything but. Her stomach was hollow. Her mouth wanted to bite. Her tongue wanted to lick. She looked over at the boy and he was watching her intently. She would let him get on top of her and slide his cock into her and when it was in as deep as it could go, she would bite his throat and swim in his blood while he thrusted into her.

Stop it, stop it, stop it!

Chloe shook her head, pressing her hands to her face. What was wrong with her? Her own feelings and impulses were like those of a stranger. It was as if she had mutated into some lascivious beast. Her natural rhythms were way off. Despite the trauma and terror of the night, there had been no panic attacks or intimations of the same for some time now.

And what did that mean?

What did it really mean?

She looked over at the boy and she had to mentally restrain her body from going over to him and giving him everything he wanted in a way he'd never guess. Sweat beaded her brow. Fires burned inside her.

The bare truth of the matter was that Chloe no longer knew who she was and maybe *what* she was. Ever since waking up in the shack, she'd been conflicted and confused, just beside herself trying to keep up with her own rioting emotions. She'd gone from being scared to being angry, resentful to joyful to bestial to horny. Nothing made sense and maybe in the context of this lunatic asylum of a night, maybe nothing could make sense.

She looked over at the boy and he was staring at her with wide, lonely eyes. There was still lust there, but it was tempered now with sorrow and maybe even despair. He was like so many boys she knew from dances and clubs, the good ones that were not conceited self-inflating bags of hot air, but just ordinary boys trapped by a loneliness and a lack of self-confidence that just needed a little encouragement.

Like me, she thought, *just like me. A wallflower that wants to be so much more.*

She offered him a smile and patted the bed beside her. "You can sit by me if you want."

Sheepishly, he came over. He was as nervous as she knew she should be, but was not. Something had been altered in her and she knew that whatever it was, there was no going back. Whatever chrysalis she'd been hiding in for the past twenty-one years, she had now emerged and not as a beautiful butterfly but as a winged predatory thing that knew exactly how to get what it wanted.

Still smiling, and amazed that she could under the circumstances, she reached out and held his hand. It was a strong hand, rough and calloused from hard labor. He said they had worked him like a slave and she believed it.

"Why?" she asked him. "Why did you save me? What made you take the chance of bringing me up here?"

It was an honest question and she expected an honest answer. The fact that he took his time in replying, first studying the floor and then her face, made her certain she'd get one.

"You reminded me, I guess, of someone I knew once, a long time ago." He shrugged. "They were corrupting you. I could see it happening. That's what they do with everyone. Bring out the animal in them."

"Did they do it to you?"

"No. Not me. Not yet."

Chloe swallowed. The anxiety began to spike in her. *That's what's happening to me. That's what they're doing to me.* She could feel it taking hold of her, inch by inch and cell by cell. It was digging in deep, anxious to exploit something immoral and crude and cunning at her core, release some primitive thing from antiquity that would live only to hunt, feed, fuck, and spawn.

The title of a book from her childhood popped into her mind—*Where the Wild Things Are*—and she knew: they were buried deep in every man, woman, and child, beneath the sludge and detritus of 10,000 years of civilization, but not buried deep enough.

"Tell me what it's about," she said, staring into the guttering candle flame and imagining a world lit only by fire, a world where you covered yourself in the greasy, blood-smelling pelts of your prey and lived by instinct and appetite and violence.

The boy sighed. He looked at her and the sadness in his eyes was depthless. "This is Blooding Night. Once a decade, the unwary can find this forest, this village, this place out of time. Just one night: Blooding Night," he said and she was sure he was just reciting something that had been told to him again and again. "It's the night that the tribe increases its stock. New blood and new life. Girls like you are brought in and hunted, but the point isn't to kill them, just to terrify them, torment them, see which one is smarter, tougher, stronger, and more adaptable than the others. Which one can outwit the pack, fight and kill, but avoid the temptation of reverting to a beast. One that can rise above the others and prove herself worthy as the Bride of Blooding Night."

Oh Jesus, Chloe thought. *We—Emma and Steph and Yvonne and I—were chosen to see who would be the best breeder, the one with the characteristics they desire. They want our genes, our heredity.*

"That's the one they want, new breeding stock, a female that can prove herself worthy to wear the skin and bring forth children that are clever and fierce."

The very idea repelled her, yet another part, the sly grinning animal inside her, liked it. Licking. Sucking. Fucking. Breeding. It filled her with heat and desire that was barely manageable. And a voice rising to the surface like a bubble screamed in her head, *the bride! The bride of Blooding Night! I want to be the one! The chosen one! The best one! Let it be me and me alone!*

"Stop it," she said out loud.

"What?"

"Nothing…just nothing."

He might have commented on that, but something began to happen. A smell filled the room that was coarse and dirty like a subterranean rat's warren, acrid and vile. The stench of urine and filth.

The boy tensed.

Like Chloe, he recognized the smell of the pack.

"We're going to die," she whispered.

There was a bumping outside the door, then the sound of sniffing around the sill. The doorknob rattled. Now the frenzied sound of scratching claws like a dog that wanted to get in. But they weren't down low, but up high. The door trembled in its frame. It was hit and then hit again and with such force it seemed to bulge. There was a growling in the corridor, then a splitting bestial roar as something out there beat against it, tearing at it with its claws.

"The window," the boy said. "Go out the window. It's your only chance."

"Come with me."

He shook his head and Chloe sensed from him that this was it, this was his last stand. He'd fight and die to protect her, to give her the time to escape. She wanted to fight with him, but she knew it was hopeless. You couldn't fight what stood outside the door. Not with your bare hands. She slid up the window. In the moonlight, she could see a flat roof about eight feet below.

The door was coming apart.

Huge cracks appeared in its surface like branching lightning. The beast out there shrieked with rage and then the door exploded in a storm of shrapnel. And in stepped the wolf—a huge, feral beast that stood well over six feet, an evil shape from an evil nightmare. Its lethally fanged jaws opened and closed, its putrescent breath filling the room in a gagging sickly-sweet mist. Its translucent yellow eyes looked from the boy to Chloe at the window. She expected it to vault at her with claws and teeth, but it didn't.

It waited.

It was then that she noticed that it was not a male but a giant she-wolf. Its head and back were shaggy with thick gray-black fur, as were the backs of its arms and hands. But its torso was nearly hairless and she could see a double row of milk-swollen teats running from breast to belly. It appraised the boy first with unbridled, salivating ferocity, its jaws yawning wide to engulf his head…then they closed and the head cocked to the side like that of a dog that was confused. It made a garbled, barking sound in its throat as if it were trying to speak.

"I'm sorry," the boy said and there was genuine grief in his voice. "I just didn't want her to be the one."

The she-wolf cocked her head again and made a low whining sound. There was desperation in it and maybe even sadness. It reached out a hand. Although heavily furred on the back, the underside was decidedly feminine. It looked almost soft, the fingers long and tapering. It stroked his cheek lovingly, claws retracted.

Chloe was not sure what she was witnessing, but she knew that she had to get out of there. She moved to climb out the window and the she-wolf growled deeply, her lips curling back from her teeth like a mastiff getting ready to fight.

"Just go," the boy told her.

But Chloe knew that if she did, he was dead. The she-wolf would slaughter him. Instinct took over. She threw a leg over the window jamb and the she-wolf responded just as instinctively. She let out a piercing howl that was pure unearthly wrath and whatever tenderness or humanity she possessed, vanished as quick. She seized the boy by the head and the sound of her teeth penetrating his skull were like knives into a pumpkin. He screamed with agony, limbs flailing as she lifted him off his feet, shaking him back and forth like a terrier with a rat. His blood spattered her teats, flowing from her jaws and she bit deeper with incredible force and his skull cracked like a peanut shell with a grinding, popping noise. And by then, her claws had disemboweled him, unraveling his entrails in bloody loops.

Chloe went out the window and dropped to the roof below. Above, she could hear the sounds of the boy being gored, his bones breaking and his flesh scattered about the room. The she-wolf bayed with a clogged, liquid sound, her mouth filled with his blood and tissue.

Chloe scrambled across the roof, jumping down to another and then into the grass below. She rolled through the dewy grass and leaped to her feet. The building behind her came alive with the sound of howling.

She'd escaped and they knew it.

The boy had given his life for her and she had to make good on that. Without hesitation she ran for the woods.

THIRTY

Hunger.

Unbelievable, gnawing hunger.

It was like knives in her belly.

Yvonne didn't dare make a sound as she laid there supine on her bed of animal pelts, clutching at the furs that covered her. She badly needed something to drink and some food, but that meant alerting Mother Streega to the fact that she was awake and she'd rather suffer than do that. The old lady was still over by the fire, stitching away at something that Yvonne feared was the skin of the man who dangled nearby.

She'll do the same to me.

The thing was not to give her that chance.

Plop.

Something wet splattered nearby.

Plop.

This time it struck her bare arm. She brushed it away and the smell was horrible. Shit. It was shit. Bird-shit or bat-shit dropped from something high above. As disgusting as it was, she told herself that it was the least of her worries.

She kept casting a wary eye about, looking for weapons. Something she could brain the old lady with. There were some logs by the fire, but to get to them would mean sneaking past Mother Streega. Maybe she was old, but there was no doubting the fact that she was also insane and vicious and quite possibly a wolf herself, if her long jagged nails were any indication.

There were lots of bones around, but little else.

Decisive action was something that Yvonne had never been good at. She liked to let others lead and then she followed happily behind. But this day, this night had taught her that there was no one to lead but herself.

Now here in what might be your darkest hour you've learned that being a follower is a bad thing, her mother's voice taunted her. *Maybe we're finally making some progress.*

She nearly told the voice to shut up in her desperation to be free of its constant nagging. Mother Streega was humming some melancholy, morbid tune under her breath. Yvonne could not only hear it, but feel it like fingernails up her spine.

The old lady was a hideous thing seen by firelight, a hunched over troll, an ancient wolf-hag whose mop of hair was silver and oily. Strands of it hung in her corrugated face, her beady rodent's eyes constantly shifting, her dog-like ears set up too high on her skull. With her hooked nose and gnarled teeth, she was every evil witch from every storybook Yvonne read as a child, the prototype of the cannibal hag from Hansel and Gretel. Her rat-skinned hands were practically claws, the flesh scabrous and scaly like the leg of a chicken.

I'll die here, Yvonne thought. *A month from now my remains will be rotting on the floor with the others.*

Just the sight of the rat-lady over there filled her with a horror beyond imagining. The fear was in her mind and in her belly, making her want to retch her guts out. Mother Streega was like some living mummy and the smell coming off her was that of plundered graves and steaming cauldrons of human entrails.

Yvonne had never been a violent person, but if she had a gun she would have shot the old lady down in cold blood. It would have been an act of mercy.

She's one of them and I know it. Sooner or later she'll become a wolf like the others.

"Eh? Eh? What is that, my child?" Mother Streega's dry, cracking voice said. It had the tonal quality of broken glass ground beneath a boot. "Still pretending you're asleep? You always were a precocious little thing. But you cannot fool Mother Streega. She listens. She hears. She knows. She senses the beat of your heart—it's like a watch held to her ear...*tick-*

tock, tick-tock, tick-tock! Your heartbeat increased when you woke, dear Nabby...did you think I wouldn't know? That I wouldn't hear? Mother Streega who has hunted her prey in the darkest of woods on the darkest of nights for so many endless years?" She laughed with a terrible brazen cackling. "Yes, she can hear your heart. The blood rushing in your veins. The emptiness of your hungry belly. Oh yes, oh yes!"

It was as if the air had been bled from Yvonne. She didn't stand a chance against this beldame that was wise from countless years. She would hear anything she tried to do, maybe even her thoughts.

Mother Streega set aside her sewing and scrambled over, moving not like a woman but a pale fleshy crab. Her narrow-lipped mouth was pulled up in the mocking charnel grin of a skull. She folded her yellow hands in her lap. They mated like intertwined spiders.

"Listen, my Nabby! *Listen!*"

Somewhere beyond the cleft-like opening of the cave, the pack was baying into the night with a low mournful sound that echoed morosely through black ravines and over desolate hilltops and into the darkest thickets.

"They hunt for you! It is you they desire! You they seek!" She cackled again. She inched ever closer, her voice dropping to whisper. "Have you ever seen a pack of wild ones bring down a young girl? It's not her blood they want...not at first! The pack will break her, rape her into submission! And but for the intervention of Mother Streega, that would be you! So mind your friends or you'll be given to them...do you understand?"

Yvonne trembled. She nodded. She mumbled, "Yes." It was all she could do to stay conscious. She was on the outer edge of blacking out as the nightmare of her existence grew worse and worse.

"Ah, my sweet stupid little Nabby." The old lady shook her head, making an odd sucking sound with her lips. "Those out there...they abandoned Mother Streega. Did you know that? She was too old so they cast her from the tribe! Left her to die in the woods! She who had lived and hunted and praised the Wolf Mother beneath the horned moon for centuries before those whelps drew their first breaths! I had commerce with the Lord of the Forest long, long before their mothers were born! He left his Mark upon me! He taught me the ointment and the turning of the skin and I taught them and their fathers! I am old, oh yes, but wise and crafty beyond years! Mother Streega is not the disciple of the Wolf Mother, but her sister! *Her sister!"*

Yvonne did not move. She trembled, she pressed her lips together so she did not scream, but she did not move.

"Yes, my Nabby, they abandoned me like a sick dog, but I did not die! I *thrived! Do you hear me? I thrived!"* She inched over toward the hanging, limbless carcass. "Mother Streega lives off their scraps and leavings and they think her dead, but she shall outlive them all."

Yvonne had never had a nervous breakdown (she'd always been too meticulously medicated for that), but she felt it coming on now and coming on strong. Reality had become a frayed rug whose fibers were loose and unraveling. She was stuck in this fucking cave with this demon and all around her were well-gnawed bones. It was like the warren of a graveyard rat.

The autumnal moon cast long shadows through the opening of the cave and now that her eyes were adjusted to the gloom, she could see bats roosting above, squeaking and shrilling, dropping globs of guano all around her. The fetid, nose-reaming ammonia stink of it was the only thing that tempered the vile stench of Mother Streega and the remains—animal *and* human—scattered in every conceivable direction. The uneven floor glistened with bat-shit and scraps of flesh and green moldering bones, all of which were acrawl with vermin. And the grisly epitome of it all was the human husk that hung not ten feet away, well-picked and well-chewed and already buzzing with flies that the suffocating heat of the rat-lady's lair had invigorated on this cool autumn night.

The old lady scuttled over to the husk and jabbed it with one long, bony finger. "Too fresh, my Nabby, far too fresh for our liking. My jaws are not as strong as they once were—I must have my meat properly softened, well-seasoned with age. Then we shall bite and sup together."

And before she could stop herself, Yvonne said, "I won't eat that. It's…it's disgusting."

The rat-lady crawled toward her, her ragged shift dragging over the ground. Her huge blood-rimmed eyes did not blink, her long yellow teeth ground together. Lice jumped in her hair. There was a gray-green fungous growth over her neck, like something that might infest a corpse in a sealed coffin.

"You will eat as Mother Streega tells you," the rat-lady said. "You will feed or you will be punished."

"I won't."

The old lady hopped in her direction like some furry toad, eyes blazing with anger, mouth pulled into a toothy scowl. Yvonne tossed aside her blanket. She'd had enough. There were limits and she had reached them. As the old lady reached for her with the scaly claws of a buzzard, she punched her right in the face with tremendous force. The rat-lady shrieked, rolled over, and came back with renewed vigor. Yvonne kicked her, punched her, but the rat-lady would not be denied. She fastened herself to Yvonne like a leech, her mouth suckering to her arm. She might prefer her meat soft with age and her teeth might not be as strong as they once were, but they were strong enough—they bit down and sheared away a three-inch strip of flesh.

Yvonne fell back, the pain like a white jolt in her arm. She screamed and the rat-lady appraised her with watery yellow eyes, her face spattered with blood, the strip of meat hanging from her mouth. The agony and the revulsion she felt for Mother Streega made her at first nauseous, then pumped her full of adrenaline.

The rat-lady spat out the meat and grabbed something up off the floor—a human leg writhing with worms. She clutched it to her like an infant, making cooing noises in her throat. *"The meat must be aged,"* she said, *"soft to the tooth."* The limb she held was a good example of that. The skin had been stripped away and the exposed muscles and tissue were necrotic and oozing, strands of them dangling like wet noodles, blobs of flesh dropping to the floor and splattering like porridge.

"You will eat now," Mother Streega said, biting into the thigh of the limb and sucking up the gelatinous flesh like oatmeal. Gore and green decay dripped from her mouth.

Yvonne made a wild dive toward the fire. She didn't even know why. But she sought the light and heat and something to fight with. Logs. Branches. Bones. A flaming stick. As Mother Streega descended on her, she reached into the fire for it. It burned her hand, but she yanked it out of the blaze and swung back with it, bringing the red glowing end to bear and—as luck would have it—right into the rat-lady's face. In fact, not just into her face but sinking it right into her left eye. It sizzled like a cigarette extinguished in an egg yolk. But this was barely audible above the hysterical screams of Mother Streega herself. Yvonne pulled the burning end of the stick from her eye with a gruesome sound of suction, a long and stringy ribbon of goo attached from it to the old lady's blood-pooling socket.

On a night in which she had seen the most appalling sights, this made Yvonne cry out...yet she did not drop the stick. The rat-lady, out of her mind with pain and pure animal wrath, slashed at her with jagged nails. Yvonne nearly fell into the fire avoiding them. When the shrieking, slobbering human rat that was Mother Streega made another snarling lunge at her, she jabbed the smoldering end of the stick right into her mouth with every ounce of her strength and weight behind it. It scraped a bleeding trench in the old woman's tongue, spearing through her uvula, and puncturing the back of her throat.

Mother Streega, seriously wounded now, pulled back with a perfectly horrible hissing sound. As her skeleton key fingers clawed at the stick, she made choking, gobbling sounds as freshets of blood poured from her mouth. She could not work the stick free. She whirled and stumbled, making horrible gurgling noises, gagging and spewing out more blood. Her good eye rolled in its socket, her bad one like a soup of mucus bubbling from a blood-oozing pocket of meat. The pupil stared off toward the ceiling of the cave.

And in Yvonne's head, she heard her mother's voice again. But this time it was not lecturing or scolding, it was shouting at her, *You've got her! You've got her! Now press your advantage! Now! Do it! If she gets that stick free, she'll tear your throat out! She'll make your death last for days!* Yvonne was threaded with terror, nearly incapacitated by it. As the rat-lady scuttled about like a stepped-upon spider, she looked for a weapon. Something. Anything. She picked up a log, but it was too heavy, too ungainly to get a good grip on. Against the far wall, she saw more heaped pelts stained with bat guano. Another skin hung above them—a wolfskin. It was huge. The beast must have stood as tall as she in life. The hide was complete with head, tail, and paws...except the front pair were like human hands.

The skin began to move.

Yvonne gasped in horror, but it was no delusion. The wolfskin was alive. Mother Streega saw her standing near it and crawled forward with rage and maybe even fear. Yvonne reached for the skin and the old lady moved toward her faster, reaching out, frightened, making a gurgling cry in her throat.

She doesn't want you touching that! It's precious to her as if it's her life!

Yvonne yanked the skin from its hook of bone. Coming into contact with her, it became even more alive, seeming to pulsate in her hands. It was warm and undulant, the fur standing on end, it's limbs crawling over her own. Luminous yellow eyes opened in their sockets, the jaws grinding together, saliva dripping from them.

Yvonne fought with it as it tried to glue itself to her, attach itself like some writhing parasite. She screamed and tore at it, finally peeling it free, an alien and wicked voice in her head whispering perversely, *wear me so that I can wear you! Let us dance together in the same skin—*

But she would not listen. The voice whispered and hissed in her brain with the blatantly evil voice of a pedophile trying to lure a child into the woods. It offered things. It promised others. Sweets and treats of the most abominable kind were hers for the taking if she would only let the skin wear her.

"NO!" she shouted, grasping it with everything she had and pulling it away from her. Before it could reattach itself—and she could feel worm-like strands of connective tissue tickling her arms as it attempted to join itself to her—she threw it into the fire. It let out a pained yelping as she did so. The flames rose up and enveloped it, hungry to burn it to ashes. And as they did so, the most horrifying and perfectly insane thing happened. Though the wolfskin had no bones to support it nor muscles to work it, it pulled itself up in the fire pit, a grisly animate hide, its human-like hands flaying at the air, its jaws opening to expose sharp teeth and the backward-curving ivory fangs of a rattlesnake. As it burned and blackened, it squealed with a high-pitched cry of agony and bestial anger... then it collapsed into the fire, burning brightly, popping with sparks and putting out plumes of churning black smoke that stank like burning bales of human hair.

By then, Yvonne was on her ass.

She fell to the floor of the cave right into a fetid pool of corpse drainage and beetle-infested bat-shit. Her left hand slapped down, disturbing a rancid heap of human excrement that burst open with looping roundworms. But she was not even aware of these things. The horror of what she had witnessed drained the blood from her and she went down. And what she saw then made her woozy with fright, hysterical laughter echoing in her skull.

Mother Streega.

The wolfskin was more than a prized possession to her—it was totemic to who and what she was and she was organically linked to it in a symbiotic union: her life force kept it alive and its malefic dark energy allowed her to live a hundred depraved lifetimes.

But no more.

As it burned and curled in the flames, she literally came apart at the seams, splitting open and crumbling, blood and liquefying viscera bursting from her mouth and gushing from her torso as it was reduced to a boiling, suppurating, loathsome swamp of anatomy. Her bones clattered dryly as if they were trying to escape and her skull—part human and part canine—opened its jaws one last time, letting out an eerie, hollow cry that sounded as if it echoed from a subterranean well.

Yvonne, deeply in shock, covered in filth and slime, her lips forming words that came out as a dry rasping, began to crawl toward the opening of the cave.

And it was then, as her sanity dangled from one rusting hinge, that she heard the sound of something dragging itself from the charnel depths of the cave.

THIRTY ONE

Somewhere in her blind, hopeless flight through the dark woods, Emma came to a halt. She stopped dead. This was ridiculous and she knew it. She couldn't hope to outrun the pack; there was just no way. And particularly in her current condition. She had to stop playing into their hands. They *wanted* her to run herself right to death. It was how they hunted, probably how they'd always hunted. No, she needed to use her brain, formulate a plan, throw something at them they did not expect.

There were only two possibilities: first, instead of running away from them, she ran *at* them and took the fight to them; second, she circled around behind them and went back to the house.

The first was suicide without some heavy-caliber weapons. The second was more practical, but still dangerous as hell.

But better than letting them run you like this.

She moved through the trees, plotting how she would get around them and then the answer was right in front of her: a creek. It was about ten feet wide, thick brush growing on its banks. She followed it until she found a break in the undergrowth. Then she stepped in. Its floor was firm with flat stones. That was good. The water was bitter cold, but she had to tough it out. She followed it down about fifty or sixty feet until the overhanging tree limbs and scrub brush became very thick.

In the distance, she could hear the pack, screeching and yelping. They were coming fast now. The water was up to her hips and already her legs were beginning to feel numb. She submerged herself until only her head broke the surface, then she ducked under the overhanging scrub. There was a nice pocket in there where she could wait it out, a fan of grasses hanging before her face.

She waited.

Though the pack was moving fast, it seemed to take forever as she waited there, shivering.

Finally, after what seemed an hour, she heard them approaching the creek. They were savage and undisciplined, like a wild dog pack with no leader. She heard them snapping at each other, yapping and growling. It sounded like several of them were fighting, snarling and clawing, rolling on the ground. The others let loose with a chorus of staccato yipping and barking.

Six plates, Emma thought.

Meg put out six plates.

Six plates for the children because they would be hungry when they returned from the fields.

That meant unless another joined them, there were six werewolves hunting her. They were children, yes, but equally as cruel, vicious, and bloodthirsty as adults. Maybe in some ways, even worse. The way children could be so cold, so innately sadistic at times. Thinking these things, made her remember the wolfskins hanging in the vestibule. Were there six? She couldn't be sure. She didn't like thinking about those godawful hides and how it was they could be living things, animate and breathing, and particularly how the other one she found in the woods seemed to telepathically uplink with her mind.

She thought of all the movies she saw where people changed into werewolves. How could someone possibly become a hybrid wolf monster? There were no wolves in the human evolutionary line, no canid genes. The skins were the key to it. They covered you, becoming you as you became them. There was a symbiosis there, a mutually beneficial parasitism. But one so incredible, so fantastic, it was pure madness.

Don't worry about that, she warned herself. *There's only one thing you need to concern yourself with—getting to the house and getting to that shotgun. If you can get your hands on it, you might have a chance.*

If it was loaded, that was.

The wolves had crossed the creek now. She could hear them running wild in the forest, trying to pick up her scent. They were young, probably inexperienced. They would run and run, track and sniff, going in circles as Meg had said. Many miles from here and many hours from now, maybe they'd realize that she had outwitted them.

Then again, maybe not.

Slowly then, feeling stiff as a corpse, Emma pulled herself out of the water, lying on the ground, shivering and gasping. She needed to move. It was the only thing that was going to get the blood moving in her limbs and bring her core temperature back up. She moved off in the direction of the farmhouse, cutting through the woods, trying to stay on her original path. In the dark that was nearly impossible, but she trusted in her instincts to keep her close to it. Soaking wet and shivering, it was hard going.

After about twenty or thirty minutes, she saw the farmhouse. It was still lit up. Meg would be there. She wouldn't be expecting her to come back and that was about the only thing Emma had going for her.

She crept slowly, very slowly up to the house. The kitchen was still lit up. Emma wasn't very tall so she had to grip the window ledge and hoist herself up to get a look in there…and she had to do this very quietly. She got her eyes above the ledge. There was no one in the kitchen. She dropped down and approached the back door. Her heart was thumping in her chest. She climbed the steps, reaching out for the knob.

It was locked.

She wanted to scream and cry and kick the door, but that wouldn't help a thing. Did this mean Meg was onto her? That she had foreseen this? But Emma had trouble believing that.

She expected me to run. Not to come back.

Emma moved around the side of the house. There was the window of the room she had been in. It faced the side yard. She crept up to it. Standing on her tiptoes, she took hold of the sash and, to her relief, it slid up easily. Holding onto the ledge, feet dangling in the air, she pushed it up all the way. Quietly as she could, she pulled herself up and in.

Right away, she could smell her dirty clothes in the corner. They were undisturbed. Listening and hearing nothing, she stripped out of the clothes Meg had given her. She pulled on her dirty shirt and pants. The smell of them made her want to vomit, but at least they were dry.

And the smell will confuse the pack.

She tied her shoes and went to the door.

She heard nothing out there.

Carefully, trying not to shake, she opened the door. Her skin was covered in goosebumps and it had little to do with the chilly creek she submerged in and everything to do with this damn house. It felt alive around her just as it did when she tried to sleep here earlier. Alive with malefic intent. As she stepped from the room, it was as if the house was watching her. She could almost sense it growing uneasy again, as if it did not like her there, as if she was a diseased germ in its body and it was scheming, plotting of how she could be eradicated. The beat of its heart had picked up to a low gallop, matching her own. The blood flowing through its veins and capillaries increased.

The kitchen was empty.

The kettle still steamed on the stove, boiling, forgotten. She moved past it, made it maybe three feet when the hairs at the back of her neck stood on end. The kitchen was filled with not just the offensive, mephitic stink of Meg's bubbling soup, but another odor that Emma knew well—the gamey reek of the wolves, a stink which was equal parts wet fur, raw meat, breath hot with blood, and acrid glandular secretions.

She turned and one of them was standing there.

It was about the size of a twelve-year-old boy, a mangy beast with piss-yellow eyes and red-brown fur that was filthy with dried blood from snout to belly. Its lips wrinkled back from sharp white teeth that had been sharpened on bones. Its tongue dangled from its mouth, curling and twisting like a worm at the end of a hook. And what was most disturbing, it had a prepuce sheath between its legs like that of a dog, a pink and glistening penis jutting from it erectly.

Though she was terrified, Emma did not flinch. She did not shake. Her eyes did not blink. Something had taken hold of her, amped her up into fight mode. The werewolf was but ten feet away. One careless move on her part and it would leap on her, teeth snapping and claws slashing. She was, at that moment, both within and without herself. Inside, she was tense, muscles bunching for combat. But outside, as if viewing herself from above, she saw not herself but one animal facing down another. Which was more powerful and dangerous was a given; but which would prove to be more shrewd and crafty remained to be seen.

The werewolf was uncertain of what to do. That much was obvious.

The front she showed it was not the one it was used to. It expected screams and cries, it expected her to run like prey, but she did neither of these things. She stared at it, meeting it boldly on common ground. It smelled her fear, but not the kind of fear it understood. This was more along the lines of caution, as it would show when meeting one of its own kind. It smelled something else, too, something unsettling: aggression. It was concealed, but it was there and the werewolf, despite its age, had had enough run-ins with human beings to know just how dangerous and wily they could be.

It took one faltering step forward, trying to trigger her into a behavioral pattern it could understand. She still did not move. Her breathing was deep and even. She was alert, tense, ready to fight. It sensed this, too. It feared that she was drawing it in, trapping it.

It fell back on eons of threat display—it snarled at her, barked, flashed its teeth and claws. It hunched over, readying itself to leap. By nature, its kind were not patient creatures. They did not do well on the defensive. It had to attack and attack now, even though its lingering human perception warned of danger.

Emma waited.

She wanted the beast to make the first move. As scared as she was, she knew she had the advantage as long as it moved first. Trembling with rage, it vaulted at her. A split second after it moved, she pivoted, grabbed the boiling kettle of soup and threw it right in the beast's face. It had been boiling so long, it was scalding. It struck the beast like acid in mid-jump. The agony made it shriek and its aim was deflected. It launched itself past her and collided with the cast-iron stove which did not give a centimeter. It was like hitting a brick wall. The beast sank to the floor, dazed, knocked nearly unconscious by the power of its own attack and the collision with the stove. The boiling soup blistered its eyes, its tongue, burning its skin beneath the fur.

When it made a sign that it was coming to, whimpering and injured—three fingers if its left hand were broken by the stove—Emma lifted the kettle above her head and brought it down with all her strength. There was a hollow *crack!* as its skull was fractured. The kettle, like the stove, was old and cast-iron. A formidable weapon.

The werewolf was damaged, but hardly done in. Its eyes rolled in their sockets, its jaws opened. It was in pain and pain, in its kind, was a great motivator. It clawed about on the floor, trying to get its legs under it.

That's when a voice from the vestibule said, "Stand back."

Emma jumped, startled, the kettle falling from her hands and clattering to the floor. It rolled on its edge and came to a stop. A man was standing there with a shotgun in his hands. He was an old, tough-looking woodsman in a green army coat, his beard silver as frost. It was the hunter she'd met earlier.

"It's you," she said.

"Step back, girl."

The wolf looked up at him with bleary eyes. It attempted a snarling noise, but it was half-hearted. One eye stared at him, the other seemed to roll in its socket. It extended a hand-like paw, the nails scratching over the linoleum.

"It knows it's in trouble," the old man said. "Seen it before. They can be sweet as an old hound when the need strikes 'em. But soon as our backs are turned, its teeth will be in our throats. You can trust me on that."

The werewolf slowly raised its head. It did not show its teeth. It acted inoffensive, harmless as a whipped dog. The old man wasn't having it, though. Without emotion, he aimed the twelve-gauge and fired. The side of the werewolf's head disappeared in an explosion of gore, blood and brains splattering against the stove front. Some of it ended up on the burner, sizzling and smoking.

"That's one," he said. "It'll do for starters."

"How did you know where to find me?"

He sighed. "Because I know this night and what they do, the ones that orchestrate it." He looked from the dead thing on the floor to her. "I'm…I'm glad you're still alive."

"I've fought werewolves before," she said.

THIRTY TWO

The thing that had once been known as Steph moved through the forest, breathing in the primal joy of the woods and becoming part of it. She looked up at the moon above, reaching toward it with bloodstained claws. She could hear things moving in the brush around her, small creatures out foraging. They hungered as everything in the night hungered. She had glutted herself on the meat and blood of the child-wolf, discovering that once the hide was peeled away there was a deliciously soft, pink-skinned treat waiting inside to be eaten.

She could not seem to remember who she was before she donned the wolfskin (or it donned her). Her memories were vague and misty. She saw faces that confused her because she thought she should recognize them. There were strange feelings attached to these images, but they were fading fast. Who she had been didn't seem to matter any longer. She had been living in a dark pit and now she had escaped, now she was fulfilling her destiny.

Such higher concepts, of course, were beyond her simple animal-human hybrid mind, but she knew that what she was doing was the right thing. When she had fed on the wolf-child, the pack—all children—had seen her doing it and scattered.

They were afraid of her now, but that didn't mean they wouldn't come for her. She was rogue. She was dangerous. She was the child-eating ogre that haunted the woods and filled their minds with terror…at least the human parts of their minds.

There was a sound.

She crouched down.

Was the pack coming? There were many of them and only one of her. She knew she must not get too confident in her dominance of them. They were still deadly, still sly and fierce. She sniffed the air. What she smelled initially confused her. It was not the pack; she knew their odor well. This was something else.

It smelled similar to the pack in a very generalized way, but much wilder and primitive, leaving a musky trail behind it that was incredibly strong, nose-reaming. With her heightened olfactory sense, she knew it was a male, but little else than that. The pungency of it disturbed her. It made her crawl into the brush and whimper.

What was this?

What in the hell was this?

The chemical signals of its odor made her frightened. By that point, she feared very little…but this, this was a lethal odor, a deadly odor.

It was coming.

The forest went silent.

It passed about thirty feet from her, snapping off saplings and knocking down dead trees, crunching through dead leaves with a resounding purposeful stride that told her it feared absolutely nothing. It had no enemies, hence there was no need for stealth. It moved up a rise to a ridgeline and for one brief moment she could see it outlined in the moonlight—massive, shaggy, an immense wolf-like head set atop squared shoulders. Then it was gone. Gradually, hesitantly, the wild lands came back to life. Things skittered. Peeped. Cried out in the sky.

And the thing that had once been called Steph bounded away into the darkness of the forest.

THIRTY THREE

Some bit of time after she escaped from the she-wolf into the forest, her mind fraught with guilt for the boy who forever would have no name and sacrificed his life for her, Chloe stumbled out of the underbrush and found a trail before her that was silvered by moonlight. She was hesitant about stepping foot on it, because nothing in this forest was what it should be and all paths led to horrors of varying degrees.

Her mind told her that this was exactly what she was looking for: a trail that led out. Better than wandering in the dark, haunted woods for hours. But another part of her mind, the fearful part, the superstitious primitive part of her brain that saw menace in every shadow and open jaws behind every tree, told her that the trail would not lead her out but deeper into the maze of this malefic never-never land of a forest.

If you take this trail, you're playing right into their hands. Nothing good can come of it...can't you see that? It's a trap laid for the unwary.

The difficult part was that she neither trusted her rational, thinking brain nor her instincts. She was not who she was before. Everything about her had undergone some radical alteration. She did not think as she did before, uncertainty and paranoia underlying every thought and action. There was a strange, near mystical motivation to her thinking, a confidence that she was forever doing the right thing, the thing that would bring her to her ultimate destiny. Even her body felt different—strong, sleek, well-muscled and lithe. As if being in such close contact with nature had morphed her from a scared, scurrying mouse to an agile panther, a sensual machine that no longer feared its own hungers, but actively courted them.

Oh please, please stay off the trail!

Ignoring the voice, she stepped onto it and a shudder passed through her flesh from toe to scalp. It was a wonderful electric jolt that made her skin tingle and her thighs tense. Her mouth filled with sweet-tasting saliva. So much so, that a warm droplet of it coursed down her chin. She felt that other in her—the one that had been activated by the hot salve massaged onto her—wake up and stretch. She could almost picture this other in her brain: it was her and not her. Naked, well-oiled with the salve, it laid on a heap of animal skins, sucking on its fingertips and sliding fingers into itself. Its body bucked with orgasm after orgasm. And when she pulled back in shock from its lecherous image, it laughed at her with an animal-like braying.

And immediately, she thought: *The Bride...this is The Bride of Blooding Night. This is who I must become.*

"Enough," she said under her breath. "Enough."

Whatever was in that salve, it was fucking with her brain, making her think crazy thoughts and imagine things that just weren't there. Some kind of hallucinogen, maybe. She remembered being in high school and wanting to be a cool Goth Wiccan like some of the other girls. She read a book on witchcraft and it said that witches (or those who were deemed to be so by ignorant peasants) didn't really fly around on brooms or hazel branches, of course, they just *thought* they did because of ointments they rubbed themselves with which contained strong psychoactive agents.

Maybe the salve was like that, she considered as she walked the path, knowing she shouldn't but feeling she must. Like a metal filing to a magnet, she was being drawn down it and even though no good could come of it, she didn't fight it; she encouraged it.

I'm going on a wonderful enchanted journey like Alice going down the rabbit hole.

Yes, that was it exactly.

Or, said the leering scarlet-lipped mouth of The Bride of Blooding Night, *like Little Red Riding Hood following the dark woodland path to grandmother's house, actively seeking the wolf that will deflower her.*

The path twisted and turned through the shadowy woods rather like the sinuous body of the serpent that tempted Eve. Huge, gnarled trees grew at its perimeter, crowding in with thick furrowed boles and spidery branches that intertwined high above, making the path into a secret tunnel that passed from the here and now into the bewitched world of nightmares. The trees excited her because there was something fey and otherworldly about them. They also scared her because they reminded her of the animate trees in *The Wizard of Oz* that captured Dorothy.

But they've already captured you, chaste little Chloe.

The voice, which she knew was her own, was trying to tease her, to annoy her, but it was powerless because the further the path took her to her ultimate destination, the more impervious she was to her own barbs and criticism. She saw and knew many things now. Grand things and minuscule things. Magnificent things and esoteric things. She was able to look at herself from above and objectively understand all those many insignificant details that made her up.

She felt happy and carefree, divorced from all the societal constraints that kept her a wallflower and all the cultural biases that made her weak and uneasy. In her mind, she skipped and sang, a basket of goodies slung from the crook of one arm.

There were things about Chloe that no one knew. Things she kept even from her closest friends. Emma and Yvonne and even Steph did not know about them. One of them, and perhaps the most closely-guarded, was that though she had dated many boys, both in high school and college, she had never slept with any of them. She was still a virgin. She was untried and untested, *virgo intacta,* an unbroken egg, unchurned butter, untasted cream. There were deep dark secrets in her loins and a playful magic in her womb that no man—or woman, for that matter—knew of. Between her legs there was a treasure chest of heat and need, but she kept it locked with crossed legs and had it not been for this night she might have kept it so for ten more years or until spinsterhood.

Maybe it was the idea that this would soon change as all things changed in this forest of delights and damnation. Maybe this relaxed her, put a spring to her step, a lightness to her being. Soon she would be free of something that she had thought of as neither a curse or a blessing, but simply a burden.

She followed the path for a long time, sliding down its serpentine back like a player in Snakes and Ladders, drawn forward but feeling as if she was really descending into the netherworld of this unnamable place. When the trees opened and she saw the cabin crouched in a pocket in their depths, she gasped. In fact, her head whirled and her belly grew weak and she sank to her knees. She could not catch her breath.

And in the confines of her brain, The Bride, hot-breathed, lips swollen with the reddest of blood, whispered, *And in the cabin in the secret wood, my lover doth wait.* The voice made her feel warm all over. The other inside her quivered beneath her flesh. Like a snake, it was anxious to shed its skin and make itself known, present itself to the world.

The cabin was small and quaint, pine logs meeting pine logs, the roof thatched and sharp-peaked. It was every cottage from every fairy tale she'd read as a young, impressionable girl. Golden light filtered through the shutters and a wisp of smoke extruded from the high chimney. This was the place that wanted her, this was what had called her down the path and summoned her to its side. This and only this.

I'm here, I'm here. Just as you wanted. I've come to be with you.

Slowly, gathering herself, Chloe approached the cabin. The door was a simple plank affair, but it looked sturdy as if it could hold back an army. Even in the wan moonlight, she could see the great scratches running down its face. At the sight of them, something inside her flinched. *Look at them! This is a warning! This is the last one you'll get!* This practicality fought against the drive within her to get through the door.

She reached out and undid the latch.

THIRTY FOUR

Yvonne wasn't sure by that point if she could trust anything: what she saw, heard, felt, even touched. As she crawled from the cave, she heard something moving behind her and was certain it was her imagination. Mother Streega, the rat-lady, the hag-wolf was dead…yet, she could feel her eyes watching, staring, eyes connected to a monstrous brain that could never truly die in the accepted sense of the term.

In her highly-agitated state of mind, Yvonne decided she would not turn around, not give into her fear. The old lady and her wolfskin were gone now, destroyed. That was a fact. She needed to get out. That was all. There was no more to it.

Listen. You better listen: this is real.

She paused.

Something was indeed moving in her direction, dragging itself forward.

As the thing crept closer, she began to sweat. She knew if she tried to make a run for it, it was going to leap on her and sink its teeth in her throat. She had to be cool and calm. That had never been so important. She kept slowly moving toward the entrance, already smelling the pines and balsam, the clean pure air of the night. But as she did so, she looked on the ground for a weapon. A rock. A stick. A stray bone. Anything.

And then—

Something jumped out of the shadows at her, its rotting hands like chicken claws grabbing hold of her hair and yanking her back.

Yvonne uttered a strangled cry, fighting herself free and scrambled toward the entrance. But the thing wouldn't let her leave—it leaped out of the shadows, springing like a frog—a long-armed wraith that jumped on her back, encircling her with bony limbs. She screamed and tried to toss it off her, but it clung tightly, wrapping itself around her like a blanket, legs scissoring her hips and splintered nails digging into her chest like a cat climbing a tree. It squealed and hissed, nipping at the back of her neck with nubby teeth.

She whirled and fought, doing everything she could to rise up from her hands and knees, but the creature forced her down again and again, pressing her to the cave floor with its weight and strength as its nails cut ruts into her chest and its constricting legs squeezed harder and harder until it felt like her pelvis would snap.

Regardless of what she did, the creature clutched all the tighter, riding her, giving off a fusty, stagnant odor like mouse piss and mold. It was incapacitating, growing stronger by the second like poisonous gas, as if it was a secretion designed to overpower an enemy.

Yvonne tore at its hands which were cold and pebbled with scabs and open sores. They were scaly and skeleton-fingered. As she pulled at them, sheets of loose flesh came free. Then it bit deeply into the back of her neck and she could feel its icy, swollen tongue licking at the wound greedily. Screaming again—and maybe she had never really stopped—she reached back and took hold of the creature's hair which was oily and seemed to move in her hands like worms. She yanked out handfuls, but her rider would not relent.

Finally, she threw herself backward, crushing the creature beneath her. With a great whoosh of air, it released her.

She rolled away, hurting and breathless, scrabbling about with her hands in the dirt and filth, seeking a weapon. She came up with a long yellow bone: a human femur. The blurring form came at her again and she swung the ball-end of it, cracking the creature in the face with it. It squealed and pulled away.

"GET AWAY FROM ME!" Yvonne shouted at it. "GET THE FUCK AWAY FROM ME!"

The creature circled around her carefully. What it was exactly was hard to say. It was a hunched over goblin-like shape wearing the ragged, threadbare remnants of a long dress. It was not exactly human and not exactly wolf, but some grotesque hybrid of the two. Its flesh was yellow and seamed, bulging eyes pink as fresh meat. They were globular like those of an insect, its puckered jaws pushed out in a vulpine snout, crooked teeth not long but exceedingly sharp. It's nose was the triangular cavity of a skull.

It hissed and snapped at her, long ribbons of drool hanging from its mouth. Yvonne held the bone above her head, ready to strike. The creature moved around her with a distinctly inhuman hobbling motion. It sprouted mangy tufts of hair like dry straw, bones protruding from its hide in yellow staffs and rungs. It looked, if anything, like a woman that had died in the process of becoming a wolf.

It kept trying to speak, its voice garbled and croaking. But finally, Yvonne could hear what it was saying, *"I...I...I am Nabby...not you! Never you! I am the one hunted on Blooding Night! I was to be the bride!"* she said, the words coming out of her fast and hot like vomit. *"Mother Streega promised me! I am the one, the cherished one, the eternal...not you! Not you!"*

Jesus, this was Nabby!

This creeping…monstrosity.

"Keep away from me!" Yvonne warned her.

Nabby was not only physically degenerate, but mentally unbalanced. She was getting herself worked up, shaking and quivering with muscular contractions. She kept trying to dart in at Yvonne, but Yvonne threatened her with the femur and she pulled back again and again. Though her face was more skull than skin, more wolf than woman, there was still something remotely human about her as there had been with Mother Streega. Yvonne sensed trauma, pain, a despair beyond depth within her.

Blooding Night.

Blooding Night.

Elizabeth had referred to that, too. But what did it mean? What was any of this about? *It's obvious, isn't it?* her mother's voice said. *Blooding Night is tonight. You and your friends picked the worst possible night to come to these woods. Whatever Blooding Night means to these beasts, you are now part of it. That's why you're being hunted.*

Yes, there was a logic to that. Maybe Yvonne could never really know what Blooding Night entailed, not really, but this was it. *Tonight.* From the drugs in the dandelion wine to waking up in the body bag to being hunted through the woods, this was it. And this pathetic, revolting creature was Mother Streega's Nabby, her daughter or granddaughter, who had gone through Blooding Night long ago and it had reduced her to...*this*. Maybe Mother Streega had been insane or senile, probably both, but she was right that something infinitely terrible had happened to Nabby on Blooding Night.

And that same thing will happen to me if I don't escape.

She remembered what Elizabeth had said to her. Maybe she was a werewolf, too, and the mother of a pack of flesh-eaters, but her words rang true. She had spoken them not to frighten Yvonne, but to educate her.

Yvonne, she said, *you need to run. You must learn to hide, to cover your scent, to fight when needed and flee whenever possible. This is the only way you'll survive this night and reach your goal. Do you understand me, child? Tonight is Blooding Night and only the smartest and strongest can survive.*

The beast known as Nabby was still trying to get at her, so Yvonne threatened her again with the femur. "Nabby," she said, astounded at how sturdy her voice sounded when she was little more than white pudding inside. "I don't want to hurt you. I'm leaving now and if you try to stop me, I'll split your fucking head open."

With that, she began backing her way toward the entrance of the cave. Nabby first made growling noises, then something between a sobbing and the whining of a dog.

"Not...not...not there, not out into the Blooding Night...never go there..."

Yvonne looked back at her once, then slipped through the crevice opening, scrambling up into the night. Now she was free and she had to stay free. Now she would fight and flee and learn to survive so, as Elizabeth had said, she could reach her goal.

THIRTY FIVE

The old man's story was soon told. His name was Hal Lamont. He was sixty-nine years old, a retired firefighter. He had a place over in Copper Springs. He lost his brother in Vietnam and his son in Desert Storm. The latter was a point of great pain to him, though he did not outwardly admit it as he drove away from Meg's farmhouse. His wife had never quite been the same since it happened and neither had he (Emma suspected). As he maneuvered his pickup down the dirt road, over hills and down gullies, he spoke freely like a man on his deathbed who had nothing to lose.

"How far is it until we're out of these woods?" she asked him.

"A long way."

"How long?"

"Ten, twelve miles."

"God."

He lit a cigarette and blew his smoke out the window. "Sure. Ten or twelve miles, but it'll seem like fifty. We have to go at it slow. Lots of twists and turns. Some parts get flooded, washed out by creeks and rivers. Sometimes trees fall and…"

"What?"

"Sometimes they get pushed over."

She swallowed. "You mean by *them.*"

"Yes. If they don't want us leaving. If they figure out what I'm up to, they'll try to stop us."

She looked at the shotgun on his lap. That was it. That was all they had to fight with. The other one in the vestibule of the farmhouse was old and rusted, hadn't been fired in years, according to Hal.

Emma studied the moonlit road, the black encroaching forest. At any moment, the werewolves could come leaping out at them. She did not pretend it wouldn't happen. She anticipated it, knowing it was only a matter of time.

"I don't suppose you have a phone."

"Out here?" he said. "Wouldn't do you any good."

As they drove, she thought about this night, what it meant and what it didn't mean, how she could survive it. And the more she thought about it, the more she thought about herself. Who she was. Maybe even *what* she was. Her memories of the Cupps and what happened during those terrible months had never been repressed like in books or movies. It was not a trauma she had conveniently forgotten about. Quite the opposite, the memories of it always hovered just at the edge of her conscious mind. She *wished* she could forget about it all, but she never did. She simply forced it into the back of her head where it could do the least amount of damage.

She had survived it.

And I'll survive this, too, she told herself.

Inside herself there were things that scared her, pockets of darkness she had never dared explore, gray areas she had never set foot in. There was something in her, something dark at her core, like an egg waiting to hatch and it frightened her.

"So why did you decide to help me?" she asked. "Why did you come and get me?"

"I figured it was the right thing to do."

"Aren't you worried about your wife? What they'll do to her?"

"Yes, I am."

"Then…"

"Sometimes you have to do the right thing. Getting you out of this mess and away from those *people* is the right thing to do." He pulled off his cigarette. "Besides, Sue is armed and she's a good shot. If they get her…then I'll die fighting them. Ever since my boy died, I've been dying a day at a time. Let's just say I'm moving things along."

"If you have a death wish, leave me out of it."

"It's not a death wish."

"Then what?" she asked.

"I need to do something right, as I said. Most of us spend our lives turning a blind eye to things we should have intervened in, should have set right. We don't because we're comfortable and lazy. We don't want to interrupt our easy lives by taking on things that are foolish or dangerous. I don't want to die thinking I did nothing. You're young. Maybe you can't understand that. But when you get old like me, you look back and you see all the mistakes you made, all the bad choices and missed opportunities. More so, you see all the things you should have done that you were too afraid to do."

"I understand that."

"No, you don't. Not completely. But one day you will. When all the fun has gone out of living and you're in a rut spinning your wheels. You'll know then. You'll ask yourself what was the point of it all and you won't have an answer."

Emma wasn't sure if she believed that or not. She wasn't sure about a lot of things. "Where are they from? The werewolves. They haven't always been here."

"For a long time they have. Originally, I think they're from somewhere in Europe."

"Why hasn't anybody rooted them out before?"

"You'd have to find them to do that." He sighed. "I can't explain it exactly. But one night a decade, Blooding Night, they're as much a part of our world as we are. But other than that…well, you can roam these woods for days and never find them. They have a village out here and cabins… but you won't find them, not unless it's Blooding Night."

"Are you saying this is an enchanted forest? That it's magic?"

He shook his head. "No, not exactly. I wish I could explain it to you, but nothing I could say would make any sense."

The forest was thicker now, huge stands of pines crowding the road and climbing up hills. It was impossibly black out there. Maybe he was right, Emma thought. There was something fantastic about it all, something darkly enchanted, a place of witchery and primal belief. She had trouble believing that such a place could exist in the light of day.

He was silent for a time, but she knew there was something on his mind. Finally, he said it: "Why did you say you had fought werewolves before?"

Bad memories filled her head like winging bats. She felt her stomach roll over. And in her mind, that same voice that she'd been hearing for years—*Tell him, Emma, tell him all about your secret, the big secret, the one nobody knows.* She cleared her throat. She could not be owned by her past, she could not let it gain control and weaken her. Not now.

She opened her mouth and it spilled out. "I don't have any family. I was an orphan. I grew up in a Catholic foster home, the sort of place that used to be called an orphanage. It was bad. The girls there abused me constantly. When I was twelve, I was abducted from the mall by a man and woman. They were crazy. They said I was their daughter." She broke off here for a moment, gathering her strength. "I went with them. I was glad to. It had to be better than the home. It was, at first. They treated me just like a daughter. Then…well, they changed. They became monsters. They beat me, tortured me, humiliated me, and raped me. But I escaped. I killed them both."

Hal was silent for a moment. "You poor thing," he said, reaching out to take her hand because it was the human thing to do.

She pulled it away. "I don't want sympathy. They were werewolves. They were monsters. But I fought them and I won. I survived. I can survive anything."

It was amazing how telling the tale (as painful as it was), was liberating. It immediately shut down the voice of Mrs. Cupp in her head that had been baiting her for years.

"I wish there was something I could say," Hal told her.

"There isn't."

"I know, but—"

"Look out!" she cried.

A tree had fallen across the road. It was a massive pine and she bet that the both of them couldn't have circled their arms around it. Later on, she would think how conveniently placed it was. The road came down a winding incline and unless you were riding your brake the entire way down, you would naturally pick up speed. At the bottom, the road cut to the right around a blind corner and that's where the tree was.

Hal put on his brakes, the pickup skidding. But there was no way to avoid the tree, not unless you turned toward the left and went off the road. Which, instinctively, he did. Then the truck was skidding down a hillside of saplings into a low, swampy valley of birch and alder. They hit stumps and jumped over logs and crashed into a deadfall, the windshield spider-webbing and falling into their laps.

"Are you all right?" Hal asked.

"Yes," Emma gasped, her heart pounding. "I think so."

"Lucky we didn't roll."

They stepped out into muck that sucked their legs down right up to their knees. Using the truck, they pulled themselves up onto higher, drier ground. Then they were standing together. Hal had the shotgun in his hands.

"That tree was no accident," he said. "They'll be coming now."

Emma looked around fearfully in the darkness. "What'll we do?"

"There's a place a mile or so from here. We'll be safe there. Now follow me and don't lag."

THIRTY SIX

About four miles from Hal and Emma as the crow flies, Steph was growing excited.

The overriding desire in her life now was to kill and feed. It was an addiction that was utterly insatiable. It owned her and directed her every movement. Crouched on the hilltop, leaves drifting down on her from the trees, she sighted the cabin below. She could smell meat. It electrified her senses. Made her eyes dart in their sockets and her nares widen. Her flesh quivered.

And that was enough.

She had to have it. She had to sink her teeth into it and swallow it in great half-chewed gulps. In her mind, she pictured herself going down there, just walking to the door like an ordinary person and knocking. She did not see herself as a beast.

Carefully, quietly, she crept down toward the cabin.

Now she stood before the door, tense with excitement. Her breathing was rapid, her heart rate accelerated. Inside, her heightened senses were picking up telltale clues of prey in distress. Intrigued, she sniffed around the door. The prey was an older woman who was nervous, worrying over something. Her agitation made her weak, made her easy for the taking. She was ignoring the signals her senses were telegraphing her that she was in danger.

That was good.

Steph liked this. It made tremors of excitement roll through her. She drew her claws gently over the door. The woman heard this as Steph intended. She stepped slowly over to the door.

"Hal?" she said. "Is that you, Hal?"

Steph, or the beast she now was, knew there were several ways to do this. She could force her way in with brute force which would mean battering the door down (and possibly injuring herself), or she could simply draw her prey in. She chose the latter. Like any predator, she preferred an easy, clean kill over one she had to work for. She raised her hand, resisting the savage urge to claw at the door, clenching it into a fist and knocking three times.

"Hal?" the woman's voice said again.

Steph heard footsteps moving lightly toward the door. She grew excited. Saliva that was hot and sweet filled her mouth and foamed from her jaws. After devouring half of the wolf-child, she shouldn't have been hungry. But she was. In fact, she was ravenous. It was an earmark of her kind that if food was plentiful and readily available, she would eat again and again…even if she needed to purge her last meal to do so.

The woman was directly on the other side of the door now. Only a few inches of wood separated them.

Steph could barely contain herself.

All her life the beast within had been so very close to the surface. She fought against it constantly, keeping it chained up in its cage so it did no real damage. But now that was no longer necessary. Letting the animal out—liberating it via the wolfskin—was like emptying a very full bladder and, perhaps better, releasing the carnal joy of the mother of all orgasms. A wonderful relief. Like opening a pressure valve and releasing all that bottled-up steam. A delirious climax. She wanted to scream with the sheer rapture.

But she didn't, of course.

The prey was coming to her. It would offer itself and she would accept it with blood-dripping claws. The anticipation of that moment was like foreplay leading up to the big event.

"Hal? Are you out there?"

There was desperation in the woman's voice now. Steph could sense her rising apprehension. It made her heart beat faster, her lungs suck in quick fearful breaths, and filled her veins with rich blood. Steph could practically feel its heat. She trembled at the idea of opening those veins and swimming in red lagoons of blood. She would tear the woman's heart from her chest in all its pumping, meaty, well-muscled glory. Its cherry-sweet juices would fill her mouth and gush down her throat.

The woman called out for Hal again and Steph cocked her head at the distress in her voice. It touched something human in her. Her high pointed ears twitched, her bright yellow eyes momentarily lost their neon luster. *Please, oh please do not open this door! I am not Hal! I am a slinking dirty monster! Can't you feel the evil radiating off me?* The humanity faded, winking out like a distant star and was replaced by a voracious appetite in her belly and a sadistic, ravening mind in her head. The woman gripped the deadbolt on the other side. *Open it, my dear, so that I might open you.* The deadbolt was unlatched.

Steph shivered with delight.

The knob turned and the door was opened warily. An inch, then two. No, no, no. This was not how Steph visualized it. It had been thrown open so the woman could see her grim shape and evil form. The pure terror of what she perceived would make her heart pound and fill her carcass with blood, sweetening the meat.

The woman, despite her age, was very agile. She caught a glimpse of Steph, tried to slam the door shut but the quick-thinking she-wolf that lurked there in feral glory stuck its foot between the door and jamb.

The woman cried out in pure delicious terror.

Steph roared with triumph.

One clawed hand reached for the woman, but quick as a rabbit, she ducked away and jumped back. She moved with grace, with purpose. This was not the old and infirm from the city that Steph was used to. This was a country woman who'd spent her life in the sun, working with her back, hands in the soil. The sort of woman that was not separate from the good earth and its indomitable spirit, but part of it. She was used to encounters with wild animals of all sorts. And she was also a crack shot and had dropped more than one buck in the autumn woods and popped her share of ducks flying over woodland ponds.

She jumped back not so much out of shock, but with a definite plan in mind. She whirled, skirted the sofa, and reached the fireplace by the time Steph lunged through the doorway. She snatched a 30.06 from its bracket over the hearth and brought it to bear. When Steph was but five scant feet from her, she worked the bolt, chambered a round, and fired.

The 30.06 was a devastating weapon at any range and was for many years the choice of snipers because of its knockdown power. As Steph leaped for her, the bullet caught her in the shoulder. At such close range, it was like being kicked by a draft horse. She was thrown six feet, crashing into the dining room table and collapsing in a shivering heap, her blood pooling on the flagstone floor.

The woman did not run screaming into the night. Weapon sighted, she moved toward Steph, ready to fire again. "So," she said with great calm and self-control, "you are real after all. I heard the stories...but I never really believed them."

Revelation had taken years off her. She circled around the she-wolf, knowing she had a trophy that was like no other.

"I'm willing to bet you'll fetch a good price, won't you?" From the tone of her voice, it was obvious she was considering this carefully and methodically. "Wait until my Hal gets home and sees you."

Steph realized she was in a bad fix here. This had not gone as she had planned. In fact, it couldn't have gone much worse. This woman was not what she expected at all. She never guessed she could be this resourceful, this dangerous. The shoulder wound, though it bled freely, was no real danger. Steph knew this. But in the woman...well, she had found an able adversary.

Steph looked over at her and growled. She rose a few inches and then dropped to the floor, feigning weakness.

"I shouldn't if I were you," the woman said. "I once dropped a five-hundred pound black bear with this very rifle at thirty yards. I'm pretty certain I can core your skull at ten."

The words she spoke were difficult to comprehend. Steph felt feverish and confused as she tried to make sense of them. Her language was the language of the wolf—guttural barking, snarling, and baying. She could read the secretions and chemical signatures of animals. Her senses were hyper-acute, practically supernormal. But spoken words confused her. Her human mind recognized them, but her animal brain would not process them. Still, she was smarter than a canid and she understood that the woman was toying with her, daring her to attack.

But she would not.

On the floor, she waited for opportunity. Patience was not the strong suit of either werewolves *or* Steph, but fear was teaching her a new way to play.

"When does it happen?" the woman asked. "When is it that you change back to a human being? When the moon goes down? When the sun comes up? You can be sure of one thing: I'll be here waiting. I want to see who you are. Are those teats?" The woman drew in closer. "Why, yes they are. You're a female, are you? I'll be damned."

Steph did not react. She laid there, eyes open, glazing over. She barely breathed. She constricted her blood vessels so she did not bleed. It was an old trick. Using the physiological gifts of her kind, she employed a form of biofeedback, gaining voluntary control over her body. She appeared dead. It was an ancient survival mechanism.

Still, the old woman was not easily fooled.

But she would be. Sooner or later. The hide that Steph wore was as much a part of her as her own, yet for all that, it possessed an intelligence all its own. It communicated with her through imagery that her mind translated in its own way. *Practice patience, little one. The woman is old. She is tired. She must rest soon. Her bladder is full. Her kind do not like to relieve themselves before others. Your chance comes soon. Do not hesitate. Fill yourself with her life. It is old and weakening, but not without some vigor.* So, Steph waited. And then waited some more. The old woman was tired, but she worried about Hal. Her anxiety was high. It made her bladder feel fuller than it was.

"I'm not convinced you're dead," she said. "But I know a way to make certain of it."

Gun in her hands, she stepped within five feet of the she-wolf. Her aim was true. She would not miss. She hesitated. If she shot the creature in the head, the trophy would be badly damaged. This gave her pause. She stepped closer. In the dimness of the cabin, she did not notice the milky-white membrane over Steph's eyes roll back to reveal sinister moon-yellow orbs. She jabbed Steph with the barrel. When that got no reaction, she jabbed her again, finger ever-steady on the trigger.

Nothing.

She studied the pool of sticky blood. "Maybe I hit an artery," she said under her breathing, relaxing somewhat.

She cracked the she-wolf in the head with the barrel. Nothing. Steph did not flinch. She was dead as far as the eye could tell.

"Well, then, so much for you."

As she straightened up, her back protesting, she lowered the rifle and straightened her spine.

And Steph leaped.

Her jaws closed over the woman's gun hand, coming together with devastating force. The woman screamed as her bones crunched and the teeth came together, grinding and tearing. The rifle was dropped. The woman, in a last-ditch attempt to save herself, beat at the head of the wolf with a flurry of blows. But the invasive trauma made her metabolism rush all available sugar to the wound site to begin repair. Woozy, a black fog swirling in her brain, her legs went out from under her and she fell, striking the table. The only thing that held her up was the she-wolf's biting grip on her hand.

Sensing its advantage, the wolf bit down again and again like a shark chomping at a swimmer's legs. The badly worried hand was macerated, reduced to a pulp of bones, flesh, and strings of tissue.

With a final shriek of agony, the woman went out cold. Shock, trauma, and loss of blood incapacitated her.

But Steph was hardly finished with her.

Like a dog with a chew toy, she savaged the hand, yanking on it, twisting it until the wrist bones sheared with a wet snapping. By then, the hand was connected only by tendon and ligament. The blood spraying over her muzzle from a severed artery and splashing into her mouth drove Steph into a rage of excitement. She tossed the woman to and fro almost playfully until the hand was torn free. Then she leaped on her, opening her throat with her claws, her teeth ripping out soft tissues in great, gory chunks. Her snout red with blood, she eviscerated her prey, glutting herself with mouthfuls of spurting blood, coils of intestine, and the soft pulsing mass of stomach.

But even this was not enough.

The she-wolf jumped up and down on the woman, smashing her, breaking bones and pulverizing organs, forcing blood from her ass and mouth. She gobbled her breasts and snapped her sternum, breaking ribs, clawing and biting until she could get at the heart which still beat, pulsating weakly and filled with blood. The she-wolf seized it and split it in half with the shearing motion of her bloodstained teeth. And as the woman shuddered one last time, her arms and legs thumping against the floor, the wolf swallowed both halves, red juice spurting from her mouth and spraying the white face of the refrigerator with Rorschach blots that ran like tears.

Panting, Steph fell on her.

Laying on her mutilated carcass, she took her time now, pawing through the bounty of the corpse, feeding daintily, seeking out the rarest sweet meats and the most tender blossoms of well-marbled flesh. She nibbled on rib bones and licked droplets of blood from the vertebral column. When she was finished with these delicacies, she stretched, yawned, and seized the woman's head in her jaws, bearing down until it cracked like a robin's egg. Removing the scalp and shattered plates of bone with her talons, she slit open the dura mater with a single claw, revealing the buttery folds and globs of gray matter within.

Making a very un-wolf-like sighing noise, as an epicurean will when contemplating a gourmet meal, she began dipping her fingers into the skull like a child with a bowl of custard, nibbling soft convolutions and sucking the sweet juice from her fingertips.

It was in this way that Steph carried on for some time, oblivious to the world around her. By the flickering orange firelight, she indulged herself like any fine gourmand, considering each bite carefully and completely. She ate leisurely and gently, the savage beast in her fully glutted and snoring off its grisly repast.

Then something happened.

Something that was not supposed to happen.

Rolling in the remains of the slaughtered woman, seasoning herself with the perfume of the kill...the wolfskin that she wore (and, of course, wore her) began to loosen its hold. Perhaps it was full, too, drunken with the butchery and gorged with fresh meat. Whatever the reason, its possession of her, its rapacious domination of her, slackened. Her human mind reasserted itself by degrees and with it came a horrifying claustrophobia as if the werewolf skin had eaten her, swallowed her. She fought and struggled until the skin opened. One bloody hand emerged, followed by another. Finally, she worked her head and shoulders free.

With a blinding brilliance, Steph remembered going camping. She saw the faces of Yvonne, Chloe, and Emma. She remembered waking in the well, hanging by her wrists. She remembered escaping. She remembered the woods and the wolves and...and...

What what what the fuck is this? Where am I? What the hell is this all about?

Then she saw the wreckage of the woman all around her and screamed, fighting to get free of the wolf hide like a fly trying to escape a spider's web or a mouse trying to squirm free of a cat's jaws. The hide became aware of her struggles and gripped her tightly like a constrictor. It's jaws opened to emit a low, coarse growling. And as easily as she escaped its embrace, the wolfskin reabsorbed her, engulfing her the way a corpuscle will a disease germ. It grew into her, its tissue connecting with her own, her blood becoming its blood, her heartbeat its heartbeat, their desires mating and becoming one.

Communing with the hide once more, she forgot all about someone named Steph and began to lick at the salty depths of the carcass. There was no *her* and no *it*, there was only *they* who walk the night and hunt the shadows with teeth and claws.

It was destiny.

And she had an appointment with it.

THIRTY SEVEN

When Chloe stepped into the cabin, she smelled pine sap and burning embers. It was just like the sort of place she'd read about as a girl—the rough-hewn furniture, the heavy oak table, the log walls and bed heaped with soft animal skins. There was a great fieldstone hearth with a fire blazing away, a kettle dangling over it, steaming and bubbling.

Here. This place. This is where I need to be, she thought.

She was drawn into it, made part of it. Being inside those walls was as comfortable as being in her own skin. Her mind still felt trippy as if it was operating on a level above or below what she was used to. It was as if there were a dozen voices in her head, all trying to tell her something. But none of it made sense. She felt beyond it all, above it, plugged into something not only bigger than herself but much older as if she'd finally tapped into the nature of life itself.

In her head, one voice kept repeating itself: *You don't belong here! This is not your place! You must run! You must get away before it's too late!* She recognized this voice as the old Chloe, the one who was afraid of everything in life. Being alive. Being alone. Being with people. Being a girl. Being not enough of a girl or too much of one. The old Chloe was given to panic attacks, nausea and dizziness, racing heart and shortness of breath, hot flashes and numbness and passing clean out. She wandered through the narrow corridors of her life, certain that she was losing control, becoming disconnected from this world and herself. Sometimes the fear simply could not be contained. Only the medication helped.

But you don't need that anymore, said the Other, the new Chloe, the reinvented and remade Chloe who was The Bride. The one who reveled in her own nakedness, her firmness, her youth, the savage appetites in her brain and the beautiful, dark secrets between her legs. *You're going to get an injection of a whole new drug soon, little Chloe, and when you do, you'll never want any other.*

Chloe believed this because The Bride offered her a way out. All her life she had longed for a way out, the ability to step out of her skin and into another where there was no fear. Soon, she would have it. Though she trembled with the need to pull her clothes off and lie naked on the bed of skins like The Bride, she didn't. Not just yet. She knew she couldn't give in too easily. She sat on the bed. She warmed herself at the fire. She removed a large wooden ladle from its hook and stirred what was in the kettle over the flames. It bubbled and boiled. The smell of it made her ache inside. She knew what it was—the same greasy salve that she rubbed herself with earlier. Her skin begged to be oiled with it.

Not yet.

Not just yet.

"But why not?" said a voice.

This time it was not in her head. It was the voice of a man and he stood in the doorway, perfectly wonderful and perfectly naked. His body was firm and hairless, his lips bee-stung and sensual, brilliantly red as if they were smeared with the juice of berries. He was well-muscled, his eyes dark and smoldering. He smiled and she noticed that his canines were long and sharp. This did not frighten her; it increased his allure. His penis dangled delightfully, shamelessly.

Chloe felt something inside her soar to new heights. Why, he was perfect! From his six-packs abs to his broad shoulders and piercing eyes. And she recognized him. That was the perfectly insane part—he was the hot woodsman who gave them the dandelion wine.

"Yes," he said. "It's me again."

He's in your thoughts. He's part of you.

Chloe swallowed down a pool of saliva. Just the sight of him made all her juices run. "Who...who are you?"

"I am the Huntsman," he said, grinning.

Shiny black hair fell over one shoulder and over the other were a brace of rabbits strung together with a leather thong like a stringer of fish. The ripe poison fruit between his legs made her blush.

"Any who are you?"

"I'm Chloe."

He set his rabbits aside and came to her, the firelight playing over his smooth, unblemished skin, sculpting his face in shadow, and winking off his white teeth. He went down to his knees before her. He wrapped his arms around her legs and kissed her thighs. Then her belly. Rising, he kissed between her breasts and then his lips brushed her mouth.

"No," he said, brushing her lips with his fingertips. "You're Annabel and Juliet and Gwendolyn. You're timeless and perfect and I love you. And you love me, too. You called to me and I called to you. Now we're together."

Chloe felt like she was filled with soft, white fluff. She had all she could do to stay on her feet. Her knees were full of Jell-O, her limbs weighty, a curious warmth rising inside her. Was this a dream? This particular scenario was too much like the fantasies she'd had as a teenager. She dreamed of a boy like this that would sweep her off her feet and lift her high above the drudgery and doldrums of her adolescence.

But such things didn't really happen...did they?

And men like this, hot woodsmen from teenage wet dreams, lived only on the covers of romance novels and in magazine ads. They weren't real. They couldn't be real.

Yet, he felt so very real as he held her in his arms and his mouth was on hers and her hands explored his sculpted body with trembling fingers (just as she had done so many times in her dreams). And he certainly felt real when his tongue was in her mouth, doing a slow luscious dance with her own and his fingers unbuttoned her shirt and then her pants, gently removing everything beneath and her flesh was pressed to his own and they began to melt into one another. And when he laid her on the bed and got on top of her, he was undeniably real. The pain made her cry out and there was heat and need and she was out of her head and maybe in his and they were welded together until she came again and again.

Later, they were spooned on the warm animal skins and he was pressed up behind her, still tasting her, his lips on the back of her neck and his tongue licking at her earlobes. It was all perfect just as she'd imagined such a thing must be. She closed her eyes, falling asleep for a time. When she woke her mouth tasted like blood.

What did you think he would taste like? a voice asked her and she knew it was her own: the voice of the *old* Chloe who was a scaredy-cat on a good day and a complete basket case on a bad one. *He's a monster, a predator, a blood-drinker and flesh-eater...what did you think his lips and tongue would taste like?*

Chloe shook her head angrily because none of it was true—he was not a monster. He was a man. A lover with poetry in his soul and sensitivity in his heart. He had taken her virginity, but softly, with great care and attention to her needs.

Then why do you hurt so much? Why is there blood between your legs? Why do you ache like you've been torn open? And why are there deep, bleeding scratches on your shoulders and breasts and belly? Why are your lips split open and why are there bite marks on your neck? You look like you've been mounted by a mad dog...

No, that was crazy. That's not how it was at all. He was so considerate and gentle. He did not bring pain; only joy. And he told her he loved her again and again. They lived in each other, they were one, joined not just physically but emotionally and even spiritually.

But the voice just laughed: she laughed at herself, at her own puerile naïveté. *Then why is there a memory of pain and violence in the back of your head? Why are you suppressing the very real memory of being raped by a beast?*

No, that's not how it was. It was beautiful. It was soft and gentle and loving. It was two souls intertwined. A depthless, timeless storybook love. The sort of thing romantic sonnets were written about. *But. . .forced down on the bed. . .the piercing. . .the growling. . .claws scratching and teeth biting and the beast laughing like a hyena as she squirmed and cried and begged for mercy.* No, she had to put that away, stuff it in the back of her mind, because that was just a nightmare.

Something was amiss here, something askew. Her brains felt scrambled and when she tried to think, to remember, to picture things clearly, her memories were elusive, dreamlike. She hurt, everywhere she hurt...as if she had not been made love to by the sweetest, kindest man in the world but punished, brutalized by a sadist. Her legs hurt. Her arms hurt. Her body was scraped raw. With her fingertips, she could feel terrible ruts in her belly and breasts as if she had been clawed by an eagle. There were sores in her flesh as if she had been punctured—*bitten*—and whorls of dried, scabby blood.

She reached down to grasp his hand at her blood-scabbed belly and it was the hand of a beast. The back of it was thick with dirty fur, the fingers long and leathery and tipped with black talons. As she moved, they scraped beneath her belly button, opening fresh wounds.

She could feel his grotesque hairy body pressed up to her, his muzzle at her neck. His breath was hot and fetid as if he'd been chewing on corpses. As she whimpered, he clutched her tighter. She could feel him growing hard as if her fear and disgust excited him. He was going to have her again and she knew it.

And in her mind, The Bride who was no bride but just a cheap whore, laughed at her. *You've failed tremendously, Little Chloe. You'll never be the Bride of Blooding Night. You've already been rejected. Don't you see? You strayed from the path. You gave in too easily. You offered yourself to the wolf and he broke you as he's broken so many others. Silly, stupid little slut.*

Chloe screamed.

She could feel all the anxieties and phobias of the old Chloe reasserting themselves. All of them converging in her head and owning her, drowning her in a whirlpool of terror and mania and self-loathing. The Bride was right and she knew it—it was all a test and she had failed, giving into temptation too easily. Like many stupid women that had been brought here she had given in. She did not fight. No, she gave herself away with spread legs.

She thought he would rape her again, but he didn't. He had already deflowered her and that had been the thrill, the contest, the game. *The ritual.* He pushed her off the bed onto the hard floor and stood over her, huge and shaggy, a deranged and baleful yellow glow to his eyes. He made a sound that was half-laughter and half-barking. When she tried to get away, he kicked her. And when she tried to worm her way toward the door on her stomach, he stomped a foot on her back, slamming her hard against the floor.

Although he could not speak as such, save a garbled, growling sort of noise, his thoughts seemed to ring out in her head. *You will crawl all the days of your life. You exist to serve me. To give me what I crave when I crave it. You will not deny me. I own you and you exist to please me. I am your god and you are my toy.* He let her slip away and when she got to her feet, he slapped her down. When she tried again, he laid open her scalp with his claws, licking the blood from them like a cat that had just disemboweled a mouse.

"Please," she sobbed. "Please just let me go…"

It was pointless to ask mercy of a monster and she knew it. But the terror that ran through her now in hot spasms did not understand things like pride or futile, inane attempts at sympathy. It was survival instinct, pure and simple. It would grovel. It would crawl. It would promise anything, degrade her in any way to save her life. If the beast asked, it would bathe in his shit to save itself and her.

The werewolf motioned toward her with one outstretched finger. He beckoned her to come closer. When she tried to rise to her feet, he growled. When she tried to slide forward on her hands and knees, he howled angrily at her. He wanted her to come to him, but he wanted her to wriggle across the floor because her subservience, her humiliation, meant worlds to him. So she slunk forward on her belly like the lowliest of shit worms, not daring to raise her head until she was within inches of his taloned feet.

"I'll…I'll do anything," Chloe heard herself say, broken completely now. *"Anything."*

And in the whirling vortex of her mind, she could hear him say, *Yes, you will at that.* He motioned for her to rise to her knees until she was at eye level with what hung between his legs, which was extending, thickening.

"Oh no, please…no…*please…*"

But even as she muttered this, the groveling, cringing thing inside her that was only interested in saving its skin, was already opening her mouth and shaking as the wolf's penis filled it. Madness tickling at the base of her brain, a shrieking demented laughter echoing in her skull, she began to suck on what was offered. When she began, she was cringing, tears rolling down her face, but by the time the wolf's hot, foul-tasting semen gushed down her throat, she was perfectly insane, a cackling, mindless thing that grinned as it wiped its mouth with one grubby fist.

And as the wolf looked down at her, she was not the beaten and whipped slave it wanted, but a skulking animal that had nothing left to lose.

THIRTY EIGHT

After what she went through in the cave, Yvonne was not coping well. Something very important had shut down inside her and whatever it was, she couldn't seem to get it cranking again. This awful night. The pack. The cave. Nabby. How much could the human mind take in before closing up like a clamshell? Particularly a mind like hers that had never been strong to begin with?

She walked on through the forest, going round and round for all she knew, tripping in the dark on roots and rocks, splashing through a brook. She was never sure if she was even awake. The only thing she was certain of was that she was afraid. Constantly afraid. It was a deep, instinctive fear of the unknown. The way prey felt.

You don't really think they're through with you, do you? her mother's voice asked her. *Or that this night is anywhere near toward being finished? After all this, you surely have more common sense, dear. Intuition tells me the worst is yet to come.*

The thing was, Yvonne could feel it, too. Something terrible was on its way to her. She could feel it building like a thunderstorm. As if a curse had been placed on her and it was nearing fruition.

It's near. Very near, she thought. *Closer all the time.*

She knew she had been feeling it for some time now and that's what kept her moving. She had to distance herself from it...yet, the further she went, the more she feared she was getting closer to it.

In her mind, it had no name, it was a ghost that haunted her, yet she did not doubt its physical reality or its menace.

It's coming.

It's coming for me.

Maybe it's been coming for me my entire life.

The idea was ridiculous, of course, but once thought it could not be un-thought. Hadn't she worried as far back as when she was in grade school that there was something behind her? Something slowly creeping up behind her? Every day, every month, every year, that much closer? She knew she had. It had never been a conscious fear, but something vague, half-formed in the back of her mind, a secret terror that lurked in her dreams, drawing nearer, a bogey of her subconscious.

Maybe there's something to that, dear, her mother said. *Maybe it was the root of all your problems, the inability to commit yourself to anything or anyone, your weird imagination with its leanings toward the macabre, your incessant need to blur reality with copious amounts of drugs and alcohol. Maybe you've been running and hiding, always on the move for fear it would catch up to you.*

Yes, that made a certain amount of sense. She had made a good run of it until tonight. But now, here in this dread forest, she could run no more.

It was coming and there was nowhere to hide.

She told herself the very idea was ludicrous, but inside she believed it because tonight had taught her to believe in all kinds of things that rational minds rejected. The idea that it was fated to happen was *destiny* and the idea that she knew about it was *prophecy.* Two things that rational people laughed at, but two things she had believed fervently in since she was twelve- or thirteen-years old.

It's coming and I know it.

Even now, standing there in the dark indecisively, she could smell it on the wind—something like moldering pelts and fusty bones, black dirt and sweet decay, the charnel stench of subterranean earth. It was the odor of something old, something impossibly malevolent and purely evil.

That is, if evil can have a smell, her mother's voice said, annoying and over-analytical as usual. Yvonne shut her down because she knew evil indeed had a smell. Ask someone who worked in a cancer ward. Ask some kid who'd taken a ride to hell in the back of a child molester's sleek black car. Ask a soldier who'd toured ground zero after civilians were incinerated in a napalm attack. Ask a prison guard who worked death row or a nurse who worked a ward for the criminally insane—it was real: the stink of blackness, of atrocity, of simmering human madness.

And as she stood there, shaking, tears rolling down her face and vomit rising in her throat, she could very definitely smell it. And maybe even worse, she could see it like there was some untethered all-seeing eye in her head that could see what was and what was yet to be. And what it showed her was an immense black shape striding through the forest in her direction. Whether it was a werewolf or a demon or some primeval pagan horror, she did not know. But this was its place. This black seemingly endless forest was its church, its altar, its sacrificial stone. It was lord here and everything that walked, crawled, slithered or hopped was under its dominion. All roads led to it and none led away from it.

She could see it looking through the trees at her with huge snake-slit eyes the color of fresh blood that not just watched her, but looked right into her beating heart which it would tear from her chest in a bleeding offering.

Every second brought it closer.

She sank to her knees, nearly insane with the vision, her entire body hurting as if it had been pierced by hot needles. Her brain felt as if it had been stabbed by a cold blade and her jaws ached as if every tooth in her mouth had been yanked out with pliers. She threw up, but even this did not make her feel better. Whatever was coming for her, had already entered her and it was growing in her like a malignancy.

THIRTY NINE

Hal was beside himself once they reached the river. The cottage he'd known all his life simply was not there. In its place was an open meadow and a grassy slope leading down to the rushing water. The river gurgled and foamed as it pushed amongst huge boulders probably laid down during the last ice age. A fallen tree created surging eddies and swirling black pools in the moonlight. On the opposite banks, a pine forest, impossibly dark and primitive encroached.

"This makes no sense," he told Emma. "It's here. I know it's right goddamn well here."

The enchanted forest, she thought. *Nothing is where it should be and as it should be. Reality ended for me and the others when we went camping. It ended for him when he intervened and tried to help me.*

"Blooding Night. You told me yourself everything was different. Have you ever come out into these woods on Blooding Night?"

He shook his head. "Nobody comes out here at night."

"It's pointless, it's hopeless," she said, feeling as if she was breathing her last breath. "There's no way out of this. The cottage you knew is gone and the roads won't lead us out, just deeper into it all."

She felt like a puppet on a string. She was not in charge of her destiny. From the moment she and the other girls got here, they were worked deftly by unseen hands. Things like chance and coincidence never entered into it; everything was carefully orchestrated. Even the ending of this horrible night was a foregone conclusion. The climax of this nightmare had already been scripted.

"I'm not ready to give in that easily," he said. "The River. We'll follow it out. It'll take us out of here."

"No."

He turned and looked at her. *"No?"*

Poor stupid, well-meaning Hal with his simple mind and his relatively pure heart. He just didn't understand. He wasn't plugged into it all the way Emma was. It wasn't running in his veins and gestating in his belly and riding the electrical pathways of his neurons. He stood there in the moonlight in his old tattered army coat, the shotgun in his hands. He had involved himself in this nightmare and it was the worst mistake he had ever made. He was in so deep now, the blackness was sucking him down into a bone-strewn netherworld where Death waited for him with a skull grin and a bloodstained scythe.

But how to explain it all to him?

How to make him understand the evil portents and malevolent omens that circled them now like hungry dogs...or *wolves.* How to make him understand the gravity of the situation, that she had never been herself since the Cupps took her, how their grip on her had only increased through the years despite her efforts to nullify it and marginalize it. On some essential level, they had tainted her. Forced her into doing things that had forever ruined her. Inside, she was cold. Maybe even cruel. She had no use for romance or hands to hold or shoulders to lean on. At her core, there was only survival and she would survive this one way or another.

How to make him understand that there was a third eye in her head that she had shut when she escaped the Cupps or that through the years, it had only been half-opened, and now it was open wide and seeing, knowing, telling her all those things she had so carefully repressed. She knew where they had to go and what they would most likely find when they got there. This third eye was untethered and could drift up into the sky and give her a bird's eye view of what had happened, what was happening now, and what was yet to come.

"We have to do something," he said. "We can't just stand around and wait."

"I killed them. I killed both of them. I killed them because they needed killing."

She listened to her own voice and marveled at how cool and detached it was. It was like someone else's voice, the voice of the survivor inside her. With dawning horror, she realized that this other in her would kill Hal if it had to. It would have have killed Yvonne and Steph and Chloe, too, because it was an animal and viewed things with an animal's calculating mind.

"We need to go," he said, having little interest in her psychobabble at this juncture.

They're everywhere.

This was what she knew to be fact because her third eye had shown it to be true. The werewolves were in the woods. To the south and north, east and west. There was no escaping them. It was like the situation with the Cupps. She had survived because she realized she couldn't oppose them. And since she couldn't, she *became* them.

But I won't become what's in the woods.

But weren't there worse things?

Yes, yes, there was death and it was much worse than anything else conceivable, at least while you had life and fight left in your body.

She pressed her hands against her face and tried to think, tried to find a way out of the darkness, because there was always a path if you could think of it.

She let her mind open all the way (something that scared her) and right away it showed her the answer: the west. She had to head to the west because that's where the others would be heading. If Steph and Chloe and Yvonne were still alive, they would hear the call and let it guide them to the west, too. That was the place. That was the arena. That's where the ending would be.

But she had to move *now.*

Never had it been so important.

These woods were dangerous beyond earthly comprehension. She could not be caught out in them. The hunt was still on, only now there was another involved. She could not see it or him or her…but they were there and they were closing in. The winner of this deranged footrace had to make it to the west before they were caught.

"What is it?" Hal asked. "You're shaking."

But how to explain it to him? How to tell him what she knew without him thinking she was crazy? How to make him understand the dire truth of the situation, that something was coming through the forest to claim her, something worse than the monsters they already knew. A horror that was scarier and more devastating than anything they could imagine. A huge shaggy thing, a voracious monster with eyes of blood and the teeth of a shark. Something nocturnal and ancient and completely nameless, a hideous progenitor that had haunted the primeval woods since the dawn of time seeking its blood offerings.

"We have to go," she said.

"Where?"

"Just follow me. I know the way."

FORTY

Steph was both shocked and amazed that she could get out of the wolfskin, that although it was most certainly a part of her—as much as her own skin—she could actually shed it. She had tried earlier to escape it, to pull herself free of its confining mass, but it was too strong. Its will was dominant. It wanted them to be together to hunt and feed and run wild so it swallowed her and she knew no more.

But now slowly, very slowly, her mind was returning. Like a ray of light breaking through the forest canopy and shining down into the murky undergrowth, she began to remember who she was and what she was. And with it came that same claustrophobic terror that she was a mouse in the belly of a cat, prey in the stomach of a monster. Being digested, absorbed, assimilated. The wolfskin was strong. It was unyielding. She stretched her limbs and rolled in it, trying to get it to loosen its hold on her.

But we are the same, we are one, it seemed to whisper in her head.

She wouldn't accept that.

I wear you! You don't wear me!

And the wolfskin laughed. It laughed hysterically and deliriously, the way a rabid dog might laugh if you tried to talk it out of biting down on your hand with its white foaming jaws. *You'll die without me. I am your armor, your flesh and muscle and strength. Without me, they'll tear you to pieces and if they don't, the guilt of what you have done will make you kill yourself. I claimed you, I took you, I chose you as my host. You answered the call of the wild because your mind is sick with lust and inhuman hunger and your heart is black with primeval sin. If you look in a mirror, little one, you will see me grinning back with a brace of blood-dripping teeth because I am what you are at your core.*

"No…I'm not you! I'll never be a thing like you!" Steph cried into the night. She could hear her voice echoing through the trees that were the first roof her kind had ever known.

The wolfskin laughed again, booming in her skull. *I've worn you as I've worn a hundred others! And you like to be worn! You like me all over you, owning you, touching you, making you strong and full-blooded, ripe and ready for the Lord of the Forest!*

The skin crawled on her, it crept over her, it tightened its embrace like a lover that was fearful of being abandoned. It clung to her tenaciously. Its tongue seemed to be licking in her ear and its hormones juiced wildly inside her, making her shake with lust and hunger, the need to tear and rend her prey to bones. She was horny for the taking of life, for the taste of blood in her mouth and the feel of it gushing hotly down her throat. Sex and death were intricately knotted inside her like vines climbing a fence—there was no difference between the two.

Yes, it teased her with what she wanted most: what the beast inside craved like a junkie craves a needle in the arm. It was tangled inside her, turning everything from muscle to organ, ligament to neuron black with its meat-hungry, loin-slapping hormonal appetite.

It owned her.

She would never be free.

Because at some essential level where the primal things lurked and sharpened their teeth on human bone, she didn't want to be free even though she knew that the coupling of herself and the wolfskin could only terminate in a ceaseless cycle of horror.

But in her mind, struggling weakly, gaining momentum, there was a single overriding impulse and that was to be free of the skin at all costs. She needed to reassert her dominance. If she didn't, the wolfskin would never let her go. And in the back of her mind, she knew that if she didn't get it off her, she never would.

The longer you wear it, the longer you must wear it.

In the subterranean darkness of her mind, her will clashed with that of the wolf. It didn't understand why she'd ever want to take it off and go naked into the world. Mad thoughts and impulses collided in her head.

She fought and pulled and squirmed. And when she screamed, it was not with her voice but the guttural baying of a wolf.

She was smothering in it.

It was squeezing her, locking itself to her. She could barely breathe. Her body was slick with sweat. It was like being zipped inside a sleeping bag on a sweltering July afternoon.

The wolfskin kept whispering in her ears with a growling voice, promising her wondrous things, joyful things, and delicious things. It tempted her with the odors of raw meat and blood. It showed her the feasts that were not always above ground, but below it—plundered graves that could be dug down to, soft, greening carcasses pawed from rotting boxes, how they boiled with plump maggots and were feathered with mold and seasoned by age. How it would be to smell those appetizing odors and seize corpses tender with putrescence in her jaws, crunching bones and gnawing on jellied brains and pulpous faces and throats yellow with sweet slime.

No! No! No! I'm being called! I need to see!

Now the wolfskin was invading her brain like hundreds of hungry grave worms, burrowing in deep, chewing and feeding and spawning in her skull. It was desperate to hold her. It filled her mind with images of the hunt, the scents and flavors of butchered prey.

But Steph fought.

She worked her hands free and tore at the underbelly of the wolfskin until her fingers poked through. She pulled until the skin ripped free and the wolf howled in agony. She writhed and wormed, peeling her way from it, severing the multiple attachments of the extracellular matrix, fibrous threads and elastic strings snapping, adipose greasy in her hands.

Then she was on the ground, naked and convulsing. When she tried to raise her head, she vomited out a gruel of human remains. The wolfskin kept trying to inch its way toward her like a huge, hairy spider. She knocked it aside and it squealed and whimpered. She kicked at it again and again, so it would know that she was master and not it. After a few moments, it stopped moving entirely, its pathetic cries fading.

She was dizzy and disoriented, nausea warm and sluicing in her belly. There was blood in her mouth and on her hands. She was oiled with it like an infant pulled from a womb.

With great effort, she got to her feet and stumbled weakly forward. She splashed through a leaf-covered puddle and then sank to her knees in the moist loam. The moonlight filtered down brightly and she stared at her distorted reflection in another puddle. She was twisted and shrunken, splattered with blood and ooze. Her mouth tasted like grease, a strand of human flesh caught between her teeth made her ravenous. She spit it out. Then vomited again.

Breathing hard, she crawled forward again, knowing she had to get away from the wolfskin or it would cover her again. Her stomach sloshed with gray water. She froze as a sound came from the tall trees before her—a growling that was not just loud, but titanic. She wanted to scream, to sob, to crawl inside herself. There was something coming out of the woods, a huge and hulking shape. Through bleary eyes she saw moonlight winking off long teeth.

It growled again and the wilderness around her seemed to tremble. Slowly, it stepped into the moonlight.

The Lord of the Forest, she thought. *This is the Lord of the Forest.*

It was a gigantic, unnatural shape, a demon wolf that stood at least eight feet on its hind legs. It wore a stitched mantle of human skins that had blackened with age. It growled again, its mammoth mouth opening, drool flying from it. One eye was a scarified, infected pit, the other bulging and huge, red as an open wound. It glistened like fresh blood. Its head was more wolf skull than flesh, canid and revolting, tufts of gray hair sprouting from a canvas of skin that had shriveled and burst open, yellow bone gleaming beneath.

Steph began to scream as the creature stepped forward to claim her. She was out of her mind with fear because this was the zenith, this was the point of no return. The Lord of the Forest had summoned her from the wolfskin and it had been calling to her all night. Now here he was, the apex predator, the carnivore incarnate, and she could not run. As he looked down on her with that single bleeding eye, she was mastered at every conceivable level. She was a convert, a disciple, she was burnt offerings and entrails, meat offered at his feet and blood in a soft pink sacrificial vessel.

She waited for his claws, but there was only his hand. She threw back her head and screamed again, raising her hands to the moon above. He reached out and placed his mammoth hand very gently against her breasts. It was scaly and rough, hairless, but it burned like a branding iron. Her flesh sizzled and smoked and with a final cry of agony, she went out cold and lay at his feet like a dead fish.

She was his now.

She had been initiated.

She bore his mark and there was no going back.

FORTY ONE

Whimpering, naked, and hurting, Chloe crouched in the corner near the hearth. She wiped blood from her eyes, realizing that she was now the thing she feared to be her entire life—a victim, a kept animal, a slave to a wicked, warped mind that would use and abuse her until nothing was left. This was where her dreaming mind had led her: into the ogre's cave.

After the thing she had done for the wolf that still made her guts roil, she tried to stand, but he wouldn't allow it. He grabbed hold of her and flung her aside until she struck the wall. *You will crawl all the days of your life,* his voice echoed in her mind. *You are my dog, my pet, my beast of burden. But that's all you are.* She had pissed herself, but her sanity was so far gone by that point, that she didn't even notice. She was a grubbing, dirty animal.

He turned away from her, staring into the fire.

Her hands scrambled about, searching for a weapon. She only wanted two things by that point—to spill his blood and to escape. If she could wound him sufficiently, it would give her the time to get away and this was all her simple brain desired.

There was nothing on the floor to be used as a weapon. The only thing she could see at all was the axe leaning up by the hearth. It would be perfect…if she could get to it. Which was a very big *if.* It would be impossible to get to it before he got to her. There was just no way.

Knowing this and knowing she had to bide her time, Chloe crawled further into the corner where he had tossed her like something unwanted, cast-off rubbish. She waited there, hunched over, knees pulled up, playing the part of a broken, beaten thing which was no large stretch of imagination. He had dominated her, subjugated her. She was no threat. He turned his back to her because she was weak and harmless.

But in the stewpot of her mind, things were brewing and bubbling. *I know who's inside that skin. I know very well,* she thought. *You called to me, you told me you loved me, you seduced me. Then you beat and degraded me. When I pull you out of that wolfskin, you will die.*

As she sat there, watching him watch the fire, she tried to bring back the old Chloe who was nervous and panicky and phobic, but a person she liked despite this. That was the real Chloe before all this, before the salve was rubbed on her and she lost her mind. But try as she might, the old Chloe would not come back. She had crawled into a crevice like a frightened spider and she would not come out. And maybe that was for the best. Because the old Chloe wouldn't have the guts or mettle to do what she contemplated.

The beast looked over at her and his lips pulled away from long killing teeth. He uttered a shrill, staccato laughing noise like that of a hyena and she could sense him trying to make contact with her. His voice was that of the Huntsman. *You just wait there, my little sow. When I feel the need, I will use you again.* He offered her a grisly grin and she knew the only reason he didn't tear her apart was because it was Blooding Night and he was not allowed, not yet. But the time would come and she could sense his hunger even across the cabin.

He moved to the window and opened the shutters, letting the moonlight in. It covered him and he bathed in it. He sighed and closed his eyes. It seemed to have a narcotic effect on him because he stretched and yawned, then laid down on the bed. His thoughts came again, crowding out her own. *I'll rest and when I wake, you will be ready for me. We'll do it doggy-style.* There was another eruption of that awful laughter and then he slipped off to sleep.

She would not let him touch her again.

She would kill herself.

After a time, she rose silently to her feet. He did not stir. She took one step, then two toward the axe. He slept on. She moved closer to it, reaching slowly down for it until she felt the handle in her hands. He made a grunting sound in his sleep. His arm moved, but he did not waken. She waited a few more moments, then she stepped toward the bed. He shifted and she thought he would wake, but he rolled over, his back to her. That's how much he feared her. She was cowed. She was a hog to be beaten and raped. Nothing more. He would use her as he saw fit.

She stepped within feet of the bed.

He slept on.

She raised the axe above her head. Her hands trembled, every muscle tightened in preparation for the act. In her mind, there was only white-hot rage. At that moment, the wind picked up and one of the shutters knocked against the side of the cabin. He shifted again, rolled back over and his yellow eyes opened a crack.

But too late.

The axe came down with everything she could put behind it. She actually came off her feet to deliver it with every ounce of strength and weight she had. It nearly severed his head with the first blow. An arc of blood shot up into the air, splattering against her face and shoulders. He squealed and barked, then let forth an agonized cry that gurgled in his throat as he drowned in blood. He threw himself to the floor, his fingers going to his blood-spurting neck. His head hung at an unnatural angle.

Chloe let out a cry of her own and bounded after him. The axe came down again, sinking into his back. And then again, splitting the crown of his skull. Two more good whacks to the head and he didn't move at all. He lay there in a spreading pool of gore.

Then—movement.

The wolfskin seemed to be dead, but something in it still moved. There was a grunting and groaning from its depths, then a tearing sound. The Huntsman crawled free, blood-slicked, wounded, his breath gurgling in his lungs. He looked up at her, trying to speak, but only blood came from his mouth. It came out in rivers.

Chloe didn't hesitate.

She hated the Huntsman even more than she hated the wolfskin itself. He was asking for mercy and she knew it. Something human in her pulled back, not wanting to hurt him anymore, but the new Chloe swung the axe with everything it had. She sank it into his face five or six times until his masculine beauty was a fragmented horror.

Still clutching the blood-dripping axe, she stepped out into the night, ready for battle.

FORTY TWO

It was utterly impossible for Emma to explain to Hal where they were going and why they had to get there. She was being called, summoned, drawn somewhere and she did not really feel that she was in control of herself. There was only the forward motion that carried her deeper and deeper into the black forest as Hal lagged behind her, crying out for her to slow down. He was not as sure-footed as she. He tripped over stumps and rotting logs, finding every dip and hollow. It was a wonder he didn't snap a ankle.

In her mind, she relived her escape from the Cupp house, dashing madly in any direction that would carry her farther away from that terrible place.

She moved faster and faster, something in her prodding her on. There was a destination and she seemed to know where it was if she didn't necessarily know *what* it was. Her third eye had blanked out. It couldn't tell her anything she didn't already know. Behind her, in the distance, she could hear the feverish, excited howling of the pack. There was no going back. The exhilaration of it all built and built in her. She felt that if she didn't reach her destination and reach it quickly, all would be lost. She would fall and strike the earth and she would never get up again, becoming one with the rot and loam.

The moon was descending and when it fell beneath the horizon, dawn would come. The very idea filled her with a sense of nervous tension that was nearly unbearable.

She heard Hal call out again and she shouted back to him, *Hurry!*

Hurry! We don't have much time! Except she never used her voice, she just sent her thoughts out at him and that was the best she could do under the circumstances.

She rushed down into a muddy dell and then scrambled up into the forest again. It was close. She could feel it. She was almost there.

By that point, she was running and Hal was forgotten. His voice faded further and further in the distance. He did not understand any of this and there was no time to make sense of it for him.

She kept moving until she saw something jutting up above the trees, something like a crooked, skeletal finger. It was etched in moonlight. She did not know what it was, but she knew it was her destination and nothing in this world could keep her from it.

FORTY THREE

Chloe no longer really knew who she was and, maybe, what she was. She stormed from the Huntsman's cabin, feeling invigorated, renewed, refreshed in a way she had never been before. The axe was still in her hands, sticky with blood. The blade was clotted with gore, bits of flesh and strands of hair. It had become part of her now and she would never let it go. If someone or some*thing* tried to pry it from her clutching hands, they would have to kill her and she decided that she would not die easily. She would fight to the death now because her survival instinct was a red-hot knife anxious to bisect flesh, to cut and slash.

Let them come for me, she thought, *so that I can show them that I'm not a victim anymore.*

The trauma and torment of this night remade her into a killer, a warrior, a lean and dangerous predator. And as she walked the woods that once scared her white, she felt no fear...only excitement. She was covered in drying blood. Where once she might have been disgusted, now she felt a demented sort of pride. The blood was a badge of honor. She killed a werewolf and in doing so, released the primal woman at her core.

This is my night, she thought. *I'll see it to its end. I'll do what it takes to be the one, the special one.*

Her hair was caked with the Huntsman's blood. A mask of it had dried on her face. It was sticky on her lips and she could taste it on her tongue. The very flavor of it fired her neurons, filled her muscles with power and vitality. She saw clearly, heard every sound. This was not just any forest, it was *her* forest and she was queen here.

Although some struggling fragment of the old Chloe kept whispering nonsense in her head about murder, it made no sense to her. *Murder, murder, you have committed murder.* She could no longer conceptualize such things. The concept was alien to her because to the animal, such things do not exist. It was just another cumbersome trapping of civilization like guilt and remorse and she no longer felt those things either. The new Chloe—who was as much a product of the shock and suffering of this night which shattered her mind as the salve which released the beast within—hated the old Chloe and if she were standing before her, she would have killed her.

I kill because I must survive.

I take life because that is my purpose.

The blood is the life.

It is the sweet joy of the hunt, to immerse yourself in it and taste it.

Ever since leaving the cabin, something had been tugging at her, pulling her in a particular direction. It was like a voice calling to her. Whatever it was, she could not shut it out or deny it. Its magnetism was both irresistible and inescapable. She was like a doll on a string being towed along, drawn to a place where it waited for her.

In the back of her mind like an echo she heard *Blooding Night, Blooding Night, Blooding Night,* and although to her simple conscious questing mind these words really meant nothing; to her subconscious mind, they meant everything. They were the ultimate truth preparing to reveal itself and she would not miss it. She must not.

So, onward through the woods she trudged, a naked girl sheathed in dried blood, an axe in her hands ready for the using. The path was easy to follow. It was as if she'd walked it a hundred times or more, day and night. There were no wrong steps. Each foot was placed carefully and she moved faster and faster as she was effortlessly pulled forward like an electrical charge down a copper wire.

She knew she was not alone.

There were others that watched her, but they didn't dare reveal themselves. They were part of this, too. They were, in a sense, one with her, knowing as she knew that this night had been leading all along to what lie just ahead. She navigated the trees and soon enough, they began to thin in the moonlight and then there was a clearing. And in the clearing, she saw a structure. An old school, perhaps a church. It was ancient and leaning, a rotting edifice that looked like it was ready to fall. Trees pressed in from either side, clutching at it like fingers. It was two-story with a decrepit cupola at one end and a crooked steeple at the other. In the moonlight, bats winged about it like moths circling a streetlight. Lights flickered in its lower windows, which were like the hollow sockets of a skull.

Chloe's knees were weak. Her head spun. It felt like all the blood in her had drained down into her feet. She stumbled forward, drawn toward this relic in the forest without knowing why. Her feet were no longer sure. She could barely move without falling. Struggling, fighting for every step, she crossed the clearing. Finally, near to it, the breath evaporated from her lungs and she fell to her knees, panting.

This is it.

You've found it.

You've reached the place that called to you.

And as she contemplated the wonder of this, what it meant and abstract concepts like destiny and fate, a voice called out to her.

"Chloe."

That voice. She recognized it. It was a voice she knew very well. The old Chloe and the new Chloe fought a pitched battle for dominance in her head. The former recalled faces and names, but the latter rejected them. It did not want her going back to all that, because if she did, she would be weak again. She would be helpless. A victim. A prey animal waiting for the teeth of an aggressor.

A form stepped out of the darkness. "Chloe, you've made it," it said. "I've been waiting for you. You're the first."

Chloe slowly lifted her head, fireworks going off in her brain. At that moment, it all came rushing back to her, every dirty, horrible detail of the night and she cried out, dropping the axe into the grass. She felt violated. As if for many hours, she had been nothing but a spectator in her own body. Something else had possessed it, moved it, made it do its terrible bidding. The knowledge of this made her scream at the moon above.

"It's okay now," the voice said. "Everything's okay now."

"Steph?" she said as her memories cemented into place.

"Yes. You've made it. You've reached the end," Steph told her. "We've all had a rough time of it, but now it's over and you don't have to worry anymore."

Chloe wanted to believe that, but she found it impossible. Things like this just didn't end and you went on your merry way. This was what her rational mind told her. But another part, her instinctive sense, was even harder to convince. It sensed something very wrong. Its hackles were up. It urged her to turn and run while she still could. The air was suddenly thick with the odors of urine and rotten meat, dank hides and wet pelts, the high, evil stench of putrefaction brought about by putrescine and cadaverine seeping from decaying animal matter.

"The Lord of the Forest is here. He has come for you," Steph told her. "He has come to take his offering. You are the weakest of all. The softest of all. You gave in to impulses and lust and desires much easier than the rest of us, so he has chosen you to sanctify this night."

The stink of what was waiting in the darkness, breathing with a rattling noise, made Chloe look around, her mouth agape, terror tapping along her spine like fingers on a keyboard, exciting ganglia and creating an absolute horror beyond anything she had known. She stared at Steph, realizing she was naked and blood-spattered, too.

"But you...you gave in so easily! You did! I saw it! I saw the animal coming over you! You're no better!"

Steph laughed. "The Lord respects that, he understands the beast inside and how I let it loose. But you...no, he sent a pretty boy to romance you and seduce you and you fell from grace without so much as a whimper."

Chloe's mouth was filled with words, but she couldn't seem to speak them as Hell stepped from the shadows. She looked up at the Lord of the Forest, needing to scream but unable to do so. Everything inside her had seized up. Nothing moved. Her heart seemed to stand still. Her breathing stopped. Her blood did not flow. She was a shank of meat waiting for the butcher's saw, an offering, a sacrificial lamb, a writhing infant awaiting the dagger of a pagan priest.

"Oh...God...oh please..."

But the Lord of the Forest was not interested in her supplications. He strode forward to take what was his and when she screamed, it only excited him more. One slight blow took off her scalp in a gout of blood.

She fell face-first into the grass. And the Lord, braying with delight, placed one of his rear feet atop her head and pushed down with his weight and strength, shattering her head to pulp.

By then, Steph had been engulfed by her wolfskin once more, communing with the beast, becoming a single entity. Growling, snapping her teeth, her glands juicing with unbridled excitement, she went down on all fours, sniffing the pulped head of her friend. And then, at the Lord's bidding, she began to lap greedily at the sweet jelly that had squirted from Chloe's crushed skull.

FORTY FOUR

Much like Chloe, Yvonne was overwhelmed by something she could not put a name to. Something that drew her deeper and deeper into the forest. Something that had taken hold of her with inexorable influence, owning her body and soul, pushing her ever forward to a destination that was both unknown and, perhaps, unknowable.

The path was laid for her and all she had to do was follow it, let it take her to someplace that she must be. She moved with agile grace, avoiding roots and potholes and jutting stones. And on those rare occasions when she did fall, she crawled on her hands and knees, not even bothering to pull herself up. Afraid of the time it would take.

And in her head, there was a ceaseless, booming voice calling out to her. It was not the voice of her mother. In fact, she was almost certain that it was the voice of Steph. But why this would be so, she had no idea. The voice kept calling and she was drawn to it, maybe out of familiarity and maybe because the idea of ignoring it filled her with terror.

Hurry, Yvonne. You must hurry.

And, yes, she knew she must. Never had it been so important. The voice of Steph was bewitching, seductive, hypnotic even. It and the desire to reach her destination had even eclipsed the cold fear she felt not that long ago that something hostile and maleficent was stalking her. She still felt this to a certain degree, but the faster she moved and the further away she got, the more she was certain that the hulking, evil shape of her nightmares would not get her.

The place has been prepared, Yvonne. We're waiting for you because it can't begin without you. You are part of this night. We need you. Hurry! Hurry!

And she did.

Now she was running full out, leapfrogging fallen trees and vaulting logs, swinging around huge oaks and climbing deadfalls in the dark like a monkey. She splashed through creeks and ponds and swam across the tributary of a river, dragging herself up the bank. The blood rushed hot in her veins. Her heart hammered and her lungs gasped for air. If she had not been twenty years old and well-toned from fencing and swimming classes, she would have collapsed.

But she pushed on.

The voice of Steph became more and more insistent. It was no longer calling to her, but shouting. She could hear it in her ears. It reverberated inside her skull.

YVONNE YVONNE YVONNE

She climbed a rise on hands and knees that were cut and scabbed. At the top, she could see a flickering light. There. That was it. That was where she must go. She leaped to her feet, running, falling, rolling down the hillside.

YVONNE YVONNE HURRY HURRY

Her friends would be there. She could see their faces in her mind, each one crowding out the other. She could hear their voices in her head, begging her to move faster for the culmination of the night, of all things known and those that were yet to be, lie just ahead. Through the trees she went, the trees, the trees, the trees. Then they thinned and she could see the edifice with the fire flickering in its lower windows.

"Oh God," she panted. "Oh God."

Emotions and images collided in her brain. She saw blood and felt terror. She saw the faces of her friends and felt comfort. Then she saw the shape of something huge and dark and primordial, and bristled with fear.

The girls were in her mind. They were camping. Sitting around the fire, passing that bottle of dandelion wine around and it all led here, to this place. Now.

And then when she was barely forty feet from the church or school or whatever it was, a voice called out of the shadows, "You've made it. You've finally made it."

It was Steph's voice.

Here.

At last.

And Steph stepped from the shadows, only it was not Steph at all. It was a wolf. It was one of *them.* What was left of Yvonne's mind broke completely at the sight of her. She was shaggy and sleek, rank with what she had been feeding upon and rolling in. Yvonne screamed and Steph showed her long, sharp teeth. But her arms were held out, not in a threatening way, but to hold her.

Don't be afraid, we've come too far, the Steph-wolf told her in a voice that was at once guttural and ragged, yet oddly smooth and silky. *We've known each other before and we'll know each other again. He wants it that way, Yvonne, and we must please him on this special night.*

Shaking her head from side to side, her eyes glazed and her mouth forming silent words, drool running down her chin, Yvonne moved toward her. Her legs carried forward; her brain seemed to have little to do with it. Her will was soft and warm like clay made pliable and easy to mold by hot hands. Steph shaped it and Yvonne simply took on the form she was pressed into. As she got closer, the moonlight—which was so bright it was nearly silver—showed her her old friend in graphic, unpleasant detail. The fur at her mouth, neck, and breasts rigid with dried blood and marrow-fat. Her leering eyes which were just as yellow as infected, pus-filled sores. Her jutting triangular ears. And her snout, jaws opening to display a brace of teeth stained pink from her feedings, how long and sharp they were, her black tongue quivering in her mouth like a blood-fattened worm.

The arms that reached out to enfold her were hairy, straining with taut muscles, the fingers skeletal and long, the knuckles knobby, the claws at their tips black and shining and sharp enough to slit throats. At the sight of them, Yvonne screamed. It was involuntary. It rushed from her with a dry, screeching sound.

Come closer, the she-wolf insisted. *Here where you belong, in this place where you have been before. Remember how it was? It'll be that way again.*

Then the arms held Yvonne close, crushing her against the bristling pelt of the she-wolf and inside, she melted. She was hot taffy and cream. She wrapped her arms around the wolf, running her fingers through the luxurious hair of its back, feeling the muscles and warm flesh beneath. Her lips went to Steph's and their tongues found each other. The she-wolf's was hot in Yvonne's mouth, circling and slavering her own. Yvonne had never felt so excited before, her blood ran boiling just beneath her skin. Her hips bucked against those of the monster that held her and easily seduced her. Then the she-wolf's tongue was retracted and she made a low growling sound in her throat...and her jaws clamped down, seizing Yvonne's tongue and shearing it off, ripping it free by the roots.

Screaming in agony, her mouth gushing red, Yvonne went down on her knees as the wolf chewed her tongue like a cutlet of tender, raw beef. Blood ran from its jaws and dripped to its chest.

A sweet offering, the Steph-wolf said as it swallowed her tongue. *But no one enters his house without an offering. Chloe gave her life and I gave my soul. Now you have given your voice.*

Yvonne was mindless with agony, blood running from her mouth in streams. And it was at that moment that the thing she feared most and had dreaded her entire life, stepped forward. The Lord of the Forest stood there, gigantic and monstrous. His huge clawed hands reached down and took hold of her, hoisting her into the air as easily as a child picks up a rag doll. He held her at arm's length so that she could gloat upon his accursed, lewd face in revolting detail.

Yvonne went limp in his grasp, the piss running between her legs. The Lord found this pleasing—anointing herself with her own urine. She trembled with horror and he would have found nothing less acceptable. Ropes of saliva dangled from his huge jaws, moonlight glinted off the knobs of bone that burst through his leathery, dark skin.

In the echoing drum of her mind, Yvonne could hear his voice—it was deep and rasping, wizened by the ages and just as dry and scratching as rats clawing about inside a buried coffin. *You will grovel in my shadow, you will crawl behind me but never walk.* He studied her the way a cat studies a mouse before disemboweling it. One eye was sucked into a seamed pit of scar tissue, the other a bright red bleeding egg, glistening in a soup of discharge. Her fear gave him great pleasure and he threw back his skull head and laughed.

Yvonne was dropped.

She immediately took on the prostrate form and body language of a groveling, servile dog whose highest achievement thenceforth would be to pick lice from its master's pelt.

FORTY FIVE

As soon as Emma saw it up close, she knew it was a church. It had existed in her mind for a long time, maybe for years, just out of sight, but its dire influence had always been felt. This was where *they* gathered, this was where they held their unhallowed rites and dark rituals. It was a place of horror and tonight, it was just for her. The consummation of Blooding Night would happen here and she was powerless to walk away from it.

Even if I ran, she thought, *where would I go? All roads will lead right back to this place because it's destiny. I can't escape it. I can't pretend that it hasn't been here, waiting for me my entire life.*

She stared in awe at the church and it seemed to stare back, enticing her to enter it. Daring her to plumb its secrets, its madness and aberration, to lay herself bare before it.

She was not alone and she knew it.

The wolves had come with her, gathering around her in the shadows but never daring to come any closer. They growled and whined and snapped at each other. She could smell their musk. The blood on their hides, the rank but not unpleasing odors of their glands. When she turned to look at them, they lowered their heads and backed away. She had a power over them and she could feel it.

She thought: *Once I was abducted by some very bad people and kept like a slave, a pet, a toy. Something to be played with, beaten, whipped, broken if need be. But I escaped all that by killing them. I offered blood and blood was accepted. But I've been asleep ever since. I was rotten and deserted inside just like this church. I ran everyday from the Cupps and from myself and now I'm here. And finally, I'm awake again.*

There was someone kneeling on the porch, head bowed, whispering strange things that made no sense. Emma climbed the steps.

"I'm here," she said.

The figure stood up and faced her. It was Meg. "I knew it," she said. "I knew you would be the one because it couldn't be anyone else. It just had to be you. Even when you sat at my table, I could feel the power coming off of you."

Emma wanted to laugh at her, call her a stupid old hag that knew nothing, but she didn't. Earlier, at her house, she'd been afraid of her, but she wasn't afraid any longer.

"So what happens now?"

Meg reached out and took her hand. "Now is Blooding Night. Now we worship and give praise to the bride."

And with that, she led Emma inside.

FORTY SIX

It was time for the culmination of Blooding Night. It was time for the ritual and the turning of the skin. Steph led Yvonne into the desecrated, rotting church by a rope noosed around her neck. She was a dog now, an obsequious, cringing toad whose mind was completely gone. She crawled happily, mindlessly along, unable to remember who or what she had once been. What she was now, she had always been and she could not think of rising above her subservience anymore than a packhorse or a sled dog could. She did not know what would be asked of her now, only that it would be important and just. That in the end it would serve the Lord of the Forest and the Bride of Blooding Night, and thus, it was something she would offer and offer freely, praise the moon and praise the woods and praise the night.

FORTY SEVEN

Yanking on the rope, Steph led the lamb into the church. It pulled back, frightened of crossing the threshold, but she pulled it forward into this wondrous place that smelled of the hunt, of blood and meat and wildness.

She thought of the fear she had once known, the fear of her primal nature, of becoming something like she now was. She wanted to laugh at the very idea. In fact, she tried, but all that came out was a strange woofing sound.

Behind her, the others were filing in now. They had waited a long time for this night, for the change and the renewal and it made them excited, happy in the way usually only a fresh kill made them happy.

The lamb strained at its leash, perhaps sensing the sort of place this was and the things that would happen here. Steph yanked her forward because there was no turning back now. The lamb could no longer speak so she made a gurgling, garbled noise.

Clawed hands reached out and stroked the lamb.

They were all eager to touch her, to make contact with her, to be part of the dark cabalism she signified, as if maybe some of it would rub off on them.

Steph pulled the lamb away from them. It was not time yet. She was a holy object and had to be treated as such. The time would come, but not just yet. Steph took her up near the altar and tied her there. She whimpered and Steph stroked her so that she would not die of fright before the ritual began.

FORTY EIGHT

Now you'll know.

Now you'll see.

In the back of Emma's mind, she feared that she was still a prisoner, a kept thing of the Cupps. Still locked away in that gray room in the cellar, waiting for the scratch of the key in the lock which would tell her that the games were about to begin again. She was not convinced that she had ever really escaped or that she had really killed them because they were werewolves and werewolves didn't die like people do. Maybe she was still there, still in that room, her mind gone, reality shattered, a flesh and blood toy to be taken out and played with roughly when the urge struck her captors.

I'm not real because I can't be real and none of this can be real because things like this can't really happen.

Meg was not real either.

She couldn't be.

A woman who lived in an old farmhouse in a lost forest who had werewolf skins that were hideously alive hanging from the walls and who brooded over a pack of wolf children and heated kettles of human stew on the stove and could see into your mind to gauge the depths of your pain—

How could she possibly be real?

She's not Meg, she's Mrs. Cupp and you've been a prisoner all these years. You've been brutalized and tortured and carefully broken by it all. You're mad. You're living in your mind in some enchanted woods in a fairy tale never-never land.

Yet, beside her walked smiling, friendly, old Meg. She had Emma's pale hand in her own and she held it tightly. She had her just as surely as the Cupps had had her and she stood about as much chance of escaping.

Emma looked at her, her eyes glazed and dreamy. "Who are you?"

"Now, now, child, it's a little late for that, isn't it? You know who I am and you know who you are and why we're here." She gave Emma's hand a gentle squeeze, the way you would to a favored child. "Let's just say that I'm your sponsor. That doesn't sound so bad, does it? *Sponsor.* Why, it sounds kind of nice. Like this is a private club or a lodge and I'm the one who will walk you through the process. I'm an old friend who has your best interests at heart, hmm?"

Meg tried to understand that, make sense of it, but it was difficult because the walls of her mind were closing in. She was spinning on her axis, wobbling, reality and fantasy equally balanced. Her memories were mixed up. She saw her friends and then the woods and running and the Cupps and school and the foster home and a million confused images in between.

Her mind was overloaded. There was too much input that did not fit within the parameters of the reality she knew. It could not be true...yet as she looked around with wide eyes, she knew it must be.

Meg led her forward. Inside the church, there were no pews or furniture. All of that had been gutted ages ago, maybe centuries. The werewolves, dozens and dozens of them, were gathering, watching her like a congregation watching a bride. Fires burned in barrels and there were ancient, dead leaves on the floor, along with dust and grime. The floorboards were splintered and there were bird's nests up in the rafters along with colonies of bats that squeaked and stretched their wings. The air was smoky and one wall had a huge hole rotted right through it.

The wolves were growing agitated, excited. They growled and huffed at one another, exchanging short howls that rose in pitch and frequency. Some of them were male with unsheathed phalluses dangling between their legs. Some were female with rows of teats at their torsos. There were children running about, barking and snarling. And there were even babies held to breasts, dark and hungry canids with bright green eyes.

But all of that was to be expected...wasn't it?

What was not to be expected were those things up on the ruin of the altar. Emma saw them and gasped despite herself. Skeletons. Articulated, yellow skeletons held together with sticks and wire, things that were not necessarily wolves or humans, but horrors in between. They looked brittle, incredibly old like relics in a museum, prehistoric monsters extending clawed metacarpals and yawning jaws to show their savage dentition. The flickering firelight made them seem to move and shift as if they were rising from their tombs and graves. Eye sockets seemed horribly aware. Skulls cracked by time and fractured by battle and violent wild hunts jumped with shadows, guttering with a dark sentience that even death could not disrupt. As she neared the altar, the skeletons rose above her, voracious and grotesque horrors standing on the powerful staffs of their hind legs, their footpads spread out with the talons of vultures.

"Our forebears," said Meg, gazing up at them with twisted delight. "Their remains are here for us to admire, to worship, to emulate. Long dead but ever vigilant."

Emma believed it because this awful place was crawling with spirits, alive with an eerie and unnatural presence. It seemed to haunt the bones of the forebears, creeping with tenebrous vitality as if it wished to make them move and kill again.

Beyond them was the ultimate horror—a corpse strung by its wrists from a crossbeam overhead. It had been a young woman, her hair fair and plastered to her face with blood. Her head had been crushed like a grape and she had been gutted. She swung slowly from side to side.

Although her face was pulped, Emma knew it was Chloe. Poor, frightened, paranoid little Chloe whose life had been a series of self-inflicted traumas.

Emma just stared, her eyes huge and wet and seemingly painted on. Her head spun and she went to her knees, heaving out what was in her stomach. When her voice came at last, it was shrill and broken. *"Oh God... oh no...oh Jesus Christ..."*

Meg reached down a hand and patted her head like that of a dog. "It was rightly done, my child. The altar had to be sanctified with blood and meat. She feels no pain now."

Emma's head shook back and forth, as if to negate what she was seeing. Because this was reality, this was real. *I'm not dreaming, I'm not fucking dreaming at all.* Chloe had been sacrificed to consecrate the ceremony that was now to take place. She was a bottle of champagne broken over the bow of a ship or a pullet whose throat had been slit to sanctify a pagan marriage.

Now Meg clapped her hands together. “LET IT BEGIN! LET US WELCOME THE BRIDE!”

FORTY NINE

A clutch of she-wolves appeared from the shadowy recesses behind the altar. They were not sleek and darkly beautiful animals, but weighty, swollen sows that stank of urine and blood and meat scraps. Their pelts were wooly and tangled, filthy with dried blood and various unwholesome excretions and foul bits of what they had been feeding on. They appraised Emma with blanched yellow eyes and then charged in, woofing and yipping.

Emma cried out, reaching for Meg who stepped away. The congregation of wolves howled with glee. The she-wolves seized her with all the tenderness of a coyote to a rabbit. They were powerful, slamming her to the floor, then dragging her up onto the altar as she squirmed and kicked. One of them stuck its snout in her face, revealing speckled gums and dagger-like teeth stained brown with age. It breathed hot, rancid breath on her. It ran its hands over her, roughly squeezing her breasts and then painfully clutching what was between her legs. Droplets of milk dripped from its distended teats.

While the others held Emma down, it made a gurgling sound in its throat that became garbled words. *"Pretty and ripe, pretty and ripe,"* the voice said. Then made a high-pitched giggling sound.

Though she was riven with terror, anger boiled in Emma. She fought loose and smashed her fist into the she-wolves mouth. The lot of them barked and whined and squealed with delight.

They knocked her back down, then attacked her with a flurry of claws, tearing her clothes off, reducing them to shreds, and laying open her flesh in dozens of places.

There was a pot of some steaming, rank-smelling brew bubbling away. They dipped their hands into it and slapped a greasy, burning unguent onto her skin. It burned into her cuts and abrasions, bringing a pain that made her scream. But they were not to be dissuaded. They covered her with it, oiling her with the fatty substance until she glistened with hot grease.

Emma fought, but slowly, very slowly, her defiance drained away. *What is this shit? What the hell is it?* Where seconds before, it had burned her like acid and made her cuts sting like rock-salt...now she was tingling from head to toe.

Her muscles were taut as bow strings under her skin.

She could feel a lovely heat at her breasts and between her legs.

Her mind took wing in her head, assailed by colors and textures and sensations.

On her tongue, she tasted honey and blood, sugar and raw meat, sweet and sour, salty and bland, seared flesh and human fat.

She felt prey in her jaws.

She crushed its writhing body in her teeth, trembling at the feel of pulped bone and gallons of blood washing down her throat.

She felt males pushing into her, sliding into every orifice and a multitude of tongues licking her the way a dog licks a bone. Her body shook with orgasms and she felt more alive than she ever had before.

The fields and forest were hers.

She could leap up into trees and fly through the sky.

She was a daughter of the moon, a carnal child of nature, an omnipotent beast with slavering jaws and blood-dripping claws.

She was the wolf and the hawk, the snake and the mantis and the black widow. She rent flesh from bones and seized still beating, blood-gushing hearts in her jaws.

She was the pagan queen of the forest.

She was the huntress.

She was a stalking horror.

A nocturnal monster whose breath was sweet with human carnage.

She was the beast within unleashed, the original woman, the apex predator in a world of sheep waiting for the grisly benediction of her claws.

The only thing that brought her out of it was the sound of squealing. It was as if a hog had been branded. The cries were strident, screeching. They sounded human, but just barely. Emma tried to clear her eyes, to see what was really before her and not just in her mind. A wriggling form had been tied-up expertly and now it was being hoisted above the heads of the werewolves, dangling by a rope. It shrieked madly, but its cries were those of a dying animal.

Emma looked at it.

Some trace of memory told her that she knew this person. The face. The hair. It was…was Yvonne. Yes, it was Yvonne. She had been trussed up and now she swung above the crowd like a piñata. The wolves could barely contain themselves. They barked and snarled and howled like starving dogs in a kennel. Some part of Emma knew she must intervene, she must put a stop to this, but as she raised her voice what came out was the growling cry of a beast.

The werewolves attacked Yvonne, leaping into the air, slashing and biting her, tearing out strips of meat and covering themselves in a mist of blood. They hit her like piranhas, savaging her, gutting her and ripping off limbs. She swung back and forth, back and forth, less of her dangling every moment. Within minutes, there was nothing but a rack of bloody bones, ligament and cartilage on the rope. Blood had saturated the wolves and they fought amongst each other for the best cuts of meat, bones, and entrails.

Emma went to her knees.

She was horrified.

Appalled.

Repulsed.

Sickened.

And…excited.

Now Meg stepped forward. She had dipped her hand into the slaughtered lamb and there was blood right up to her elbow. She left a trail of red droplets as she approached. She reached up and painted a symbol on Emma's forehead. The blood felt very hot. It burned deep into her skull. And she knew, she knew—this was The Blooding. The blood of the first kill was sacred and ensured good luck and prosperity. Yvonne had been sacrificed for her.

"ALL PRAISE THE BRIDE OF BLOODING NIGHT!" Meg called out, falling to her knees before Emma. "SHE IS THE CHOSEN ONE, THE ADORED ONE! PRAISE THE LORD OF THE FOREST AND THE MOTHER OF ALL THINGS! BOW DOWN BEFORE THE DAUGHTER OF THE HORNED MOON! THE MAKER OF THE WILD SALVE WHOSE LOINS AND WOMB WE VENERATE! LET IT END AND BEGIN! LET THE BRIDE DANCE IN HER SKIN!"

The wolves howled in a chorus that was shrill and baying and unbroken. Emma could feel the power of it, their worship of her. It made goosebumps run up and down her spine. The energy of the congregation entered her, flowed in her veins and increased with each beat of her heart. They were joined and made into a single entity that raised its head to the moon above and the world shook with the howling.

Meg climbed to her feet, still looking upon Emma with complete adoration. Her eyes seemed to twinkle. She stepped out of her clothes and proudly exposed her nakedness to the wild congregation. Though she was on in years, she was well-kept, her skin smooth though blemished by a few ancient scars. Her body was rawboned, flexing with thongs of muscle at the arms and legs.

"On this night," she said, "we replace the old with the new. We call on fresh blood for the tribe. We honor the new and revile that which is old and leeched dry of purpose."

Now something crawled up the aisle between the gathering of beasts. It moved with a creeping undulation like an enormous slug, inching ever forward. It was another werewolf, but one that had been badly used, degraded and broken. It moved with shattered limbs. Its jaws were sprung wide, tongue lolling from its mouth. It breathed with harsh, wheezing, phlegmatic respiration. Now and again, it emitted a broken whining.

The other wolves looked down on it with what appeared to be indignation if not complete outrage. *What is this worm that slithers amongst us and disturbs this holiest of nights?* Emma looked to Meg and she, too, viewed this interloper with contempt. The other wolves bristled with rage. They began to growl and snap at it. One of the males stepped forward, lifting a leg and directing a stream of urine at it.

Meg ran her nails down her chest and belly, opening her flesh and letting the blood run. "Let the turning of the skin be seen by all," she said.

What happened then was another atrocity in a night of plenty. The crawling werewolf moved ever forward to the altar, leaving a trail of ichor behind it. The company of wolves howled and roared with bloodlust. They began to kick at the crawling thing. First beating it and pummeling it senseless, then tearing at it with their claws. It became a frenzy of violence as they crowded around it, biting and slashing it, making it shriek in agony as they drew blood. The younger ones jumped up and down on it, breaking bones and ripping out globs of bloody meat.

"Turn the skin!" Meg commanded.

It was a communal effort. The crawling thing was rolled over in its pain and humiliation. Claws dug into its belly, shearing open its pelt and peeling it like the skin of an orange. This was not a simple act of divesting the creature within of its wolfskin, no, this was a flaying. They peeled the hide free and what was beneath—the broken, bleeding body of a woman—had her skin sheared free at the same time. Wolfskin to human epidermis were joined, inseparable, two layers of integument covering the same person and they came off in a bloody sheet.

The wolfskin was tossed aside like a squeezed-out sausage casing. The woman managed to squirm away three or four feet, screaming madly, looking like a human-shaped shank of raw meat. Then the wolves seized her. Their fangs punctured her soft body, crunching through bone, opening her up and plucking her limbs free until she was a writhing torso and then even that was reduced to pink mince.

The wolves were showered with gore. They chewed and sucked blood and meat from their claws. But mostly, they watched as the wolfskin began to tremble. As it pulled itself up, teetering uneasily, just a pelt but one that was filled with a diabolic life of its own.

Emma shook her head from side to side, knowing beyond a doubt that the woman they killed had once been the Bride of Blooding Night. The den mother, the child-bearer, the bitch, alpha female, and that she would now replace her. And in her brain, she heard the voice of Mrs. Cupp. *Tell them, Emma. Tell them how you don't want this, how you didn't know it would be like this. Tell them that you do not wish to be joined with the wolfskin. That you do not wish to be a werewolf. That you're afraid to be the Bride.* But Emma did not tell them this—she only screamed. It was the only thing she seemed capable of as the wolfskin moved in her direction. From crotch to throat, it was open and there was nothing in it but glistening blood and hanging sections of the woman's skin. Its jaws hung open, its eye sockets black and empty. It was a sagging, boneless horror that moved ever closer with a dragging, shuffling stride. It held up flaccid arms. A hollow hissing noise came from inside it.

Emma tried to get away, but she was held down by the wolf-hags. They would allow nothing to disturb the ritual that had to be seen to its end now. As the congregation of wolves rolled and fought, biting and clawing, feeding and fighting and fucking, the wolfskin fell on Emma like a blanket and Meg laughed with a high keening sound and Emma shook her head from side to side, *oh please oh dear God not this not this,* but even as her mind pulled away from it, nauseous with fear, insane with terror, her body—still under the hot, greasy intoxication of the wild salve—betrayed her. Her flesh quivered. Her nipples stood erect. Her hips swayed. Every cell in her body lusted to be joined with the wolfskin.

It attached itself to her.

Fusing itself with her own skin.

She screamed with horror, with madness, with orgasmic release as it crawled over her, engulfing her and sealing her inside its dark, bleeding depths until she stretched out her long, taloned fingers and saw the world through yellow vulpine eyes, her sharp teeth gnashing together.

Lost in the depths of what she now was, who she had been fading into the distance, Emma let out a high-pitched howl. She was hungry. Unbearably hungry. For meat. Blood. Sex. There were demons loose inside her, all fighting for dominance. Her head was filled with stars. Her eyes wanted to see the moon. She howled and howled again and a voice inside cried out, *where is the one? The one I am promised? Where is the Lord?* But then he was there, gigantic and blood-smelling, ticks crawling at his belly and lice hopping in his pelt. Drool hung from his mouth and his single blood-filled eye blazed with triumph as he entered her, spearing her like a fish. He pushed into her again and again and she screamed because he was so cold that he burned. Blood ran down her legs and his seed filled her, overflowed her, drowning her in a swamp of life and in her mind she could already feel her belly fattening with children, with the spawn of the wolf, a generation of vipers that would destroy her, leech her, suck the blood from her veins and the marrow from her bones and the life from her pumping heart…until she was worn out, used up, a crawling subhuman thing that would be flayed alive on Blooding Night.

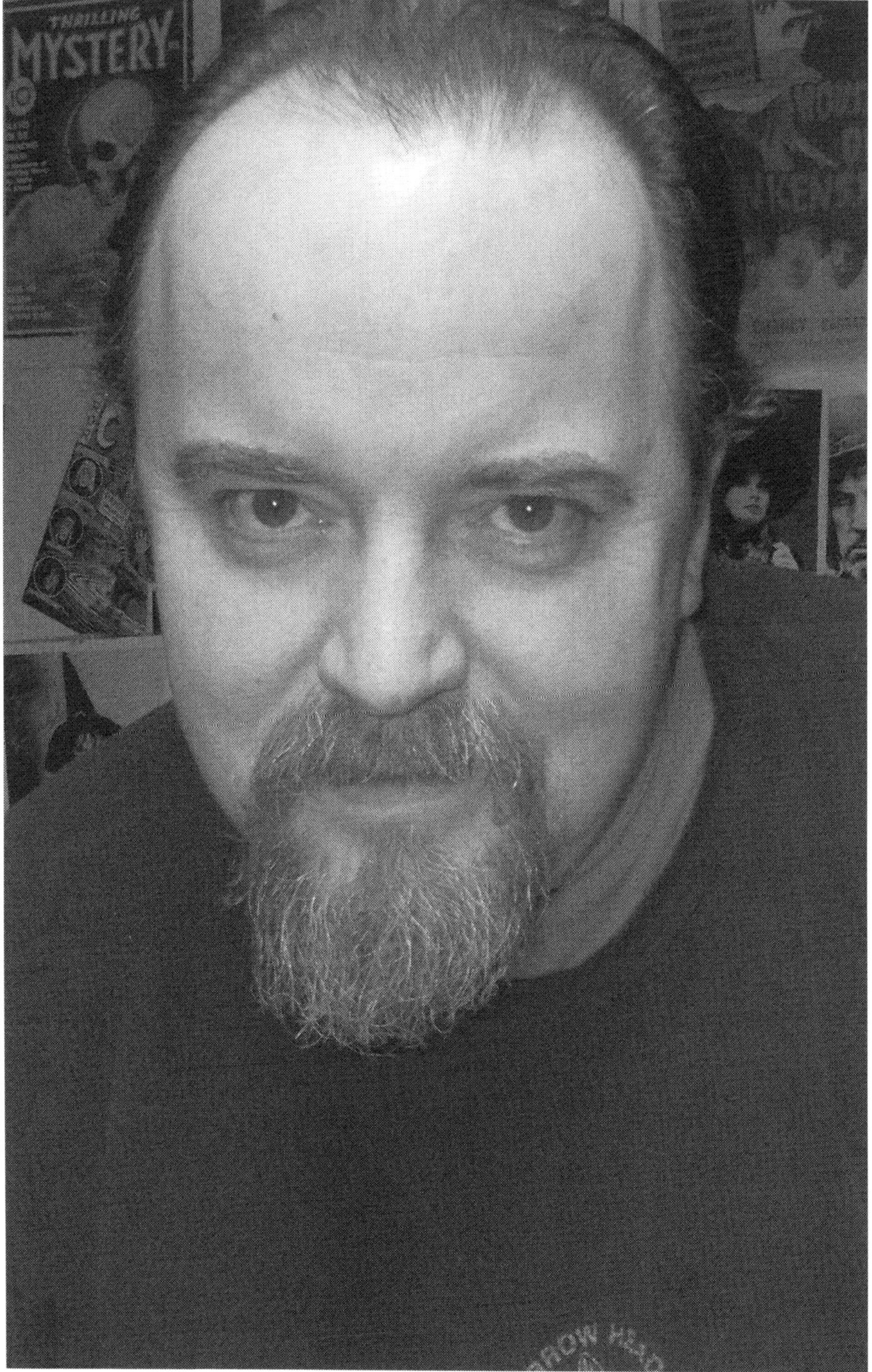
THRILLING
MYSTERY

ABOUT THE AUTHOR

Tim Curran is the author of *Skin Medicine*, *Hive*, *Dead Sea*, *Resurrection*, *The Devil Next Door*, *Dead Sea Chronicles*, *Clownflesh*, and *Bad Girl in the Box*. His short stories have been collected in *Bone Marrow Stew* and *Zombie Pulp*. His novellas include "The Underdwelling," "The Corpse King," "Puppet Graveyard," and "Worm, and Blackout." His fiction has been translated into German, Japanese, Spanish, and Italian.

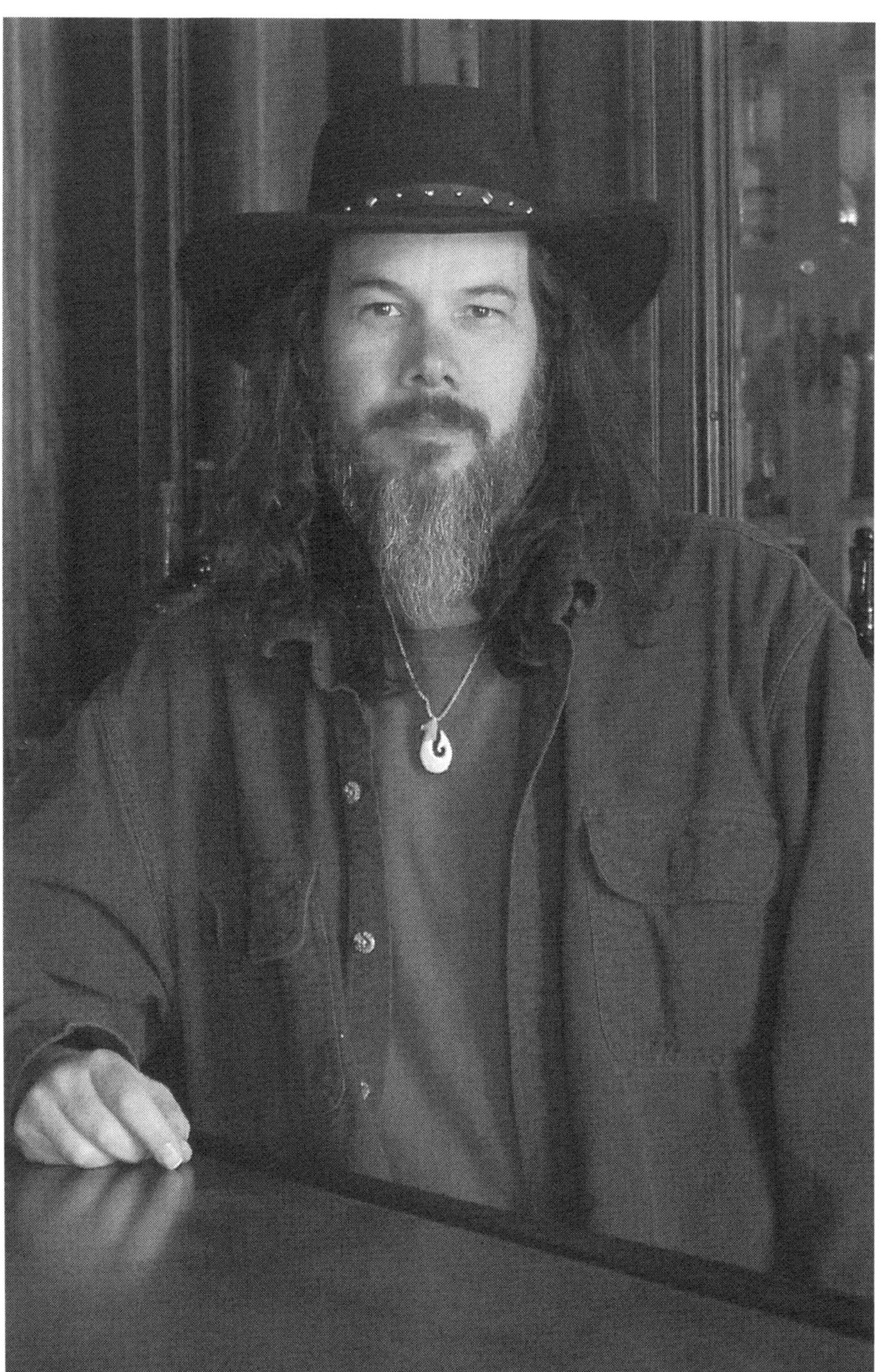

ABOUT THE ARTIST

Steeped in the enthralling fantasy and science-fiction illustrations of the 1960s, '70s, and '80s, artist and illustrator **K.L. Turner** brings a bit of old-school painterly style to today's methods. With more than 30 years of experience in the arts, he expertly brings an expressionistic style into his illustrations to create compelling works which captivate and draw the viewer in. His works are found in media and galleries around the world, and celebrated in pop culture. A versatile creative type, Turner is also accomplished in the mediums of photography, sculpture, and the fine arts. Choosing to live and work on the beautiful front range of the Colorado Rocky Mountains where he was born and raised, he continues to derive inspiration from nature as well as cultural influences both at home and in his travels.

Made in the USA
Columbia, SC
30 January 2023